A Legend in Ruins . . .

"Ordinarily, he enjoyed musing over the old wrecked village, which had once been a populous frontier city of New Spain. It had remained a place of some importance until the gringoes came and rubbed out the old without writing in the new. . . ."

But legend had it that one day the bells of the crumbling village church would mysteriously ring. And on the day they did, San Filipo was reborn, brought back to turbulent life by the discovery of silver bullion!

W9-DHS-797

Books by Max Brand

Ambush at Torture Canyon
The Bandit of the Black Hills
The Bells of San Filipo
Black Jack
Blood on the Trail
The Border Kid
Danger Trail
Destry Rides Again
The False Rider
Fightin' Fool
Fighting Four
Flaming Irons
Ghost Rider
(Original title: Clung)
The Gun Tamer
Harrigan
Hired Guns
Larramee's Ranch
The Longhorn Feud

On the Trail of Four
The Phantom Spy
Ride the Wild Trail
Rippon Rides Double
Rustlers of Beacon Creek
Seven Trails
Singing Guns
Steve Train's Ordeal
The Stingaree
The Stolen Stallion
The Streak
The Tenderfoot
Thunder Moon
Tragedy Trail
Trouble Kid
The Untamed
Valley of the Vanishing Men
Valley Thieves
Vengeance Trail

Published by POCKET BOOKS

 Are there paperbound books you want
but cannot find in your retail stores?

You can get any title in print in **POCKET BOOK** editions. Simply
send retail price, local sales tax, if any, plus 35¢ per book to
cover mailing and handling costs, to:

MAIL SERVICE DEPARTMENT
POCKET BOOKS • A Division of Simon & Schuster, Inc.
1230 Avenue of the Americas • New York, New York 10020

Please send check or money order. We cannot be responsible
for cash. *Catalogue sent free on request.*

Titles in this series are also available at discounts in quantity
lots for Industrial or sales-promotional use. For details write our
Special Products Department: Department AR, POCKET BOOKS,
1230 Avenue of the Americas, New York, New York 10020.

The Bells of
San Filipo

by **MAX BRAND**

A KANGAROO BOOK
PUBLISHED BY POCKET BOOKS NEW YORK

THE BELLS OF SAN FILIPO
Western Story Magazine edition published 1926
POCKET BOOK edition published September, 1977

The Bells of San Filipo originally appeared in serialized
form in *Western Story Magazine* in 1926.

This POCKET BOOK edition is printed from brand-new
plates made from completely reset, clear, easy-to-read type.
POCKET BOOK editions are published by
POCKET BOOKS,
a Simon & Schuster Division of
GULF & WESTERN CORPORATION
1230 Avenue of the Americas,
New York, N.Y. 10020.
Trademarks registered in the United States
and other countries.

ISBN: 0-671-81236-X.
Copyright, 1926, by Frederick Faust. Copyright renewed,
1954, by Dorothy Faust. All rights reserved. This book, or
portions thereof, may not be reproduced by any means
without permission of the copyright holder.

Printed in the U.S.A.

The Bells of
San Filipo

CHAPTER I

The Man on the Mountain

On the eighteenth of June the sun rose only a very few minutes after four o'clock to shine over Sierra La Viega. At the same moment Jim Gore rose from his blankets in the little lean-to which he had built beside his diggings, and blinked toward the east.

The red sun was like a thing of fire, rolling along the edge of the next mountain through the foresting of great pines which crowded swiftly across its face. There was only one gap in the thick woods, and just as the sun reached that open space, a man laboring up the slope under the weight of a heavy pack came into the clearing and turned, instantly, into a jet-black silhouette pasted on the face of the broad sun. It made a startling illusion, but only for an instant. Then the stranger was across the gap in the woods and lost far away in the next stretch of trees.

Even such a small thing meant a great deal to Jim Gore. For his life was composed entirely of events of two kinds. Some of them were very great; some of them were very little. When a man faces a blizzard, or when he risks his life through a frightful mountain winter for the sake of drilling away at a hole in the ground, or when he stands gun in hand and barks profane insults at another, ready to kill or be killed, it may be said that he has entered into great moments.

But there were not many such moments in the life of Jim Gore. There were so few of them, indeed, that it often seemed to Gore that his life was like the running of a still water, picking up nothing on its clear current. He was thirty-five years old, and yet his achievements were astonishingly few. Once, in a burst of passion, he had risen to such a height that he had

7

stood up to a gunman with his own weapon in his
hand and a stream of ringing insults on his tongue
—but the gunman had not chosen to fight. It had not
been fear of Jim Gore; rather it was a touch of pity,
for all men who knew Jim knew that however much
strength was in his hands, there was no peculiar skill
with guns in him.

He was a laborer, pure and simple, a cow-puncher
at times, and even a sheep-herder one summer in his
youth. But most of his life had been spent wandering
through the mountains, chipping at the more promising rocks with his prospector's hammer and looking
at the unweathered interior of the stone with a wise
eye. Or else he found some little streak of pay ore
and blasted away at it, breaking ground slowly, and
grinding up the pay dirt in a "coffee mill" as he was
doing now. In the last twenty years, Gore had spent
more than fifteen by himself. So one can understand
why that one great moment, gun in hand, oaths on
his lips, lightning in his eyes, still filled Jim Gore
with a comfortable content. For that scene was the
proof to himself that he was not a coward. He had
faced death in that moment. For if it had developed
into a gun fight, he had known well enough that he
had not a chance.

Perhaps you will feel that such a man is hardly
worthy of being the central figure of a narrative. Perhaps he was not, but we must look at Jim Gore exactly
as he was.

He was thirty-five years old, then, and he was without peculiar talent. Any Mexican could handle a knife
better than he. Any cow-puncher could manage rope
or gun better than Gore, and with a rifle he was, as
he put it, "no great shucks!"

He was neither young, nor handsome, nor particularly neat. If he scrubbed himself on Saturday night
with laundry soap and a bucket of cold water, he felt
that he sufficiently possessed the virtue which is next
to godliness until another Saturday rolled around. If
he shaved on Sunday morning, it was his nearest ap-

proach to a prayer for that holy day. He observed Sundays, moreover, by boiling up his soiled clothes, by a hunting trip through the near-by mountains, by fishing in the first promising stream, and by returning to his camp to pick up a much-worn copy of "Robinson Crusoe" which he spelled out with a never-increasing speed. When he had finished a page he felt that he had accomplished a worthy labor. Often he dwelt for a moment with a serious frown and his blunt forefinger jammed close beneath a word while he pondered its meaning. When he read in this manner, he felt that he was drawn within hail of the world of art.

Not that he pretended to culture or that he really hoped to attain to it; but when he read his one book, he was like the mariner who scans the dim, unknown shore and tingles with the delightful strangeness of it.

So it was with Jim Gore.

He was a man of middle size. He stood about five feet nine or ten and he weighed a hundred and seventy solid pounds. When it is said that he had strength in his hands, let no false hopes be wakened. He was not one of those men who have romantic possibilities even in their finger tips. But he had worked hard all his life, and having worked most of the time for himself, he had put in far more blistering, grinding hours than he would if he had worked for another person.

He was hard from head to foot. There was no fat on him. A thumb drawn over his ribs would have numbered them one by one. His chest arched out boldly; his belly shrank against his hips, and he had to draw his belt so tight to keep up his trousers that it seemed to be cutting him in two. On this morning, when we see him for the first time, his face is less heavily masked than it will be by the end of the week —for it is only Wednesday; and though his bristly beard grows fast, it has not yet thickened to the dark cloud which it will be on Saturday, say. One can draw all his features, particularly the sunken cheeks and the sad mouth. For he who works hard, even for himself, carries the story of it in his face, eventually.

Then there are his eyes which deny all the rest of the story; they are pale blue, clear as the eyes of a child, ready to smile beneath the shaggy brows. Let me tell you the whole truth of Jim Gore: He *is* a child!

If he had not been a child he would never have taken up the prospector's life, knowing as little as he did of geology. But when he was able to read the chapter heading, as one might say, of the story of the stones, he felt that he could guess at all the details. So he joined the ragged army which still explores the uplands and the deserts of this continent and finds the millions which make others rich.

If he had known a whit more, he would not have been so happy. Geology would have become a science to him; as it was it remained a rich, bookless mystery —a thing to dream over, to pray about! He lived among crowding symbols which pointed toward vast happiness, vast wealth. If he struck it rich, he hardly knew what he would do with the money, except to buy a pair of good mules to pack his outfit, and then a quantity of the finest powder, and the single and double jacks of the truest balance, and the drills which keep the best temper, and a thousand other little conveniences which would turn his camp life into a heavenly existence. For instance, if he could buy a jointed fishing rod—and a fine repeating rifle.

He did not even indulge in such dreams as these, very often. His passion was for the gold itself, and not what he would do with it. To rip the rocks apart and unlock the treasure for the world was his yearning. He wished to handle the key; instinctively, I suppose, he knew that the gold would never stick long to his fingers! Yet the love of this great adventure never died down in him. He never lost sight of it except in towns where the crowding faces and the crowding voices filled him with homesickness and sorrow, so that he fled back to his mountains in haste.

We must not consider that Jim Gore was a peculiarly sensitive man. But he was very free, and being very free, he was wild also. Perhaps you will no longer feel an interest in him when I tell you what joys made up his life—next to the gold thirst. Well, first of all, he liked to waken slowly, to lie blinking as the first daylight warmed the sky, to drink a few deep breaths of the mountain air, cold and satisfying as water.

Then to take a filthy black pipe, eight years old at least, with the stem thrice chewed away and new grips whittled into it, to fill this pipe with the rankest plug tobacco which he cut up and mixed on Sunday mornings. To inhale a few breaths of this terrible smoke, and then slowly to rise and dress—this was how he liked to begin his day!

His dressing, I should add, consisted of drawing on his trousers, and then his boots.

After that, he enjoyed a breakfast of black coffee taken from a great smoke-incrusted pot in which the supply was brewed freshly every third day, and no more frequently. Indeed, the third day's brew was the brew which he liked the best. He was a man of hearty tastes, as you may see. He made pone every second day, and ate it cold the rest of the time. It was soggy, but he did not mind that. Besides the pone, his breakfast was completed by slices of bacon. He did not cook this meat to crispness. In fact, he never could understand why finicky people insisted on cooking all the "good" out of their bacon.

When his breakfast was finished, he lighted the pipe of which he had smoked a few drafts upon waking in the morning. He smoked it through deliberately.

As a rule, he would pick out some object to be gazed on while he smoked. Since he had started his drift against the side of this mountain of the Sierra La Viega, he usually matched the ruins of the crumbled Spanish town of San Filipo, which stood on the bank of the yellow little San Filipo River, in the heart of the valley beneath him. It was a good two thousand feet down and several miles away, but the pitch of his eye reduced it to a clear-cut view. He could see everything so distinctly that he no longer wondered how the soaring owl could see the darting field mouse so far below.

Ordinarily, then, he enjoyed musing over the old wrecked village which had once been a populous frontier city of New Spain. It had remained a place of some importance until the gringoes came and rubbed out the old without writing in the new in many places. They drove railroads through the land. They hewed out new trails. And the town of San Filipo had depended upon a more leisurely time, a more leisurely people, who were content to travel a week, a fortnight—they hardly cared which. The Americans, however, reckoned time even to minutes —so San Filipo dwindled. There were still a few white drifts of morning smoke above the houses, and it seemed to Jim Gore, as he brooded over the picture on other days, that these were the last breathing of San Filipo, the last misting of the mirror.

On this morning, however, he had something better to muse upon.

CHAPTER II

Old Treasure

It was the picture of the traveler which had come across the red face of the sun. You will say that this was a very small detail to hold the thoughts of a mature man, but it must be remembered that Jim Gore had not been able to see the face of another human being for eight months. And, during eight months, he had not seen even the figure of a man as near by as he who had strode across the circle of the sun. Only, from time to time, he made out the tiny form of horse and man herding the cows in the valley of San Filipo

—cows which were dull spots of color, and whose low-ings welled faintly up to him when the wind was still. But even a breath through the trees near by was loud enough to cut away those noises.

So, having only the moldered town in the distance and the ghostly small life in the valley, this nearer sight of a human being filled the simple mind of Jim Gore.

The pack on the back of the stranger was not large, but either it was very heavy or else the man had struggled hard up the slope and spent a great deal of his strength, for he was bent low, with legs sagging at every step.

He was not an American—that was certain. An American walks with his head up, an American pauses a fraction of an instant at least on the top of a hill. But this fellow had gone on with head down like a mute beast tugging at a load, and he had hurried on without pause where the sun looked through the tim-ber gap at the top of the hill.

What manner of man might he be, then? What was his destination? And whither had he come? Was he some trapper who had risen before daylight and strug-gled up from old San Filipo with this little pack? Was he a hunter? Was he a Mexican miner, burning with new information which made him eager to take up the trail of a hint of gold?

But only some burning necessity could have made him rise so early and labor so hard. By his step and his carriage it was plain that this fellow had done his day's work even before the sun looked sidewise at him!

It was an intriguing problem for Jim Gore, but just as he was enjoying the relish of it, a bubbling in the bowl of his pipe announced the end of his breakfast smoke. Automatically his mind stopped working. He tapped the bowl out on his heel, stamped on the fum-ing refuse of tobacco, and shoved the pipe into a hip pocket where its warmth came through the jeans and burned against his flesh. Then he started for his hole.

In another moment the single jack was chiming against the head of the drill. The sun grew hotter. Perspiration began to collect under his hatband; sweat began to pour out beneath the pits of his arms, and across his back broad black stains began to come shadowy through his shirt, already dusted with white from the dried salt of this week's labors.

He knew his strength so accurately, that he was aware of just what he could do in a morning. He could gauge the number and strength of his rapid hammer strokes so that he would be completely spent at exactly noon.

When noon came he cooked his lunch, which was simply another breakfast. Then he stretched out in his lean-to and dozed until a sudden guilty stir of his spirit warned him that he had been resting for an hour. He sat up, glanced at his watch, smiled as he saw that old habit was a most accurate chronometer, and then went back to his labors.

At four o'clock he had finished, fixed his shots, and fired them. When they had exploded he went back to look at the broken ground. The vein had neither expanded nor pinched down. It was just the same—a glimmer, a streaking of hope, and no more. In his eight months of labor on this spot he had gathered not more than a scant five hundred dollars in gold. However, that was better than nothing. And who could tell? If he left this difficult ledge of hard rock where every foot of broken ground was purchased at such infinite cost of pain and patience, might not some luckier man come along and, digging deeper, open another Comstock Lode? Such things had been in the past. They would never happen to Jim Gore! He had decided that much in the early days and stuck patiently to his first ideals.

Now he took his rifle and went out hunting, but a pair of squirrels was the only result of his labors until he turned back toward his drift. Then he managed to shoot a rabbit which had crouched foolishly in a bunch of grass with its long ears cocked out. Jim Gore laughed at the silly thing until the rifle shook in his hands—but he succeeded in putting a shot through it. It meant fresh meat for supper, fresh meat for the next day. And fresh meat meant easier work, deeper, sweeter sleep.

A deep sleep indeed! For the day had been hot and the work a little tougher than usual. He remained not more than a scant hour after his supper was finished, letting the cool air of the evening bathe his body and relax his nerves. Then he pulled off boots and trousers, twisted a blanket around his body, and lay down to sleep.

This was a typical day for Jim Gore. In fact, it was rather more exciting and eventful than usual, for its annals included the shooting of two squirrels and a rabbit. Perhaps a whole month would pass, after this, without bringing so much action. During all that time he would dwell upon that pleasant afternoon!

You who live in cities cannot understand, of course. But it makes little difference what happens to make the heart swell. It is the sense of joy which counts, and not so much the cause of it. And I doubt if many of you have lain down to more contented sleep than that which passed over the mind and the eyes of Jim Gore on this night.

He slept like a child, perfectly, without a dream, without a stir of body or mind. And so complete was his rest that it was not the rising of the sun which roused him, but the first rosy glowing dawn that made him sit up in his blanket and yawn widely as he looked eastward, glad of the early beginning of his day.

He reached for his pipe automatically, but his finger froze suddenly upon it as though it had been the hot shaft of a drill. For yonder, across the open gap among the trees, dimly marked against the pink of the east, walked his vision of the morning before—the very same outline, the same hanging head, the same sagging stride of weariness, the same tugging at the same small, heavy pack.

Jim Gore glanced over his shoulder with a guilty

start, as though he had seen a ghost. He was so disturbed that he forgot his pipe and stumbled out with a frown to cook his breakfast.

Such a thing as this, such a perfect coincidence, had never happened before in all his life.

It followed him through the day. Sometimes, with a hand closing on his throat, he swore that his eyes had lied to him. And when the sun was rising high and the rock dust was churning around the shaft of his drill as he worked the hole deeper, it seemed that the morning's vision had been no more than a dream indeed!

But when the dark of the evening drew over the mountains again, the thing grew more real.

There was broken sleep only for Jim Gore on this night. A dozen times he wakened and sat bolt upright. Once a wolf was howling, a great timber wolf hunting on a blood trail. Once it was the dreary hooting of an owl. And again, it was no more than the sudden flurry of his heart.

There was an ache behind his eyes when he sat up again in the pink of the morning and fastened his gaze on the gap among the trees to the east. The minutes went by him; the rim of the sun began to prick above the mountain's edge; he was on the verge of congratulating himself because the vision had not come again, when once more the slumping form came from the trees into the clearing, waded leg deep in the red fire of the sun, and disappeared into the shadows of the trees beyond.

It was more than enough for Jim Gore. He could not work that day with such a burden on his mind.

After breakfast he trudged across the intervening ravine and found the clearing itself, and there he cast anxiously about for some sort of a trail. He was not long in finding it. In a spot covered with soft soil he found a trail worn which could not have been made by less than a score of passages of human feet—human, naked feet!

How long had this thing gone on? How many

weeks, how many months, while he dozed in his cabin? From what place did the man come, and where did he go?

He looked northward into the tossing sea of mountains. It would be useless, he felt, to try to follow that trail where it would soon disappear among the hard rocks that could have taken the falling of shod hoofs without giving a trace to anything but a microscope. But from the south, where could he have started his journey except from the valley of San Filipo? And might he not have come from the dying town itself?

Jim Gore went back to his camp to smoke many pipes and turn the matter over and over in a restless mind. In the afternoon his lack of sleep the night before was compensated by a pleasant nap. But that night was more broken than ever. Well before dawn he wakened and dressed. He could not live, he felt, unless he had deciphered the meaning of that traveler's many journeys.

He took his rifle, therefore, and trudged heavily through the darkness of the ravine and up the farther side of it to the clearing on the edge of the hill. There he found a covert in a nest of jutting rocks and waited. The cold wind of the dawn began to blow. The east turned gray, the mountains were tall and black against the growing light, the rose began, and then the full brightness of the morning fell around him.

He heard not a sound. But out of the southern edge of the trees on the far side of the clearing stepped a barefooted Mexican, head down, long black hair falling raggedly across his eyes, hatless, with his white trousers rolled halfway up his muscled calves. At his back was a dirty canvas bag, and his left hand gripped a rolled edge of it that came over his right shoulder. He was very tired. His breast heaved with the labor of his climb, and his knees sagged deeply with every step.

Yet, when Jim Gore rose from his concealment with the rifle in his hand, the Mexican leaped into sudden life. The heavy pack dropped with a thud upon the pine needles; his hand whipped a knife from his belt, and the glittering blade hissed close beside the head of the miner.

As for Gore, he had had no thought of an attack. He threw his rifle against his shoulder with a startled oath. But even then he did not shoot, for he saw the Mexican rush away through the northern trees with a yell of terror.

Gore did not need to examine the canvas bag. It had dropped upon its side and from its open mouth a bar of solid silver bullion had rolled forth upon the brown needles!

CHAPTER III

A Trip to San Filipo

Far to the north he could hear the fugitive crashing recklessly through the brush. There was a startled yell again, as though some sound behind the Mexican— perhaps an echo cast up by his own flight—had made him feel that the American was running close behind. At least there was little danger that the barefoot man would return at once, and Jim Gore rolled the contents of the canvas upon the ground.

There were five bars, each blackened by the tarnishing of long time. He weighed one in his hand. It was close to ten pounds! It was not strange that the Mexican had been spent by the burden of this pack up the long, steep slope. Fifty pounds of solid silver!

He shaved the surface with his knife. It revealed beautiful, pure silver, glistening like ice in the morning light. Fifty pounds! Hundreds of dollars!

He sat down and figured in the dirt with his finger just how much it would be. Almost twice as much money as he had broken out of the face of his mountain with more than half a year of bitter labor! And this on the back of a Mexican?

He examined the bars more carefully. In spite of their apparent age, and their black tarnishing, they seemed fairly crisp from the mold. There was no great blunting of the edges, as from much handling. The corners had not been rounded. Surely they had not been shifted a great deal since the day of their making.

Each was marked with a stamp, and over that stamp Jim Gore brooded for some time. Small trifles could hold his mind, and here was a unique trifle indeed. It was the design of an odd-looking creature with the body of a horse, erect on its hind legs, but clothed with a sweeping pair of wings and additionally garnished with a great horn projecting from its forehead. Beneath this monster lay crossed swords and over it head was arched a motto inscribed in a language which Jim Gore could not read. He had never seen such a design as this before, and why it should be inscribed on a bar of silver bullion was more than he could make out.

What was of more immediate importance, however, was that this mass of silver, with a value of nearly a thousand dollars, now lay unclaimed upon the ground. And though the Mexican who had carried it to this point might return for it, Gore was practically certain that he had very little right to it.

Otherwise the man would not have shown such emotion when a stranger crossed his path. A thief, like a dog with a bone, will fight instantly as soon as he is alarmed. An honest man carries a treasure in his pocket without suspicion of the world. The whole bearing of the Mexican had been so wild and wolfish that Jim Gore had no doubt of his own right to pick up that load of silver and cart it back to his cabin.

But when the little treasure was there, he could not help wondering how he could protect it. For yonder might lie in constant danger of the escaped Mexican's revenge. He was only comforted by the reflection that the brown-skinned carrier had not shown a more formidable weapon than a knife.

It was not the present bag filled with silver that mattered most. There were other things of more moment, and the chief food for thought was this: What was the source from which this parcel of silver had been drawn? Furthermore, how much had been drawn from that source before the load which he intercepted? And whither had it been taken?

A keener mind than that of Jim Gore would have been excited by the thoughts which these things conjured into his head. To follow up the trail of the silver carrier was not to his taste, in the first place. He could follow up signs as well as most. But a trail which wandered through a forest over pine needles which received a tread and sprang up elastically when the weight was removed, a trail which then passed on to a barren region of rocks—this was not to his liking. Even an expert scout might have shrunk from such a problem.

As for the source of the treasure, he felt that he might have some luck if he could search among the ruins of San Filipo, though how precious metals could remain in it after it had been swept by fire and successively plundered by Indians, Americans and Mexicans in turn, he could not see.

But what he finally decided upon was to hide the silver as well as he could and go down to the town to find out what he could—though how to go about it he hardly knew. His hiding spot was the raise which he had sunk, or started to sink, at the top of his little shaft. There he disposed of the silver bullion behind broken rock fragments. And after this was done he started toward San Filipo.

It was the warm and lazy middle of the afternoon when he reached the smooth bottom of the valley, and there he turned onto the old road to San Filipo. It was soft and deep with dust, but here and there a scouring of wind, or the grinding of a rare wheel, had cut down to the broken face of the stone paving which the Conquistadores had laid many and many a generation before. To Jim Gore, as to many another simple heart, those men of old seemed giants. In the West legends grow quickly. Many a man has become a half-fictitious figure before his death. Five years of adventure will establish a romantic background upon which eager imaginations can build around the camp fire, or in the long winters of the lonely crossroads towns. But for what has passed a century before—that is as far distant, as colored, as misty, as the dark ages are to present Europe.

So the picture of the Conquistadores, to Jim Gore, was composed of colorful dreams of fierce-eyed, mustachioed, armored, sword-bearing men. He saw them in velvets and in leather, in silk and in steel, with great-mouthed purses full of gold and ever emptied by the handful. He saw them on glorious horses brought at great cost from Spain and Africa—slender-limbed, tender-eyed, great-hearted steeds whose worth in the New World was the value of half a dozen lives of men. He saw them turning native princes into beasts of burden and slaves in their train; he saw them ride in blood through a thousand battles against fearful odds. He saw them building, by means of their hosts of bondmen, forts and castlelike homes. He saw their servants rip open the stout ribs of the mountains and tear out the gold ore and the silver; he saw the Indians die in swarms in the dark bellies of the mines, or clambering with their baskets of ore up the long, rotten, weaving ladders to the day above; he saw them like great and evil spirits out of a story book.

No wonder, then, that he looked upon the moldered, time-crushed outlines of San Filipo town with an interest that no tourist could have shown. The village was only a tomb now, but it was a tomb of greatness. To Jim Gore, it excited as much awe and reverence as some cloudy aisle in Westminster raises in the breast of an Englishman to-day.

A herd boy, bareback, hatless, his long hair sneaking behind him in the wind, galloped out from the town toward the pasture lands beyond. He was not changed from his ancestors, the Indians, who had watched the fierce Spaniards first come. Yes, his skin was a few shades lighter, but his soul was the soul of the Indian. But the horse he straddled, lump-headed and roach-backed though it was, showed in its fiery eye and in its slender legs of iron that the blood of the Spanish horses flowed in it. It tossed up the fine sand behind it. Time had been, in the days of the Conquistadores, when those drifting sands, pinned down only here and there by knots of bunchgrass, had been overcast by a network of little channels through which the rich waters of the San Filipo river flowed and covered the face of the valley with greenness. And in those days five hundred cattle lowed and five hundred horse pranced and played where there was one to-day.

Jim Gore thought of these things, not with a real regret for that vanished glory, but as an exciting fairy tale, something more unreal, by far, than the written agonies of Robinson Crusoe. For to him Crusoe was more a fact than was any man he had ever known!

He entered the outlying edges of San Filipo. It was a compact little town, as seen from the mountainside above, but when one walked through it, one could view its ruin and its magnitude more fully. He passed, on either hand, broken-backed houses, and adobe walls which had melted into shapeless mounds, or were fast melting now! He passed casements which had widened in ruin to great fissures. He saw walls well preserved for two stories' height, but above that shorn away suddenly—like standing corpses without heads. He saw, here and there in long-untenanted courtyards, great heaps and tangles of wreckage—rotting parts of wagons, twisted cordage as brittle as dirt, and tangles of iron junk. Yes, even a junkman could have found nothing worth salvage in this dead town.

Not entirely dead, either. There were traces of life, just enough to mark a trail here and there across the deep white velvet of the dusty streets. And through the air the sensitive nostrils of the mountaineer found occasionally streaks of familiar scents—wood smoke, or cookery.

Three things Jim Gore took note of, one by one, and found them symbols of existent life in the dead city as strange as ghostly whispers in a town thronged with voices.

Here he turned from the street by which he had entered the old place to the main thoroughfare, a wide avenue pointed toward that central plaza where once the currents of the town had drawn and pooled in noisy circles. He wandered on toward this point until he found, squatted in the dust upon his heels at the side of the street near the entrance to an old patio, a brown-faced youth with sandals on his feet, and soiled cotton trousers, and in his hat a few dry leaves of tobacco and a few corn husks for the manufacture of potent cigarettes. If he had had a sweetheart he would have worn at his breast a little package of made smokes, tied with gayly colored ribbons. Yet he was so good-looking and so amiable of eye and smile that Jim Gore knew the lack of a lady was due to the absence of girls rather than a lack in the young Mexican.

He stopped close by before the youngster saw him and started out of his dream to his feet with: "Señor, señor! Where have you come from to San Filipo?"

The miner waved toward the lofty mountainside. So crystal clear was that mountain air, that the eye could strike through the distance to the dark shadow which was the mouth of his mine and even to the tiny shack which stood beside it.

The boy understood at once.

He said, half earnestly and half smiling: "You are one of the eagles, then, señor? You have been sitting up there on your rock watching us field mice! Well, we make a small diet for great birds!"

CHAPTER IV

Ramirez Tells a Tale

Jim Gore felt the neatness of this compliment and grinned his acknowledgment.

"You live here, then," said he, rather without point.

"Forever, señor," said the affable youth.

There was just a touch of solemnity in this answer that made Jim Gore gape at the other.

"Oh, well," said he, "you are young. You'll be off, one of these days, what? You'll be off for a better place!"

"This is well enough," answered the youngster. "My people have lived here always."

"What may you mean by that?"

"Oh, a great time!"

"Well," said Jim Gore, "I've seen a year that I'd call a great time, and I've seen two hours on the desert when I could *see* water, but when I thought that I'd die before I got to it. That was a great time, too!"

The other rolled up his eyes and under the shadow of his broad-brimmed hat, he looked at the sun-flooded sky. "Consider, señor, how long you have lived, and if your father is an old man before you, and if his father that is dead was old also—that is three lives, is it not?"

"Yes."

"Then, ten times those three lives—that would be a great time, would it not?"

"A thousand years!" murmured Jim Gore, vastly impressed. "That *would* be a long time, my friend!"

"Well," said the boy, "we have lived here forever, as you see!"

And he pointed behind him toward the broken gate of the patio, and behind the patio extended the vast ruins of what had once been a huge house—a veritable palace of adobe. How wrecked it was now! One might have thought that a furious giant, in a rage, had trampled it down. Here the roof was fallen in; here the madmans' heel had stamped roof, wall, casement and all to the dust, and tumbled into the patio half-decayed bricks of adobe, fast turning into dust. Yet there were signs of life. A wisp of smoke hung above the top of the building; there was a bucket by a door; and through the unshuttered, unglassed casement. Jim Gore looked upon sundry signs of life within the place itself.

"You and your mother," said Jim Gore, "you live here together, do you not?"

The youth made a gracefully eloquent gesture, shrugged his shoulders and amiably answered:

"What should I do with a mother?" said he. "Could I keep her? Could I support her?"

"Why not?" said Gore, with an Anglo-Saxon terseness. "What's a woman to do if her own son ain't gunna work for her?"

"Ah, señor, but where shall one find work here? What is the work that is to be done at San Filipo?"

He made another wide gesture of expostulation, and Jim Gore looked into the palm of his hand. It was as pink and as soft as the hand of a child. It was the hand of one who has never bruised the flesh of his fingers with labor.

"You are your own man, then?" asked the miner.

"I am my own man."

"But how do you live if you do not work?"

"What work does a bird do in the air?" smiled the boy. "What work does a grasshopper do in the field?"

And again he made one of his eternal Latin gestures.

But Jim Gore had grown so interested that he almost forgot the serious purpose which had brought him to San Filipo—which was to ask questions. He forgot everything, except the smooth, handsome face of this lad—more sun-tanned than brown by nature, as he could afford to suspect since he had seen the pale inside of the boys hand.

"Well, well," said Gore, smiling rather sternly at the indolent beauty of the youth, "this here satisfies you, maybe?"

"Perhaps it does, señor!"

"And perhaps it don't," said Jim Gore. "Because what happens in San Filipo to keep a smart kid like you in fun?"

"What happens," smiled the other, "on the side of the mountain yonder?"

"Gold!" said the miner briefly.

"So? But here, señor, we have heard the bells!"

"You have heard what?"

"The bells, señor."

"What the devil might you be talkin' about, now?" asked Jim Gore. "I dunno what this drives at!"

The other stared at him in some surprise.

"Is it true, then?" said he. "You have not heard of the bells of San Filipo?"

"I have never heard of them!"

The boy took corn husk and tobacco from the band of his straw hat, and while he crumpled the brittle tobacco leaf in the hollow cup of his palm, he looked earnestly at Gore. The latter knew by this that something worth while was about to be uttered, for every light thing will run out from the lips of a Mexican as freely as water from a snow-fed spring in the May of the year. The smoke was made and lighted and Jim Gore accepted the token by stuffing and lighting his own pipe and then squatting in the shadow of the crumbling wall. The Mexican sat at his side.

"Three hundred years ago—" The Mexican began.

"Three hundred years!" murmured Gore. "Lemme see. That was—doggone it, that was before there was any United States."

"Before there was a white man yonder!" said the Mexican, and waved his hand widely, north and east and west.

"What might your name be?"

"I," said the youth, looking him full in the eye and speaking slowly, "am Diego Ramirez!"

"All right, Ramirez, go on with your yarn. You handle centuries as easy as I can handle a drill. Go on with your yarn."

"Three hundred years ago," said the boy, "a Ramirez came to this valley and gave it its name."

"That ain't a third of a thousand years," said Gore, a little sharp.

"Very well. But my people were here long before."

"Ah!" said Gore. "On your ma's side, then? Well, ramble along."

"He came with a good padre who founded the mission church."

He waved toward the structure. Half of its height was lost and the roof line was a wavering thing like the tops of three crowded waves jumbled together. But still the great mass of masonry loomed above the wrecked city like a prehistoric monster crowded about by pygmy life.

"He staged a right big job," admitted Gore.

"When the church was built, they brought nine great bells which had been cast in Barcelona. They hung them in the bell tower—you can see its great shoulders now, above the ruins!"

"I see them, very well."

"Well, it happened that the first day the bells were rung, the canals were opened to water the valley, and while the bells were ringing—and they rang them half a day without ending—the water from the dam up the valley poured into the canals and streaked across the desert and traced the sands all across with tangles of silver. Do you see?"

With both hands he drew mazy lines in the air.

"Think how that sand must of drunk it up!" sighed Gore. "I can hear 'em and I can feel 'em!"

"And people said, señor, that so long as the bells could ring in the tower of the church, there would be water in the valley—there would be happiness and there would be wealth!"

"Water would make it a rich place. There ain't any doubt of that," admitted Gore.

"So the bells rang for two hundred years."

"A long time, son!"

"Until there was war and there was great trouble. And the valley was filled with fighting. In that fighting, San Filipo burned, and the flames reached the church and cracked the walls of the bell tower, and the timbers were burned from the walls which supported them, and the bells fell and were lost in the ruins!"

"That was sort of too bad," said Jim Gore.

"That same day, señor—mark what I say, for it is very true—on that same day the dam was broken, and a great yellow wave went down the valley from the lake, and the canals ran dry, and from that moment San Filipo Valley has been a desert!"

"Wait a minute," broke in the miner. "There is one thing that you was saying that I don't quite follow."

"Say what you will, señor."

"A little spell back you was sayin' that you had heard the bells of the church?"

"I have heard the bells of San Filipo, señor."

Jim Gore grinned.

"Might you be a hundred years old, Diego Ramirez?"

"What I said is the truth. The other day we heard the bells of San Filipo."

"The devil! Who hung 'em up ag'in?"

"No man, señor."

"But where are they?"

"Lost for a hundred years, señor."

Jim Gore opened his eyes.

"Are you jokin'?" said he.

"I am telling you the very simple truth. I myself heard the bells ring, and so did every one in the valley—great thick notes that seemed to come up out of the ground at my very feet!"

"H'm!" murmured Gore, and scratched his chin. "And who might 'a'f ound 'em and rung 'em?"

"Señor, did you not speak of the devil?"

"Look here, Diego Ramirez," said Gore frowning, "I'm a tolerable sensible man and I'm a patient man, but doggone me if I don't hate foolin'!"

"And I, señor! But I tell you that the bells have been heard to ring. It was the very day of the earthquake. All of us heard them ring. And the meaning is that San Filipo shall be rich again!'

"Earthquake?" said Gore. "I didn't feel none!"

"Look!"

He pointed to a mass of wreckage which was strewn halfway across the street.

"It fell at the same time!" said he.

"So the bells rung?" said the miner. "And San Filipo cannot help but be rich again?"

"It is the prophecy," said the youth. "And who can tell? The Almighty does not lie!"

CHAPTER V

The Tall Stranger

It was such a legend as Gore had heard before from many credulous miners and trappers. There were even more miraculous tales to be told of the past, but this was of the present! And here was a youth speaking of supernatural things with as grave a voice and as clear an eye as he had ever heard or seen in all of his life. He could not think that Diego Ramirez was perpetrating a hoax. There is a certain open self-confidence that shines from a man who speaks what he believes to be verity. That radiance was in the face of Ramirez.

"All right—all right," murmured Jim Gore. "I'll go as far to believin' that as most folks. But I dunno that I see San Filipo showin' much signs of gettin' rich ag'in! The waters ain't flowin' in the valley, so far as I can see!"

And he could not help grinning in triumph at the boy.

"Ah, that is very true," said Diego Ramirez. "But the water did not give the city all of its wealth. Perhaps the silver mines will begin to give out good ore, again!"

Gore started violently. And he clenched his teeth upon his pipe so hard that his jaw began to ache.

"Silver?" said he, a little huskily.

"Silver? Have you not heard? Once those mines poured it out in great white rivers!"

He waved to the southern mountains which framed the valley. The sides were spotted and marred by great heaps which had been dumped there in the past ages and since then, weathered to some sort of harmony with the color of the rest of the slopes, had gradually been sinking out of easy view.

But here was the explanation of the silver which the Mexican had carried across the mountain. There could be no reasonable doubt of that.

"How long ago," said Gore, "did the mines stop paying?"

"Why, perhaps a generation before the dam across the upper valley was broken," said the Mexican.

It was enough for Gore. Five generations—in a damp place—would account for the coating of black tarnish which obscured the white metal of the silver bars as he had seen them. There were other questions which he could have asked. But they would have been too pointed. He decided to leave the young Ramirez to his place of sun and shadow and stroll on.

"And your people?" he asked. "Maybe they were mine owners in the old days?"

"In the other times," said Diego Ramirez, "there was a day when Ramirez owned great mines, and great farms, and besides that, the people of our name had half the city. Do you see the church? All the houses around it were our houses! Great places, as you see. And this ruin behind me was our home!"

So Jim Gore nodded and left him, and strolled idly through the streets of the town; but though his movements were leisurely, his glances to the right and to the left were the glances of a hawk, probing the odd corners of the ruins. Somewhere among them, he had no doubt, was the treasure hidden. No wonder if it were—no wonder if even a hundred years of searchers and plunderers had been unable to find the proper place until, perhaps, that lucky Mexican whom he had stopped, stumbled upon it by chance.

For his own heart, patient as he was, failed him at the thought of digging systematically among these houses. What a moldering wilderness they made! Ten-foot walls, for strength and for coolness, had not been uncommon in the times when San Filipo first grew and prospered. And the sun-tempered bricks had been heaped together by such a vast deal of labor that the miner was amazed at it. He knew what hard work meant. He had been a moiler and a toiler all his days. And how many days of skill and of sweat had been necessary to compose this decaying labyrinth! His work would have to be done at night and, like the Mexican, when the dawn came he would have to be on the height again.

He turned out of San Filipo, at last, and struck away toward the cabin. It was the last of the day when he reached it again. The sun was not a foot from resting on the top of a western mountain, and the first thought of Jim Gore was for his hidden silver. Night would be the time when the Mexican would return to hunt for the little treasure which had been taken from him. And Gore, feeling, like many another Western miner, that a Mexican can literally "smell" his way to silver, decided that he would take the stuff back to the shack.

So he gathered it from the mine and brought it into the cabin, where he rested the load of it in a corner of the place. Then he went out to smoke a pipe and enjoy the evening.

He had a guilty feeling. It was the first day—except Sundays—in a full six months that he had not completed a full quota of labor with his hands, and his conscience bothered Jim Gore. Besides, there was the question of that infernal silver. His final decision, just as the sun slid down behind the western mountain and the world went suddenly a shade dimmer, was that he must covertly bury it the next morning.

He turned toward the shack filled with that resolution, and was hurrying to cook his supper before dark when a wicked singing darted past his ear, like a giant hornet blown down the wind, and a split part of a second afterward the report of the rifle clanged, sounding small and far through the thin mountain air.

It struck at Gore like a hand clapped across his face. He started back, tripped his heel on a jutting rock fragment, fell heavily and rolled half a dozen turns of his body down the slope. There, with surprise and the shock of the blow, he lay half stunned and only vaguely saw the form of a man race into his shack and instantly dart out again, lunging along under the weight of the silver pack, a rifle slung in one hand.

It was a long shot—far too long for such an inexpert hand as that of Gore. But he scrambled to his knees at once and tugged out his revolver.

A nearer enemy, however, rose in the path of the Mexican as that worthy fled. For here a tall man jumped out from the edge of the woods and thrust a revolver fairly under his nose.

The Mexican did as he had done when Gore first surprised him. He dropped the canvas sack—he dropped his rifle also—and darted at full speed toward the woods.

"Stop!" barked the stranger, poising his gun with a carelessness which made Gore wonder. "Stop, or I'll salt you down, greaser!"

The Mexican merely dodged like a teal shooting down the wind. There was no bullet from the revolver of the newcomer, and the fugitive was once more safe.

"Well, old son," said the tall man, "if my damned gat has clogged, I'll get you with my bare hands."

He was off at once, at a speed which made heavy-footed Gore gasp with amazement. There was a brief crashing among the shrubbery followed by a wild screech of terror that sent waves of uneasiness through

the body of Jim Gore. He hoped that the tall stranger
had not sent a bullet through the body of the greaser.
No, there had been no sound of a gun. A knife thrust,
then——

A crackling began in the brush. Out stepped the
Mexican with his arms tied securely behind his back
and the tall youth sauntering in the rear. As he passed
the fallen sack, he gave it a thrust with his boot and
out tumbled a blackened bar of silver. At this, he
whistled softly—leaned for a single glance which, Jim
Gore felt, probably told that eagle-eyed youngster as
much as his own patient observation and study of an
hour had told him—and then marched his prisoner up
to Gore.

What the miner saw was a flat-faced Mexican with
a very dusky skin, bright little eyes—a stupid and
honest face rather than a malicious one, Gore thought.
The fellow was very frightened; he was trembling
visibly. But Jim Gore could not pay much attention
to such a person with the tall youth so near. He was
a flame of a man, tall, and as supple and strong as a
steel spring, with a face as manly as it was unhand-
some—a bold, keen, hawklike face.

Striding against the wind on an untracked mountainside, Gore had once come upon a cougar crouched
over the body of a deer, and he had jerked up his
rifle and fired—and missed. Then, as the tawny monster slid away among the rocks, a sense of terror and
helplessness had passed through the soul of the miner.
The same sensation went through him now.

"Here you are," said the stranger. "Here's your
greaser. You can serve him up boiled or fried, or
put him on a spit and roast him, or beat him up like
dough first and then bake him an a slow fire!"

The smile of Gore was rather forced, for something
told him that this wild young man was making these
remarks rather in earnest than in jest. Certainly his
expression remained serious.

"But," went on the stranger, "what's it all about?
I'm not curious, but when I find bar silver wearing

a coat of arms in its buttonhole and a couple of generations of black on its face—I begin to wonder."

In half a minute Gore had told the story. The young stranger listened with a polite attention.

"Then," said he, "I have an idea that you're on the trail of something rich. A regular treasure, stranger!"

This polite cordiality was not exactly what Gore wanted. He looked at the greaser first, and then down to the yellow curving of the San Filipo through the valley and the tiny white ruins of the town—a toy which one could put in the palm of the hand—It was a very large task which lay before him, Gore felt, and it would require for its solution a good many more brains than he himself possessed.

"My name is Gore," said he.

"My name is Chris," nodded the other.

"Chris," said the miner, "I ain't got a claim staked out on this job. But I'd like to stake it out if I could get a man-sized partner to throw in with me."

The smile of the other was like a flash of light.

"I think that's sense," said he. "You'll find I'm worth my keep before the party is over. Do we shake on it?"

Their hands closed. The grip of the young man was as light and as soft as the touch of a girl's hand. That uncalloused hand was not familiar with labor, Gore could guess. But no matter what this fellow might be, Gore felt that he already knew too much to be excluded from the mystery. Whether he was worthy of it or not, he would have to be trusted!

"The first thing," said Chris briskly, "is to find the back trail of the greaser. And the best way is to make him talk."

CHAPTER VI

The Doctor Explains

There was no doubt as to this, and Gore asked the first question.

"Where does this stuff come from, partner?"

No light came in the dull eyes of the Mexican. Chris broke into the smoothest Spanish:

"We are your fathers, my child." said he. "And we do not wish to see our children worn out with hard work carrying such heavy stuff. Tell us where you found it, and there will be no more trouble for you. We will take the labor off your hands!"

He grinned broadly as he spoke, but still the eyes of the Mexican were unlighted by comprehension. Chris winked aside to the miner. Then he tore out his gun and proved that it was now in working order by blowing the corner off a jagged rock near by. After that he jammed the fuming muzzle into the belly of the Mexican.

"Yellow-faced dog!" said he. "Our friends the buzzards are hungry and it is time that we should feed them. Do you understand?"

A flash of terror crossed the eyes of the poor man. But in an instant his face was as blank as ever. Chris shoved the gun back into its holster with an oath.

"He's a tough old egg," said he. "We'll have to put on the screws, Jim!"

"Which?" said Gore.

"Toast his feet for him. That'll make him chatter a bit!"

But Gore shook his head resolutely.

"I can't stand for that sort of a game," he declared. "It goes sort of ag'in me."

"Turn your back, then, and go up and do some housework. I'll promise you that I won't hurt him much. He'll be able to do a day's work after I'm through with him!"

It was very much against the grain of Jim Gore. But when a man has been half an inch from death he is not apt to be too tender with his would-be assassin. He turned his back obediently. But he was sweating when he reached the cabin. There he sat down and faced the wall, his muscles tensed, his jaw set.

Down the hillside he could hear the voice of his new partner talking softly to the prisoner—then a pause—then more soft talking. What was happening in those pauses? It turned the soul of the miner cold to think of it!

Presently a frightful groan brought him leaping to his feet, and he whirled with a shout.

"Stop it, man! Damned if I can stand it!"

What tall Chris had done he never knew, but he saw his new companion rise slowly from beside the body of the Mexican, which was stretched upon the ground. He stirred the other with his boot and the Mexican staggered to his feet. A touch of the knife freed his hands.

"Get out!" commanded Chris, and waved toward the woods.

There was no speed in the departure of the Mexican. He went staggering, with his head fallen on one side and a contorted face which made Jim Gore sick for days thereafter. It was a sight which haunted his dreams.

But Chris was perfectly cheerful.

"You should have held out five minutes more— thirty seconds more," said he amiably. "I was working him up to the right point. I was kneading him, you might say, and getting him just ready for the oven. He was just on the point of getting talkative when you yapped, Gore!"

Jim Gore was sweating with cold horror. He broke out: "What sort of a man are you, stranger? I've seen 'em big and little, hard as wood and hard as iron, but I'm damned if I ever seen 'em hard as you!"

He felt that he had gone a little too far, for the cold eyes of the younger man studied him gravely for an instant. Then Chris shrugged his shoulders, as though he had decided not to take offense.

"I don't mind telling you," said he, "that you ought to drop down into Mexico. When you get below the river you find that things have a different face. I was only talking to that fellow in his own language—which I understand as well as he does. I've talked—and I've listened to that sort of thing! Look here!"

He rolled up the sleeve of his left arm. It exposed to the eye of Jim Gore a surface curiously engraved with white scars, some of them short, some long, and twisting well around the surface of the arm.

"How the devil did that happen?" asked the miner, horrified.

"You'd never guess," said Chris, smiling as he rolled down the sleeve. "It would make a story that would cost you a bit of sleep—and I don't wish to shock you. But that will help you to understand me when I say that I know their language—all of it!"

Jim Gore could guess at enough to make him stare.

"All right," said he. "Maybe I yapped too soon. But when I heard that poor cayuse snort, it sort of curled up my stomach inside of me. How come you to fall out with 'em—south of the river?"

"That's too long a story," said the other carelessly. "But I'll tell you this much—that is my own country!"

"What?" cried Gore.

"My own country! I've only borrowed the States. I don't really belong here."

There was no real mirth in his smile.

"My full name," he went on, "is Señor Don Cristobal Jose Rodrigo Orthez Estaban."

"Good heavens," murmured Jim Gore. "How can a gent wear all of a name like that—in hot weather, too!"

"I like to travel light," grinned Señor Estaban.

"That's one reason I came north of the river. Partly because you might say that I was invited to travel north, and partly because I like to go with a light pack. Well, I got what I wanted. If you've ever heard any of my names up here, you know that they're short."

Jim Gore scanned him again. Every moment he had increasing doubts about this hawk-faced youth.

"I live sort of lonely," said he. "You might say that I live sort of without hearing news. I dunno that I've ever heard of Chris before. What's the last name?"

"Some people call me Chris Estaban," said the other, looking fixedly at him. "Others call me simply Chris. I think I prefer that name. Then there are chunks of the range which call me 'The Doctor.'"

"The Doctor?" echoed Jim Gore. "How come? Are you a sure-enough sawbones?"

"I'm handy in all sorts of odd ways," smiled the young fellow. "But you might say that some folks drive right at the heart of things and some folks just trim around the edges—the same way that a doctor does!"

He cast at the miner a glance of mingled amusement and recklessness.

"You see?" said he.

And, at the same time, he brought out not only the gun from the holster but as expertly with his left hand another Colt which had been hidden in his clothes.

"Some folks," said The Doctor, firing with his left-hand gun as he spoke, "aim for nothing but the bull's-eye."

He fired with the right-hand weapon and Jim Gore noted two white splotches on the face of a black stone thirty paces away.

"But other folks, like a doctor, just trim around the edges, because they don't like to take chances with the real inwards of a man. They simply cut off the spare timber—as you might say!"

While he spoke, the guns chattered alternately, at

every pause. Eleven shots in quick succession, and now a beautifully symmetrical pattern appeared on the stone. It was a perfect circle, each white splotch where a bullet had struck the heavy stone being placed with geometrical exactness at an even distance from its neighbors—eleven white spots sketching the circle on the rock.

"And so," said The Doctor, as he broke open his guns and began to reload them with a lightning speed, "some folks have called me The Doctor because they've noticed the way I operate—without any losses of life. Except," he added grimly, "a couple of times when the knife slipped—as you might say!"

Jim Gore walked slowly down to the rock and kneeled almost reverently before it. He touched those deep indentations one by one. He picked up the flattened bits of lead which were scattered under the face of the stone. He examined the truth with which that circle had been drawn. Then he rose with a sigh and walked even more slowly back toward his companion.

"I see." said Jim.

"What?" asked The Doctor, a little sharply.

"I dunno," drawled Jim Gore. "I hope that I don't see too much."

"I guess you don't," admitted The Doctor. "However, I've been in jail only three or four times, and never stayed long enough to carve my initials on the stones."

"Maybe," suggested Jim Gore, speaking with the same thoughtful slowness, "maybe you wear other names, too?"

"Only a few," confessed this talented rascal. "A good many people call me 'Colonel Dice,' however."

"Colonel Dice? You been in the army?"

"Why, they gave me that name, I suppose, because at times the ivories seemed to be pretty well under my command. But there's never been more than two in my regiment!"

He chuckled as he spoke, and Jim Gore blinked.

What amazed him most of all was the perfect frankness with which this man admitted that he was a combination of gunman and gambler. The explanation he determined to get if he could.

CHAPTER VII

The Sound of Bells

"Colonel," said he, "I dunno that I quite understand how you come to spill all the facts out like this."

"Not all," said The Doctor with a touch of grimness. "Oh, not all, Gore—just a part. And I'll tell you why. Sometimes I have a lot of crooks and slick birds around me, and then they never know me. But sometimes I meet an honest man, and when I do, I don't want to pull the wool over his eyes. Now, Gore, you've had a chance to hear the facts about me. I haven't explained them. Perhaps if you had more of the explanation I wouldn't seem such a hard chap. But I'm hard enough, at that. Oh, I'm plenty hard enough. But I give you a chance to look the whole affair over. Now that you know a bit of me as I am, you can back out of the deal that we've just made. Say the word and I pike down across the valley and into the hills on the far side, the way I was headed when I stepped out and met you. Or, if you want, I'll stay on and we'll try to work out this silver game together."

Jim Gore, like the honest soul that he was, brooded upon this matter for a moment, and then he spoke his thoughts, singly and aloud.

"If I tackle this job alone, I got an idea that I'll run into a nest of foxes with wolves' teeth. And if I take you in with me, I'm liable to work with a gent that argues with lead. I've got to put the whole game into your hands—or else have nothin' to do with you. And if I tackle the job all by myself, most likely the only thing I'll gather in will be six inches of knife stuck in my back. Take it all in all, I think that I've got to hand half the cards to you, Colonel Dice!"

"That sounds good to me," murmured the youth. "I like the way you talk, Gore. You don't dodge around the corners. You keep out in the open."

"I aim to do that always," announced the prospector.

"Now, look here," said The Doctor, "I've showed you my hand. You know what my trumps are, and how I'm apt to play them. I think you understand, too, that you haven't enough aces up your sleeve to beat me if I want to use all of my cards. But I'm going to tell you this, besides: as long as you keep in the open and treat me honestly, you'll find that I'm the straightest man that ever pulled in harness with you. The minute you dodge into cover and play fox, I'll play wolf—and damned pronto! Do we understand each other?"

Jim Gore cleared his throat and then wiped his brow. But after a moment he was able to smile again.

"After all," said he, "when a man is breaking hard ground, he has to work with high-power powder. Doctor, I guess that you and me may hit it off pretty well together!"

"Good!" said the Colonel. "Then we're fixed. And the first thing is a bit of chuck. I don't mind saying that I've eaten nothing but my belt for the last day and a half."

Jim Gore, looking down a the mid-section of his companion, saw that the belt, as a matter of fact, had been drawn to the very last notch. The tall youth was as lean-bellied as a grayhound.

So they set about their preparations for the evening meal, and those preparations were made with wonderful speed. For the stranger, though he could have known nothing about the arrangements in the cabin, seemed to guess them by instinct. It was as though he smelled out the location of the bacon and the other provisions and knew by instinct where the pots and pans were kept.

And, where Jim Gore made one movement, the stranger made half a dozen. Never had Gore seen such smooth, unhurrying activity. The fire was swept together as by magic and the flame commenced leaping until Gore cried out: "We're lightin' a pretty bright candle, partner. Maybe the greaser will come back and use it to sight a gun by!"

But The Doctor merely laughed as he worked.

"That greaser friend of mine," said he, "figures that he has had a face-to-face conversation with one of the principal devils, and unless I'm very wrong, he's going to avoid this section of the mountains as though it were the hottest part of hell from this time on. He might have come back to pot-shot at you. But now that I've arrived—and remained—I think that you won't have any more trouble with him!"

It was not spoken in vanity, but rather as a calm presentation of facts of importance, and Jim Gore straight-way dismissed all care from his mind. This young man was not apt to be wrong!

And then the cooking of supper being finished, Jim Gore sat back and watched such trencher work as he had never seen before. Yet The Doctor found time and ability to talk even as he consumed his food. All that was within reach slid down his gullet with amazing steadiness; and when all else was ended, the great pot of beans began to disappear, until finally the big iron spoon was grating on the bottom of the kettle. More than this, when the food was gone, there remained the coffee—a quart of it—of which Gore accepted one half cup and the tall stranger took the rest and stowed it boiling hot as though it were water. After that, his belt loosened to the first notch, he jumped up and scoured the dishes clean, singing as he worked. And Jim Gore looked on and helped as he could, admiring and pleased. He foresaw that this man would be an excellent camping companion. And that is the highest praise which one Westerner can give to another.

Then The Doctor stretched himself on the outer rim of the light of the dying fire with his coat rolled under his head. He uttered one deep groan of satisfaction and relief, and lay for a moment with his eyes closed.

Jim Gore had an impression that this man had not closed his eyes for whole days before this moment. And he had an impression, also, that the man could have gone on for other days, delving for his support into a mine of inexhaustible energy supplied by a well of nerve power which could hardly be drained dry.

Then Colonel Dice began to smoke, consuming a cigarette in a few swift inhalations, and then rolling another with marvelously active and sure fingers. One hand shook in the tobacco and the other hand, without the supervision of the eyes, twisted the paper into a cornucopia-shaped, Mexican-style cigarette.

How much Mexican was in this man the prospector could not tell. His eyes and his hair, to be sure, were black. But his skin was far whiter than the skin of Gore himself. Perhaps Spanish, rather than Mexican blood, flowed in his veins.

However, Jim Gore decided that it would be useless for him to attempt to understand his new companion entirely. There were sure to remain certain phases of his nature which were beyond the ken of his own simple mind. So Jim felt that he should accept the character of The Doctor just as it was unfolded before him, without attempting to guess too much at what might lie behind the veil.

In this silent fashion the next few moments passed, and then:

"You got riding boots on your feet," said Jim. "I suppose that they ain't the most comfortable for mountain travel."

"If you run on your toes," said The Doctor, "riding boots aren't so bad. Besides, you see that I don't wear the extra-high heels. Matter of fact, I've found that I've had to use the fast feet about as often as I've had to use fast hoofs, and I wear boots that serve the double purpose."

"But," said Jim, eying the boots carefully by the dim light of the fire and noticing that they we not greatly worn or scratched, "you haven't been tramping very long in those boots."

"Only half a day," said the gambler calmly.

"Your hoss give out?"

"The bullet," said The Doctor, "didn't hit him in a vital spot. The poor devil kept going for another ten miles. And by that time I had shaken them off. I took a blind trail and the blockheads behind me thought that I had run into a trap. But where the trail stopped I went right on over the rough country and turned it into a short cut. The horse dropped in the next ravine —rolled a hundred feet down into the bottom of the cut, as a matter of fact—but I managed to jump out of the saddle just as he started falling. That's how I happen to be here. In the meantime, those two posses have—"

"*Two* posses?" gasped Jim Gore.

"Oh, yes. A couple of towns joined hands in the good work of taking me in a net. But there are holes in a net, you see. And there's always a little space between *two* nets. One of those gangs rode right on behind me. The other lot took the long way round and thought that they'd head me off. But I was gone before they came up with my trail."

"Then they'll be along here?" cried Gore.

"They will not," chuckled the fugitive. "I made a little trail problem that'll keep them busy for quite some time. And what they make out of it, uness I'm very mistaken, will head them back north again to hunt for me there!"

His chuckle turned into a laugh.

"It was a very pleasant ride, Gore! But a damned hungry one. However, it's better to play a game than to eat, eh?"

But Jim Gore returned no response. He was too busy fumbling toward the ideas which seemed to be moving in the brain of The Doctor. But he could make nothing out of them. This was a sort of man beyond his ken. He was glad that he had determined beforehand to make no real effort to decipher the hidden features of The Doctor's character. Here, already, he had come to a blind wall.

"What's that?" asked Colonel Dice, suddenly sitting up.

There was a faint chattering of glassware, a fainter chiming of pots and pans in the little lean-to of the miner.

"An earthquake?" asked the Colonel.

"They come prretty frequent here," said Gore.

"Listen!" cautioned The Doctor.

Out of the depths of the valley, like a deeper, dimmer echo of the noise which had ended in the shack behind them, the sound of distant bells welled up to them—the bells of San Filipo!

CHAPTER VIII

The Start

Jim Gore was already upon his feet, while his new friend remained sitting, with his ear inclined toward the earth and one hand raised for perfect silence. But so faint was that melody of far-off bells that the first puff of wind, sighing about them, cut off the music. And when the wind died again the sound had died also.

Yet The Doctor remained in his attentive position for another moment.

He said at last: "Is there a church in San Filipo?"

"There's the wreck of a church!" said Jim Gore.

"With bells, though?"

"No! Not a bell. The bell tower went down with a smash when the town and the church was burned."

"No bells?" echoed The Doctor.

"Not one."

"Then what does it mean, old son?"

"Ghosts!" cried Jim Gore, the words fairly bursting from his throat. "That's the long and short of what it means!"

"Look here," chuckled The Doctor, "I'm a very credulous sort of a fellow. And I'm specially parital to ghosts. But what do you mean by the ghosts of bells?"

Jim Gore was busy for a moment catching his breath and mopping his brow.

"I ain't no soothsayer," he declared at last. "I dunno nothing about ghosts and don't *want* to know nothing. But I'll tell you that them are ghost bells that you hear down yonder in the valley. Yep, they come from the bells of the old church—dead bells— bells that ain't got no body no more'n a spook has! They hunted through that damn church, but they ain't found no bells left. The bells ain't there—but the voices of the bells still stick!"

The Doctor did not laugh again. He remained most soberly silent.

When he spoke again it was to say gravely: "When do we start down to have a look at the old town, partner?"

"Some other night—not this night!" exclaimed Jim Gore. "I got the creeps already, and I'm free to say it!"

"Buck up!" murmured The Doctor. "I think that this is the very night we should start. What do the people in the town say? Have they heard those bells before?"

"Not long ago they heard 'em, and they say that they's an old saying in the valley—that San Filipo is gunna be rich again when the bells of San Filipo begin to ring once more. Well, I dunno but what they's something in it. The greaser has found a bunch of silver down there."

"Where could it have come from?"

"All across the other side of the valley—there used to be a pack of silver mines there. If there was moonlight, even by the moonshine you could see the dumps from clear over here."

"Ah!" sighed The Doctor. "I begin to understand!" His hands became intensely active.

"What are you doin'?" asked Jim Gore.

"I'm chucking the bullets out of these guns and cleaning them. I hate dirty guns when there's a chance of running into a little flock of wild trouble floating through the sky like a bunch of geese. I hate dirty guns when a time like that comes."

"Doctor, d'you aim to go down to that town tonight?"

"Of course!"

"Curse it!" pleaded Jim Gore, "I tell you that I feel sort of curled up and weak inside of me! Let's wait till tomorrow!"

The Doctor laughed softly. And his laughter put every nerve of Jim Gore on edge.

"Heads up!" said the gambler. "When you see trouble, the thing to do is not to sit still, but get up—with a gun in each hand—and go asking questions. Or better still, go ready to use your own eyes. Do you believe me?"

"You may be right. But I got an idea that it would be a lot more peaceful right up here in this shack tonight."

"Who wants peace?" said The Doctor. "What do we live for? The trees and the stones and the mountains have plenty of peace. But dogs and horses and men—they live to use their hands and their heels and their—teeth, Jim! The more action, the more life. Otherwise, we might as well go to sleep and keep on sleeping till the end of time! No, no, Jim, we don't want peace!"

Jim Gore chewed a liberal chunk from the corner of his plug of Star tobacco.

"You got a nice, smooth way of talkin'," said he. "I enjoy hearin' you a lot. But I got to say that from my way of lookin' at things, I differ from you. I take off my hat to you. I wish you all the kinds of trouble that is invented or that grows natural in these here mountains—which by my way of thinkin' is plenty. One greaser floatin' around through these here hills ready to soak a knife into the innards of you—that, by my figurin', is plenty of trouble for any one man, even if he is full growed like you. But for me, Doctor—I like sleep, plenty of sleep! And as far as ghosts go—I say, give 'em room. Don't crowd 'em none!"

The Doctor was laughing again in the soft way that went through and through the soul of Jim Gore.

"Partner," said he, "I think you'll change your mind."

"Not me!"

"Well, then, do you want to stay up here in the night with the greaser, all alone? Or do you want to go down to San Filipo with me—and meet the ghosts?"

Jim Gore groaned. "That's a terrible choice to have to make!"

"I'm sorry. But take your choice. After all, partner, the ghost of a bell won't hold a knife at your head."

"You're young," said the miner gloomily, "and bein' young, you ain't particular believin'. But when you get older, and by the time that you're my age, you'll find out that they's plenty of things in this here little old world that don't bear no explainin'. They's plenty of things that has to be took hold of with gloves, and they's plenty that don't want no handlin' at all!"

"I believe you," said the younger man calmly. "The question now is, though, will you come along with me and take your chances with me?"

"Ah, well," sighed Jim Gore, "I dunno whether to thank Heaven that I'm old enough to have sense, or to wish that I was young again, and had plenty of nerve!"

"Well?"

"I suppose that I'll go along. Otherwise every time I hear a whisper in the wind, I'll figger that you're lyin' down yonder in that damned town with your throat cut from ear to ear, and that what I'm hearing out of the wind is the whisperin' of your ghost come back to tell me that I was a quitter for not goin' down—and gettin' my own throat cut, too!"

"Good!" said The Doctor cheerfully. "Then we start!"

"We start. Wait a minute till I take a look at my gat."

"Take a good look. I'll brisk up the fire for you."

He stirred the embers to a flame and by that flame Jim Gore went over his weapon slowly and carefully. When he was ended in that examination, he stood up with another sigh which was very like a groan.

"Are you ready, old-timer?"

"Oh, I'm ready, I suppose. There'll be luck on this trip, though."

"Do your old scars begin to ache?" smiled The Doctor.

"They begin to get fever and shootin' pains," sighed Jim Gore. "But, come on, you young blood lover. I'll stick to your shoulder steady enough, and if you don't take no back steps, you'll find that I'll go as far forward as you do!"

"I believe you," murmured The Doctor.

And they swung down the steep slope into the valley side by side.

There was little conversation. It seemed to Jim Gore that the traveling wind as it passed his ears carried whispers of warning, and with every step that he took his heart felt more cold. He would have turned back a dozen times on the way, had it not been for the dauntless carriage of his companion, who went ahead with his chin raised high and with a careless way of humming and of whistling. New tunes and old came softly from his lips as he walked.

"Look here!" broke out Jim Gore at last.

"Well?"

"I'd like to ask you one honest question."

"And I'll answer it honestly if I can. I don't mind questions from a friend."

"Then tell me, man to man—d'you really feel as happy as you sound and as you look?"

The Doctor did not laugh.

"I'll tell you the truth," said he. "Down in my inwards I'm about the worst-scared man in this valley— not even excepting you."

An oath of astonishment exploded on the lips of Gore.

"D'you mind tellin' me, then, why in the name of the Almighty you want to plug away at this here little game tonight—you bein' so very scared, as you say?"

"Why," said the irrepressible Doctor, "that's what really makes it fun. Because, Jim, if we weren't frightened almost to death, there'd be no game at all. It would simply be like betting on a sure thing!"

Jim Gore threw up his hands.

"Is that the way you feel about it—honest?"

"That's the way I feel about it, honest!"

"By Heaven!" breathed Jim Gore, filled with great awe. "I got to say that you plumb beat me!"

CHAPTER IX

A Song in the Night

A thin sickle of a moon rode through the eastern sky as they reached the valley bottom and approached the village of ruins. And they heard, far away, the strumming of a guitar—a pulse, rather than a musical sound —and then the singing of a gay tenor voice. The Doctor paused and raised a hand. Jim Gore stopped also, and above the noise of their heavy breathing, and the creaking of Jim's thick cowhide boots as he stirred uneasily, the song went on, soared to a thrilling climax and then died away.

"Well?" said Jim Gore, feeling that his strange companion had found something worth notice in this singing.

"Did you say that that town was empty of people?" asked The Doctor.

"Pretty nigh. They's a few lyin' around and sleepin' in the sun all day and yappin' out their songs like that in the night. Why?"

"Because that's not yapping. That is singing, and there's a difference. The fellow who sang that song may lie around during the day, but he has done better things than that in his life. He has studied music where it is really taught. He has worked pretty hard, old son, to learn how to sing like that."

"Worked?" exclaimed the miner. "Are you jokin', Doctor? How come that singin' could be work?"

"More work," said the other deliberately, as they started on again, "than you'll put in at your mine. It means working with your strength until you're tired, and working with your brains, too, all the time!"

"I dunno," said Jim Gore, "that I foller the drift to what you got to say about that, Doctor. You're a smart feller, but I'd like to have you show me how it come that makin' a noise is worth workin' to learn how to do!"

"I'll tell you," said Colonel Dice. "Some people open their throats and do what you say—simply make a noise. And others make music. And the ones who make music are very well paid for it. Very well paid! Think of a man, partner, getting a thousand dollars a week for simply singing a few moments every night!'

"A thousand dollars a week!" echoed the miner, pausing and taking off his hat, as though to let this mighty thought work more freely into his brain. "A thousand dollars a week. You ain't stuffin' me, I guess."

"Oh, that's a fact. And for the really great singers a thousand dollars a night."

"Great heavens!" whispered Jim Gore. "That'd be

three pounds of gold all worked out and clear profit. Gosh, will you think of that?"

"Or—a few of them—three thousand dollars every time they come out and sing!"

The prostration of Jim's mind before facts like these was complete. He mopped his brow and refused to walk any farther until he had grappled with this mighty problem.

"Now, Doctor," said he, "will you tell me how folks come to be so simple that they'd pay big money to hear a gent yap?"

"Do I seem like a simple man, Jim?"

"Simple? You? Simple like arithmetic, than which there ain't nothin' more unsimple. That's how simple you are, partner! Simple like a dog-gone vein that's pinchin' out and turnin' corners in quartzite. But you don't mean to tell me, Doctor, that you've spent time and money goin' out of your way to listen to yappin' like that?"

"Not very much better yapping than that!" was the reply. "Wait a minute! There he goes again!"

They were nearer, now, and though the voice was so softened by distance that the lower notes were felt rather than heard, yet there was much more body to the music he made, and Colonel Dice swayed his head in rhythm with the strain.

"No, by Jove!" said he, as that song ended in turn. "I've paid good money and lots of it to hear fellows who yapped not a whit better than our friend yonder with the guitar. That man could make a very handsome salary on the stage, I tell you!"

"Well," said Jim Gore, "he ain't gunna. Because if he's the gent that I got in mind, he ain't never been outside of San Filipo. He told me so."

"Who do you mean?" asked The Doctor.

And Jim Gore told him, briefly, how he had seen Diego Ramirez sitting idly in front of the ruined house of his ancestors.

"And you think that he's the fellow who's singing now?" asked Cristobal Estaban.

"I got no manner of doubt about it. He had a face like he could sing pretty good."

"What do you mean by that?"

"You seem a mite heated up about this greaser."

"He's no greaser, my friend. No greaser ever spoke perfect Spanish like that! Listen again—no, by Heaven —not Spanish this time, but the purest Italian."

"Is that the way dago sounds?"

"That's the way! So this fellow sits in front of his house and wastes all of every day?"

"That's what he does."

"And he's never been away from San Filipo?"

"He says that him and his folks has always lived there for more generations than I got years under my belt, almost!"

"Then," said The Doctor, "he is an admirable liar. I can tell you that. He has studied—in Paris, most likely. What's his appearance?"

"Maybe eighteen, maybe twenty-five. I don't read a greaser none too clear."

"Nearer twenty-five than eighteen, I should say. What's the look of him?"

"Mighty pretty. Pretty enough to be a girl. Lazy lookin' like a girl, too!"

"Humph!" said The Doctor, "not too lazy to study like the devil when he learned how to sing. Not too lazy to learn how to lie like a young devil."

"I dunno that I could say that he was lyin'!" said Jim Gore, remembering the apparent frankness of the ragged youth. "But he didn't look like nothin' much— I'll tell you that. He looked like pretty near nothin' at all!"

"What the devil could he be doing up here?" said The Doctor, thinking aloud.

"Settin' in the sun and hatchin' cob-webby dreams," suggested his rough companion. "He had that sort of a look about him. Looked like it would pretty nigh kill him to have to do a lick of work."

"It sounds," said The Doctor, paying no heed at all to this interpretation, "like a gentleman."

"Gentleman? He's poorer than me, and I ain't no millionaire. But I am compared with him."

"Don't you see?" said his companion. "That's the very point. Here's a fellow come to San Filipo—for it's absurd to think that he learned Italian and how to sing it in that heap of ruins—here's a fellow come to San Filipo, living like a low beggar and spending his days, apparently, sitting idly in the sun. And yet, if he has nothing else, he has a voice which is worthy of bringing him in a good living on any stage in any country."

"Maybe he don't know it no more than I do," suggested Gore.

"An idea which is not worth a snap!" replied The Doctor. "Because in the place where he learned how to sing the cash value of a good voice is perfectly appreciated. There he begins again—just the guitar, this time. And he handles even it like an artist. An artist he is—sitting here mooning through the days, talking about his decayed ancestry, and changing gossip with the loafers in the town. That's how his days are spent."

"Sure. I seen that with my own eyes."

"But what about his rights, Gore?"

"What do you mean by that?"

"Just as much as I say, and no more! While we are dodging the ghosts of those old bells, I think that we'll have to do a little inquiring into the nature of that young fellow with the fine voice and the ragged clothes. Ragged clothes?"

He shook his head dejectedly, as though this point worried him a good deal.

"After all," said Gore, "what difference does it make?"

"This difference, son. Every queer fellow in San Filipo may be hunting for the same thing, exactly, that we're hunting for! And so we have to keep our eyes open. Who's that?"

They were close to the village now, and across the field near by a fleet shadow ran.

"Hello!" called The Doctor. And then in Spanish: "Why do you run, friend?"

The shadow dodged in the thin moonshine as though it had seen a leveled gun. And in another instant The Doctor had leaped in pursuit. The boy ran fast as a darting terrier, but The Doctor leaped behind like a long-striding greyhound. Presently he overtook the shadow and came straight back to Jim Gore with a youngster of thirteen or fourteen trussed over his arm.

"He's too scared to talk," said The Doctor. "Let him sit down and get his wind."

He deposited the boy on the ground and there the youngster sat quaking and gasping in his breath.

"So," said The Doctor gently at last. "What is the matter, my boy?"

There was only a frightened groan.

"What is your name?"

"Filipo, señor."

"Are you named after the town?"

"After the blessed saint, señor."

"Quite right. And why did you not stop when I called? Why did you not answer me, my friend?"

"Ah, señor, forgive me!"

"Of course I do. I only ran after you because you tried to run away, you know. "I'm not going to harm you. Why the devil did you run?"

"Ah. kind señor, I thought it was the ghost coming for me!"

CHAPTER X

A Boy's Story

"Good!" murmured The Doctor.

"We are getting nearer to the ghost every moment, Gore!"

"I don't like it," said Jim Gore. "Joking about this sort of thing is mighty like to be dangerous, Doctor!"

"Don Cristobal is my name," said his companion, softly but sharply. "That is my name, señor."

"Sure, Don Cristobal," grinned Gore.

"But the ghost——" The Doctor spoke to the boy.

"Heaven shield us from it!" breathed the boy.

"Brave Filipo! We will help to shield you—my friend and I."

"I am no coward," said Filipo, rising from the dust and facing them in the filmy moonlight. "I can fight boys my own size. I have fought until I was all blood, and I have not cared. But the ghost——"

"That is different, of course!"

"Of course, señor! That is very different! Can you find four grown men in the village who will go to the convent at night?"

"I suppose not."

"Indeed, they will not go. And who can blame them?"

"I have never heard of this ghost, except vaguely, Filipo. Why is it so feared?"

"Because when she is seen, a man will grow dumb and never be able to speak again."

"Frightful!" said The Doctor, in his gentle voice. "Are there any dumb men in the village now?"

"Not that I have known. But my father remembers that when he was young there was an old man who had seen the ghost and therefore had become dumb."

"Really?"

"It is very true. My father would tell you."

"Did that old man talk about what he had seen?"

"Señor—being dumb, how could he talk?"

"With signs, I thought. But perhaps he wrote what he saw?"

"He could not write, señor."

"You see," said The Doctor to Gore in English, "how stories grow up. A man becomes dumb—perhaps he was born dumb. He cannot write. But it is said that he has seen the ghost. How was it learned?"

He returned to the boy.

"Let us walk on into the village together. We will guard you, Filipo."

"I thank you, señor."

"This ghost—is it known who she is?"

"She is a young nun, señor."

"That is attractive."

"She is very beautiful, men say."

"Those who have seen her say so?"

"I cannot tell, señor. I only know what is told me."

"Right. The beautiful young nun—why does she haunt the nunnery?"

"It happened many years ago, before I was born—before my father, also. But all men know that it is true."

"I shall believe you implicitly."

"When San Filipo burned, on the day that the dam was broken——"

"I think I have heard of that."

"On that day, when the flames reached the nunnery and the nuns ran away from the fire, there was one young girl who had just become a member of the order. And she was telling her beads when the flames came. Her sisters called to her:

" 'Alicia—the fire!'

" 'I have nearly ended!' said she, and continued on her knees.

"They ran out then and left her, and the fire grew,

and the nunnery began to smoke, and still Alicia did not come out."

"Poor girl,!" said Don Cristobal. "I can see it—I can see her and the cursed beads——"

"Did you say, Señor——"

"Nothing. Get on with your story!"

"One of the nuns, a very brave woman, ran back with her cloak wet and thrown over her head. She ran through fire and smoke. She came to the room and there was Alicia on her knees with the smoke rolling in and the fire leaping along the floor.

" 'Alicia! Alicia!' she called to her. 'Come with me, in Heaven's name!'

" 'I come at once, sister!' said Alicia. 'I have almost ended!'

" 'Come now, or you will burn!'

"But then a great wall of flame rose in front of the older sister and forced her to run back to her friends on the outside of the nunnery. And, after that, Alicia was never seen, but the roof of the convent fell in a little later, and they knew that she was dead!"

"A frightful thing!" said The Doctor gravely.

"Afterwards, when the stones were cool enough, they went in and they searched in that room, but there was no trace of her burned body. And they searched in all of the convent, but not a bone of her was found. It was a great mystery, for certainly she could not have escaped from the fire! Do you not think that it was a great mystery?"

"Prodigious!" said The Doctor.

"But in the next year, when the fire was long out, and a man was walking by night between the church and the nunnery, he saw a woman wrapped in a black cloak with a white cloth across her forehead, and her face as white as the cloth and her hands as white as her face. And she walked out from the church and went across to the nunnery, and as she walked she told the beads of the long rosary which hung around her neck. It was the ghost of Alicia, the nun! And it is said that that man could never speak thereafter, but he was forced to write out the thing that he had seen and to warn other men to avoid the nunnery and the church forever, because a curse would come on them and they would be made dumb if they saw the dead girl! And that is the whole story and the true story, just as my father has told it to me, and word for word, he says, as his father before him told him!"

"The Doctor paused and sighed.

"Peace to her poor soul!" said he.

"But she being a holy woman, why should her ghost walk in that place?"

"Perhaps there was a secret sin?" suggested The Doctor.

"Ah, I did not think of that. Perhaps it was that!" said the boy.

"But are you always in fear of this ghost?"

"Ah, señor, not always, but to-night we heard the dead bells of San Filipo. And after they have spoken, it is known that the ghost roams near the town. So when you called to me as I was running home from the cows, it jumped on my back—the fear of the ghost. I would not stop—it was a terrible thing to me, señor!"

"Of course it was. And I am sorry for that!"

"Not that you should be sorry. I was a fool not to have known a man's voice. Well, it is ended now!"

And he shuddered.

"Then the whole village is filled with fear?"

"Except Señor Ramirez."

"That is Diego Ramirez?"

"That is he."

"Is he not afraid?"

"Hush! He is singing again! He is afraid of nothing!"

"How can that be?"

"My mother says it is because he is so lazy that he knows not even a ghost would bother with such a worthless fellow as he is! Consider, señor, that all day he sits in front of his ruin of a house and does nothing but sing and sit, and sit and sing. And so into the night, unless it is to go inside to eat or sleep."

"Does he live on air?"

"When he came back to San Filipo he had a little money, and he lives on that, like a grasshopper living in summer. But when it is all gone, he will have a cold winter!"

And Filipo laughed maliciously.

"He had been away, then?"

"Ah, yes, for many, many years! I have never seen him in my life until a little time ago."

"How long, Filipo?"

"A month, señor? Yes, I think that he has only been here a month."

"Well, he is having a happy time of it, I have no doubt, with his singing."

"Do you think so, señor? My mother says that there is a curse on grown men who are as idle as he!"

"Well, perhaps there is. But I hope not. He sings very well."

"My mother says, 'too well for an honest man!'"

"He is bad, then?"

"No, I know nothing. Only my father says that he will come to no good end. He offered Ramirez fifty cents a day, which is much money, to help him with the herding of the cattle. And he yawned in my father's face.

"'I have still a little money,' said Diego Ramirez. 'When that is gone, then I shall begin to think of working, my friend. But do not spoil my happiness with talk of money and work now!'

"Was not that a rude speech?"

"A terrible thing!" said The Doctor.

"But my father says that when the money of Ramirez is gone he may rot before he will give him work or so much as a crust!"

"That will teach him a lesson, the rascal!"

"Will it not? Here I leave you, señor. For my father's house is down this alley."

"Good night, Filipo, and forgive me for frightening you."

"It was not you, but the thought that was in me of —but I shall not name it. When one is in the village, señor, it is better not to name it!"

"Thank you, Filipo. I shall remember!"

And the boy was gone, walking a pace or two, and then leaping off at full speed as though the fear of the ghost stole out at him from the silent black shadows that fell from the ragged tops of the walls.

CHAPTER XI

The Vision in the Church

The singing had ended and the singer retired when they passed his usual post, which Jim Gore pointed out to The Doctor. The latter did not pause, but he seemed to see enough even in passing to familiarize himself with all that had been the glory of the house of Ramirez.

He expressed his opinions to the miner.

"That was a great house, Gore!" said he. "There was a time when the people in that house lived like princes, you can be sure! In that courtyard there have been big coaches with six or eight blood horses strung out in front of 'em and fellows in livery perched on the seat and behind, and outriders togged out like dukes and earls. There have been more stirrings of silk and lace and gold and plumes and tassels in that house than you have ever seen in your life. That fellow was a little king. And now his descendant sits in the sun all day and whacks a guitar at night. That's really the devil, and I tell you that it must be working on the heart of that Diego Ramirez. He's not what he seems. He's no idler."

"My eyes didn't see what they saw, then," said Jim Gore.

"We'll see what time shows us," said Cristobal Estaban. "In the meantime, let's get on with our hunt."

"Aye, but where do we begin?"

"With the nine ghosts, Jim!"

"What nine ghosts?"

"The bells of San Filipo, old son. Here's the church. Let's duck into this alley."

He led the way, side-stepping into the blackness of the alley. Down it they went, climbing over moldering heaps of the fallen adobe bricks, gradually turning into the dust from which they had first been compacted. Jim Gore, utterly confounded by this boldness, drew his gun and walked second, his frightened eyes busy every moment with all that was around him.

Presently Gore stopped.

"What's that?" said he, pointing.

A jumble of confused, ruined walls, some fallen and some standing, but all more lofty and better preserved than any building in old San Filipo except the church itself, loomed against the sky and the dimness of the moonshine. The reason for their better preservation was not that the hand of time had fallen upon them, but simply that the substance of which those walls had been reared was hewn blocks of stone, a truly mighty masonry.

"The nunnery," said The Doctor.

"Let's get away from it," said Jim Gore, whispering.

"And yet," said The Doctor, "it frightens me enough to make me want to get inside it and look around me there!"

Jim Gore laid a resolute grip on his arm.

"We're after the bells—the ghosts of the bells. Ain't nine ghosts enough for you in one night's work, Doctor?"

"You're right!" sighed The Doctor.

And they went on together until they stood in view

of the church itself. It stood in a dignified isolation. The buildings around it, when they fell, seemed to have sagged back from the house of God. They dropped upon their own foundations, and the church perhaps seemed more huge and substantial now than it had ever appeared before. That was partly because of the dullness of the light by which they viewed it. One of the big stone-built towers had fallen and its fragments lay strewn across the open court near the building. The other tower still remained—the bell tower from which the nine silver throats which were cast in Barcelona had sent their calling up and down the valley of the San Filipo. And looking through the dark arch of the lantern in which they had hung, it seemed that their ghosts *had* been those which had sent the bell-like murmur through the night air and up the hillside where the miner and his new friend waited and watched.

"You see?" whispered Jim Gore. "There ain't anything that we can find. This here has been hunted over about ten thousand times, I s'pose."

"I don't think so," said his companion. "They may have searched it once or twice, but never very hard and never expecting to find anything. There are too many stories about ghosts and what not connected with this church and its vicinity. What did the boy tell us? That the ghost of the dead nun walked out from the bottom of the church——"

"Good heavens!" breathed Jim Gore. "You ain't going in, partner?"

"Have we come all this distance to turn around and go back?"

"Well, we know what the church is now, and we know where the convent is. Dog-gone it, colonel, ain't that enough for one night's work?"

"I think," smiled The Doctor, "that nearly all the other hunters came to the church in a frame of mind like yours—or worse! Because we don't believe in their superstition—we're simply afraid of it by instinct, you might say. But they have religion behind them!"

He added: "Come on, Jim, or else I'll go in by myself."

"Would you do that?" quaked Gore. "Would you go in there all by yourself?"

"Watch me and see!"

But Gore, as he cast a frightened glance around him, decided that it would be less awful to accompany his daring guide than to remain in the open stretch with all the black, eyelike casements of the church in front and the nunnery behind, gazing out upon him. So he freshened his grip upon the revolver and walked well behind Estaban, treading as lightly as he could, and yet making far more noise than the quick and apparently careless stride of the younger man.

They had entered through a fallen door at the base of the church and now Estaban took from a pocket a small electric torch, the light of which he cast far before him. They found themselves in what had once been presumably a cellar, but now it was filled with a vast quantity of junk. Crumbling heaps of adobe brick littered the floor, and among them the vast fragments of a wall which had pitched in. But beyond the wreckage of adobe and stone masonry there was a confusion of half-burned furniture, and there were tangles of wire—how it had come there, who could tell?

They even found heaps of broken glass. In fact, that cellar looked very much like an immense junk heap. Through this confusion they threaded their way, and gradually made the circuit of the foundations. The building had seemed large from the outside, but wandering in this manner through the interior, it was like a little world of its own.

They had reached the farthest corner of the church when the electric torch suddenly went out. They were left plunged in utter blackness, and Jim Gore whispered with chattering teeth:

"Doctor, can't you get it workin' again?"

"I'm trying," whispered the colonel. "I've never had the cursed thing act like this before."

"Is the battery run out?"

"I think not. There's a fresh battery in it. Something out of kilter, I suppose. Well, we'll have to get out by feeling our way, I suppose."

He started ahead and Jim Gore set his teeth to crush back the overwhelming sickness of spirit which had fallen upon him. A wind had raised and a thousand whispers began to stir in the blackness around them.

Luck was with them in another moment, however, for they rounded the corner of the church and stole forward saw before them a large arch from which the outer wall had fallen away, allowing a dimness of moonlight to enter aslant. This would guide them for at least a section of their journey back to the outer world of night.

But just as the heart of Jim Gore strengthened, his leader stopped short and grew rigid. And at the same time Jim Gore was aware of a black-robed figure which left the shadows at the corner of the church and stole forward into the dim moonshine of the arch. The figure was lost in the folds of a sweeping black cloak, and a white inner hood was drawn closely around the white face—the face of the beautiful nun of San Filipo!

Fear sometimes dulls the senses, and sometimes it sharpens them. It sharpened those of Jim Gore. As if in a blaze of sunlight he saw every detail. He noted the dead whiteness of that face—pale as the linen which surrounded it—the wide, blank, unseeing eyes which stared straight before, and the absence of either sorrow or joy from that dead countenance. And he saw the glimmer of the beads of the rosary, and he saw the hands, mortally white as the face itself, which counted the beads as the vision walked forward. He noted, too, that the feet of the nun, stepping among all the fragile débris which littered the floor of the cellar, made no sound. No, though all the sighing of the wind had ceased at that moment, there was not so much as a breath of noise from the sweeping cloak or the stepping feet.

Then she passed from view beyond the pillar—and with that The Doctor came to life again. He leaped straight ahead, but Jim Gore gripped him, and strove to cry out. Strove to cry out—and from his numbed throat not a sound came!

Was it not the curse of which the little boy had told them? And The Doctor himself, turning to beat away the detaining hands of his companion, writhed his lips, but made not the volume of a whisper in sound.

Next he wrenched himself free, and quickly rushed away after the ghostly vision.

Jim Gore followed, stumbling and falling every second step. And when, by luck, he saw a glimmer of light straight before him and following it came panting out in the open court beyond, he found The Doctor standing there already rooted to the spot and with a fallen head.

They exchanged one glance with horror-stricken faces, and then stole together from the wide court and through the black peril of a narrow alley, and so out onto the open street where, far away, they heard the yapping of a dog—or was it a coyote? Even that sound was like a blessing to the frightened ears of the two!

CHAPTER XII

New Arrivals

They needed no interchange of opinions to tell them what they wished to do then. But hurrying straight ahead, they left the jumbled ruins of San Filipo and strode out onto the valley beyond—the blessed open valley with the bright stars and the thin moon about them.

Then: "Thank Heaven, I ain't dumb! I can speak, Chris. Lemme hear you talk!"

"Damnation!" groaned The Doctor. "We've acted like a pair of frightened curs! Gore, why did you lay hands on me in the cellar of the church? I might have caught her!"

"Caught her?" cried the miner. "Good grief, partner, I'd as soon have seen you try to catch the devil himself!"

"Would you? Well, Jim, I didn't catch her. And why not, I can't say to this moment. I was only delayed a moment by you. She seemed to be heading straight out from the cellar of the church—but though I ran faster than any woman could have run, when I got to the courtyard she seemed to have disappeared into thin air."

"Seemed to? Why, man, she did!"

"Nonsense!"

"Can't a ghost appear and disappear?"

"Who's talking about a ghost?" said The Doctor, shuddering violently.

"I am—and you're thinking about it, too. I can see your face!"

"If there's one day that I want to wipe out of my life," said The Doctor, "it's this day. I've never acted such a part as this before. I hope by Heaven that I never act it again. Gore, there's only one way to redeem ourselves—and that's to go straight back to San Filipo now and hunt through that church!"

"Would you really do that?" asked Gore, almost mute with wonder.

"Of course I would—and I will!"

And The Doctor turned resolutely back.

"Wait a minute!" called the miner.

"Well?"

"You aim to say that that ain't a ghost?"

"I do, of course."

"Did you ever see a woman with a face as white as that?"

"The moonlight might make her face appear white."

"I seen you by the moonlight. You looked pretty pale, Doctor, but you wasn't as white as that. And her hands was the same color as her face—dead white, like paint. No blood in that flesh, Doctor. And how can there be any life where there ain't any blood?"

"Gore, it would make any man have the shivers to hear you yap like this."

"I'm tell you just the facts. I ask you, startin' in, would any real woman in the flesh have had the nerve to walk straight past us like she done—two strange men in the middle of the night in the cellar of that old church? No, sir, I say that she wouldn't, and you know that the same thing is true!"

"I know nothing of the kind," said The Doctor gloomily. "So far as we can tell, that girl may merely have been throwing a very large bluff—playing the part of the ghost that all of San Filipo knows about."

"Estaban, damned if I ain't surprised at you," remarked the miner. "You got pretty good ears, ain't you?"

"Fair, I suppose."

"Did you hear a sound when she stepped through all that noise-makin' junk?"

"The wind was stirring."

"Not when we seen her. There wasn't a breath of wind. I noticed that particular."

"You were so scared, Gore, that you forgot about the wind."

"And how about you?"

"I've never been so badly frightened in my life."

"Then when I tried to yell out to you not to run after her, I tell you, partner, that I couldn't peep!"

"It was fright. Fright will close up the throat of a man well enough. It closed mine when I turned around to tell you to let me go."

"All right, Doctor, have it your own way. You can explain everything that you want to. But you can't explain the way that she went out like a candle that the wind had hit!"

The Doctor bent his head.

"It's true," murmured he. "I can't explain that. And

yet she might have dodged out of sight. There were a hundred places where she could have hid."

"Was she walkin' as though she might of dodged quick out of sight?"

"She might have changed her gait."

"Nope, Doctor, she don't have to run to get away. She just can snuff herself out as thin as air, and by Heaven, you know it as well as I do."

"Perhaps I think so. That's the very reason why I won't admit it. There can't be such a thing as a ghost, Jim. There can't be. No, sir, that was a girl—and a howling beauty, at that! A face cut out of stone!"

"Aye," said the miner, "but more life in a piece of stone than there ever was in her face!"

"Well," said The Doctor, "we go back to-morrow night."

"Not by my advice. We've got our warning, now, and if we go back a second time, the curse'll sure get us!"

"Jim," said The Doctor, laying a hand on his shoulder, "I know that you've got just as much courage as I have. I say that I'm going back to San Filipo just as I went to-night, and I'm going straight to the church, and straight to the corner of the church where we saw her—and you're going with me!"

There was a groan from Jim Gore, and then:

"Well, partner, I suppose that I ain't gunna quit on you, but I'd rather take ten years in jail!"

"That," said the other quickly, "is because you were never in jail!"

They went on up the hillside, slowly, beginning to feel the fatigue of the long day and the frightful tension of their night adventure combined. When they reached the little shack, they had barely energy to look, to see that the silver and gold dust of Jim Gore, which they had secreted before leaving, was still safely in its hiding place. Then they turned into their blankets and fell soundly asleep.

In the middle of the night Jim Gore heard a subdued cry. He sat up and saw his tall companion, a blanket trailing from one shoulder—his eyes wide and unseeing—stalking stealthily through the dying moonlight, one hand stretched out before him as if he were feeling his way, and the other hand gripping a leveled revolver.

He stumbled over a rock and this seemed to waken him, for he straightened with a jerk and a subdued exclamation.

Turning, he encountered the frightened eyes of Gore. Without a word The Doctor returned to his blankets, rolled in them, and presently his regular breathing announced that he was sound asleep. Jim Gore, after a long moment, slept again also, but all through the rest of the night he was haunted by the sense of impending disaster from which even the courage and the fighting skill of his companion would not be able to extricate them. And he dreamed of stealthy Mexicans, knife in hand, stealing upon them, and of the walking ghost of the nun, and of tall Colonel Dice striding to confront these evils, but walking as in his sleep, feeling his way, his gun pointed at the empty air!

When they wakened in the brightness of the morning, they were almost as tired as when they fell asleep. Breakfast was cooked and eaten in silence, and then Jim Gore, by force of habit, went into his hole and started to work with single jack and drill.

His heart was not in his employment, however. Presently he came out carrying his tools with him, and slumped down in the shade beside The Doctor.

"It's all right, Jim," said the other. "You can't be interested in dragging three dollars a day out of the rock when you've got the scent of a million in your nostrils. But after we've tried and failed at this new game, you'll be able to go back to the old stand easily enough."

"After we fail?" muttered Jim Gore. "Have you got your heart set on missing before you even try to shoot?"

"We've got one chance in a hundred," said The

Doctor cheerfully, seeming to have recovered his usual spirits. "We're trying to get something for nothing, and that never works out. I've tried it all my life. And look at me now!"

"Aye," muttered Gore, "but you've had your good time!"

"Perhaps I have. Not in spending the money, but in trying to get it. And yet I've had the coin, too. I've had it in chunks of a good many tens of thousands at a time, and spent it in a whirl. But what have I left of it? A pair of guns and a good constitution!"

He laughed as he said it.

"But the game is all that is worth while, Jim. Not what you get out of the rock, but the fun of hunting it. Isn't that so?"

"I dunno," said Jim. "D'you suppose that if I ever struck my million I'd ever take to the drill and the single jack again?"

"Of course you would. They'd trim you out of your money in no time, and then you'd be back here plugging away at a hole in the stone and a good deal happier than when you were dropping thousands every day in New York! And the fun we'll get out of this hunt will be worth more than any coin we extract."

"The fun of ghost hunting?" asked Gore sullenly.

"Exactly that! What's that coming to San Filipo?"

He pointed across the valley, to a dust cloud.

"A bunch of cattle comin' in," suggested Gore.

"No, men on horseback, I think. I can make them out."

Both could make them out in another moment—a dozen or fifteen tiny figures of horsemen followed by three or four big wagons, each dragged by several spans of horses—and all so small in the distance that they needed ten minutes to cover a space equal to the breadth of one's hand.

"What's it all about?" asked the miner.

"It has something to do with our friend the ghost," said The Doctor. "You can lay your money on that."

CHAPTER XIII

Ramirez Makes an Offer

The train of horsemen and of wagons disappeared into San Filipo, but that was not the only unusual disturbance of the day. Before the afternoon had reached its hot beginning another and a different procession wound out of the village. It consisted of a long, straggling file of riders and carts and pedestrians—perhaps thirty souls could be counted by the two watchers from the height.

"What the deuce can *that* mean?" said Jim Gore.

"Some go in and some go out," said The Doctor. "A peaceable exit, however, with all their chattels. What the deuce can it mean?"

They spent the rest of the afternoon in conjectures, and when the evening turned to dark even Jim Gore had recovered a sufficient amount of curiosity to overcome even his dread of the ghost of Alicia. Down they went from the mountainside and into the valley, but they had not come to the outskirts of the town when a horseman shot up and out of the dark and hailed them in ringing Spanish:

"Who goes there?"

"Is this an army post?" snorted The Doctor to his companion. "Make no answer," he continued to Jim Gore.

And they walked on side by side.

"Who goes?" shouted the Mexican again, thrusting his horse in front of them.

Señor Estaban made answer in softest Spanish:

"Son of a coyote, carrion eater, dog of a greaser, why do you stop a man and try to talk man's talk?"

The dull moonshine winked on the barrel of the Mexican's rifle—but, as though realizing that he was

hovering on the brink of eternity, with the hand of
The Doctor ready to push him over the edge, he suddenly wheeled his horse away and darted off at full
speed.

"He lost his nerve, the skunk," chuckled Jim Gore.

"He hasn't finished his play," said The Doctor.
"We'll have another talk with that fellow before the
morning. You can do a little betting on that, Jim!"

It came long before morning. In a scant three
minutes a veritable cavalry charge swept toward them
through the dim moonshine.

"Down on the ground!" commanded The Doctor,
and set the example by throwing himself headlong
on his belly, with his pair of revolvers stretched out at
arm's length before him. Jim Gore, his heart in his
mouth, imitated that good precept.

The effect was immediate. The half dozen riders
split before them and swerved away on either side.
One gun exploded, but apparently it was merely a
wild shot, for the two did not hear even the singing of
the bullet. From a little distance, the cavalcade halted,
and one rider, advancing a little, called out:

"Friends?"

"Who in the name of the devil should we be?"
asked The Doctor in anger. "And what do you mean
by stopping two peaceful travelers? Are you robbers
—or fools?"

There was an exclamation of impatience from the
rider, but then he urged his horse a little nearer.

"Is Señor Gore one of you?" he asked.

"He's here," answered The Doctor.

"Señor Ramirez will be happy to talk to both of
you, then. It is by his orders that we stop all men
bound for San Filipo, friends."

"Ramirez, Ramirez, Ramirez!" murmured Estaban.
"You see, Jim, that your guitar-playing idler, your
boy who day-dreamed in the sun, has turned into a
leader of men. Eh? Oh, we shall find a great deal in
that same idler!"

He added, loudly: "What is the right of Señor Ramirez to stop us or shut us away from San Filipo?"

"You must know, señor," said the Mexican rider, "that on this day he has secured the control of all of San Filipo. It is his, señor, to the last foot of the last building, and all the land, and he has the power to keep off trespassers."

"This man talks like a lawyer," said The Doctor to his companion. "Confound the whole breed! Lawyers and gunmen are riding in the service of this obscure beggar, this time killer, this man of little account—this Diego Ramirez! We'll sweat on account of Ramirez before we're through!"

He stood up and beckoned to Gore to follow his example.

"We'll go in with you," said The Doctor to the Mexican. "You and your men can lead the way and guard us on the side, but I want none of you behind us. You understand?"

"It is very agreeable to me, señor," said the Mexican, and gave the directions in swift Spanish to his followers. He himself rode up beside the two to escort them into the wrecked village.

"Are you a friend of this Ramirez?" asked The Doctor.

"I am, señor. I am Pedro Blas."

"Pedro Blas, I am glad to know you. I have read an account of the travels of one of your famous ancestors."

"Ah, señor," laughed the other, "that rascal Gil! I claim no relationship to that fictitious scoundrel, I thank you! And your name, señor?"

"I am Cristobal Estaban."

"Ah! You are true Mexican, then? I thought from my friend——"

"I called him a coyote and a greaser," said The Doctor carelessly, "because he yapped like one. I hate a noisy man, Don Pedro. I hate 'em."

They reached the outskirts of the village and now they entered along the main street. At the word of the leader, all but two of the scouts fell back and returned to their work of riding slowly and cautiously through the night around the town.

"It is the grace of Heaven that I was on duty and heard the call," said Pedro Blas. "For the rest of them are rough fellows and they would have been as apt as not to open fire with their rifles. Diego Ramirez has brought up some tough rascals from Mexico, I can tell you. Here we are near his house, my friends!"

They turned in through the gate into the ancient patio and there they found a fire blazing in the center of the open space with a single man seated before it —the graceful form and the handsome face of Diego Ramirez. He rose and greeted them. What a change in this Diego! From the tattered beggar, he had become a man of fashion, in a wild way. He wore a short Mexican jacket ablaze with gold lace. Silver conchos gleamed down the sides of his trouser legs, and on his head was a sombrero which was netted around with jeweler's work.

He greeted them with a cordial wave of the hand and called:

"Jim Gore, I am glad to see you! Very glad! I have had my men looking for you. And your friend I am glad to see also."

"A Señor Estaban," said Pedro Blas.

"My countryman," said Ramirez, "you are very welcome. I am engaged in a work in which I can use strong men, señor, and brave men."

"My friend Estaban," smiled Señor Blas, "was about to exchange bullets with six of our men. Luckily I was in the party."

The fine eyes of Ramirez flashed up and down the form of The Doctor.

"I think that you have saved the blood of several of our friends, Pedro," said he. "Señor Estaban, I am still more glad to have you with us!"

And he shook his hand most cordially with the tall man.

"And yet," he added, scanning Estaban, "not truly Mexican, I think?"

"And not truly American," said The Doctor grimly. "I am afloat between two nations. A man without a country, if you wish to put it that way. But what is this work of yours in which you could use us?"

"I have brought to San Filipo," said Ramirez, "a number of brave fellows to guard the town, which I have recently bought, land and buildings."

He smiled to illustrate the last word, and waved genially toward the shattered wreck of a house which surrounded the patio.

"And what," said The Doctor, "is worth guarding in it?"

"You have come directly to the point! What there is worth guarding in it, I do not know. But I trust that I shall find out. And in the meantime, I have hopes, of course, or else I should not have hired so many first-class men—and fighters!"

"Something worth fighting for," said The Doctor, "is usually gold or silver. But that is your own affair. How could you use Gore and myself?"

"As I use the others. No, señor, as I speak with you, I see that I might be able to use you in a larger way. It is necessary that there should be some lieutenants in so many men!"

"And the pay?" said The Doctor calmly.

"Five dollars a day and food."

"Five dollars?"

"Or ten to an exceptional man like yourself, señor."

"This is very kind."

"Not at all. I intend to spend freely, because I hope to make great returns. That is a matter of course, unless I were a fool. In the meantime, what do you decide?"

"To take it under advisement," said the careless Doctor. "I have never been a hired man. But we'll think it over—eh, Jim?"

The latter obediently nodded. In this affair, which was becoming momentarily more complicated, he felt that the only thing he could do was to follow the lead of his more active-minded comrade.

"Señor Ramirez?" called a man, entering the patio.

"I am here, Gonzales."

"We have ridden the rounds to the north and found that two of the people have been trying to come back into the town."

"And you?"

"We turned them and herded them down the valley a little distance."

He laughed mischievously as he came into the light of the fire—a swart, bow-legged, scar-faced Mexican of middle age.

"And then——" He began, but here he caught sight of the face of The Doctor, and he leaped back with a cry of alarm.

CHAPTER XIV

A Friendly Meeting

"Oh, the little world!" murmured The Doctor. "We meet again, Gonzales, my friend."

"Merciful Heaven watch over us!" breathed Gonzales. "It is Estaban!"

"Old friends, then?" said Ramirez, regarding the pair curiously.

"Sacred devil," gasped Gonzales, still backing away and pulling nervously at his lone, sparse black mustaches. "This cannot be he!"

"Ah, yes, my dear Gonzales," said the tall man. "It is I. But let me prove it. When I was last with you, I made you a promise, did I not?"

"Señor?"

"I shall fulfill the promise now! I was to take you by your mustache, and wag your head for you, Gonzales, in the presence of other men. And now the time has come, *amigo mio!*"

And he glided a long step toward Gonzales.

"Señor," snarled Gonzles, "I give you a true warning—you see that I am armed!"

"Gentle Gonzales! And I, also—but keep your hand from your gun or your knife. Otherwise there will be a dead Gonzales, and not simply a shamed dog of a Gonzales to-morrow!"

"Señor!" broke in Pedro Blas. "What will you do?"

"Keep from between us!" said Estaban curtly. "It is a line of danger—is it not, Gonzales!"

And, with a sudden forward leap, he reached Gonzales with his long arm and seized the drooping mustache with a movement of incredible swiftness.

The cry of rage and of shame from the Mexican was mingled with a still greater share of terror.

"Friends—to me—to my help!" he screamed. "The devil himself has me!"

But though he gripped both his guns, and even drew them half out of the holsters, still he did not fully expose them, but let them fall back into their guards and merely caught with both hands at the strong wrist of The Doctor.

It was such a frightful thing that the blood of Jim Gore ran cold. And he, looking askance at the faces of the others, saw them fairly trembling and white with shame and disgust—and with fear also. For Gonzales was a known man. Of all the bravos who had accepted the money of Señor Ramirez to come north to San Filipo, none had a record so long and so dangerous as had this Gonzales. And yet he submitted himself, without even attempting to use a weapon, to the most horrible degradation.

For The Doctor, keeping his grip upon the mustaches of the Mexican, wagged his head back and forth with savage jerks, while he said through his teeth:

"It was by firelight that I made the promise, Gonzales. And there were other men standing near us. I, then, weak as a new-born infant, covered with my blood—I then promised you, Gonzales, that if I lived I should treat you in this fashion. For why should I kill you? Why, Gonzales? When to live and to be despised as a cur is more terrible?"

He gave a final wrench which twisted the wretched Gonzales entirely around.

"So live and be shamed till you die like a starved dog in a gutter!" said The Doctor in a great, terrible voice.

And he stepped back from his work.

Gonzales whirled back toward his tormentor—whirled with his arms flung up as though either to leap at the throat of the big man or else pour forth dreadful curses. Next he clutched the butts of his guns, but The Doctor, with his arms folded, smiled calmly upon him, and the iron of that derisive glance went into the soul of the Mexican. His convulsed face twisted to grief and to shame, and, turning again, he stumbled from the patio with sobs and moans tearing his throat.

The Doctor watched him go, and then laughed, and Jim Gore felt that that laughter was more horrible than all which he had seen in the scene before.

"It is really enough," said The Doctor. "I knew it at the time, as I lay fluttering like a bird's wings between death and life. I knew it then—that there was one way in which I could make this Gonzales repay me. Because what is death? What is blood? And what is agony, compared with this?"

He turned to the others.

"Do you agree with me, my friends?"

There was no answer.

More frightful than the humiliation of Gonzales was the knowledge that that man of battle had not dared to lift a hand in his own defense. And they stared at The Doctor with a mingled aversion and respect.

"You see?" said The Doctor to Ramirez. "It would not do for me to help you in this work of yours, Señor Ramirez. Your men look at me with an ugly eye!"

"Señor Estaban," said Ramirez coldly, "they have seen a very ugly thing just now!"

"That is as you wish to look at it," replied The Doctor. "For my part, I may say that this has been a very pleasant meeting. A new friend has been made"—here he waved to Ramirez—"and an old debt has been paid. But I suppose that the best thing I can do now is to leave San Filipo and go my way."

"Señor," said Ramirez, as coldly as before, "I shall not dispute with you in this matter. I fear that you are right."

"Adios, then, Señor Ramirez. I wish you luck in your work. I shall come to wish it to you again later on."

"Do not, if you please," said the handsome youth. "For I must tell you that Gonzales has many friends in San Filipo. And they will not receive the news of what has happened to-night very calmly. If you were to return, I might find them quite beyond any control of mine!"

The Doctor smiled.

"Although you would strive your best to contain them," he suggested ironically.

"By all means," said Ramirez, looking him calmly in the eye.

"I understand you very well, señor."

"We are clear to one another, I believe," said Ramirez in his former tone.

"Adios, Señor Ramirez."

"Adios, señor."

"Ramirez," said Jim Gore, "I'm sorry that there's been what looks like a fallin' out between you and my partner, Estaban."

The eyes of the young Mexican opened a little.

"But is he really a partner of yours?" he asked.

"Him and me are hand in glove," said the miner heartily.

"Is it possible!" murmured Ramirez. "But you are not leaving with him?"

"Me? Why, Ramirez, I got to go where my partner goes."

But here he received a swift glance from The Doctor, a look so impregnated with meaning, that it said as plainly as words: "Stay with them for a while at least—and then come after me if you will."

So, as the tall man walked from the patio, the miner lingered unwillingly behind.

"But," went on Ramirez smoothly, "I know that you are not growing rich from your work on the mountain, Señor Gore, and I have a job here which needs the eye of a good miner, perhaps. Do you understand? I could make it very much worth your while to stay with me!"

"The mine ain't much," protested Gore, playing the part which had been assigned to him by his departed companion, "but it looked to me to-day as though the vein was sort of opening up."

"I tell you," said Ramirez patiently, "that my work in San Filipo will not require more than a single week, I hope. Could you not leave the mine for a single week, my friend?"

"A week is seven days," said Gore sententiously.

"And at what rate would you hold yourself?"

"I dunno that I've figgered it out," said Gore.

"For the week, amigo, a hundred dollars in gold!"

Jim Gore started. It was higher pay than he had ever dreamed of before.

"A hundred dollars!" he echoed.

"All of that, and if we have luck which your work helps us toward, there will be a bonus—of ten times that much. A hundred dollars certainly—and the hope of a thousand, Señor Gore!"

"But," said Gore weakly, "there's the mine and my stuff in it!"

"I'll send men to-morrow—or up with you to-night, if you wish—and they shall bring down everything that belongs to you. Will that do?"

I seemed to Gore that this golden proposal fenced him round about and that there was no way in which he could withdraw from the temptation. But here a timely interruption gave him a chance to rally his scattered wits.

For a horseman came to the entrance of the patio, stopped his pony with a violence that flung the poor beast back on its haunches, and then ran into the open space with the wisps of dust cloud which the horse had raised clinging about him.

"Ah, my friends," gasped this man, "have I heard a true thing?"

"It is true!" said some one.

"It was Estaban himself?"

"Yes."

"Heaven give him to our hands. We shall overtake him!"

And he whirled about to race from the patio when the voice of Ramirez, raised to a clarion strength and clearness, stopped him.

"What is your name?"

"Porfirio Vega, señor."

"You are a friend, then, of Gonzales?"

"I am his half brother!"

"And you know this Estaban?"

"I know that devil—yes!"

"Then you shall not ride after him, but stay here to tell us a little about him!"

CHAPTER XV

The Lion

Porfirio Vega made a gesture of despair, as though the hope of a lifetime was, at that instant, wrenched away from him.

"You have bought my time, señor," said he to his leader, "but have you bought my honor also?"

"Vega," said Ramirez, dominating Vega and the rest

by his perfect self-control. "I remember you now. You were recommended to me by Gonzales himself. It was he who brought you north with the rest of the party."

"Ah, but if there were a kind fate," sighed Vega, "my brother Gonzales would never have heard the name of San Filipo!"

"Be patient, amigo," said Ramirez more gently. "I tell you now in the beginning that the troubles of my friends are my troubles. But how can I help you when I do not know what is grieving you?"

"It is true," said Porfirio Vega. "We hear that for those who serve you, you are as a father."

"My name," said the youth haughtily, "is Ramirez, and that is a sufficient proof of what I am. I am at least the son of my father. Open your heart to me, Vega. I am not one to forget. But if you rush out into the night—you will find there this Estaban."

"That is my prayer."

"Listen to me still. I have only seen him once. And you know him by some proof of what he is. But I tell you, Vega, that I had rather go out with my bare hands to attack a lion than to fight with this Estaban even with guns in my hands!"

"It is true," said Vega, his ecstasy leaving him little by little. "It is very true that he is a man! But what has this devil done to my brother, Gonzales?"

"Something that we may be able to understand," said Ramirez softly. "We shall show Gonzales in the morning that he may still hold up his head. Had I been in his place—except that I am the son of Ramirez—I should have done as he did, I think. Life is a precious thing, Vega. It is not to be thrown away lightly. And if he had stirred, he was a dead man! I, who had never seen this Estaban before, knew that much quite clearly. One can tell a lion by his paw!"

"It is true," nodded Vega, perfectly subdued by this time. "He would crush me, as he has crushed others!"

"Tell me what you know of him."

The Mexican turned and fixed a stony eye upon Jim Gore.

"There is one man here who should not stay to listen," said he.

"Señor Gore is about to become one of our friends, I trust," said Ramirez. "You may speak freely before him."

"As you will, señor."

"Sit down, Vega. Men speak better when they are at peace. Sit down, smoke, forget all your anger and your hate. Remember that the quiet mind thinks most surely. The patient hand is the hand that cuts a way through the mountain of rocks."

So Porfirio Vega seated himself by the fire and rolled a cigarette, and as he smoked it, alternately scowled at the fire and shuddered, as though the tale which he had so recently heard, or perhaps the remembered face of his half brother, so recently shamed, rushed back upon his mind.

"It is old Mexico of which I speak," said Vega at last.

"It is old Mexico of which you speak," said Ramirez and disregarding the chair in which he had been sitting, he took a place on the ground opposite the speaker. The others followed his example—all saving Jim Gore, who remained standing, partly shrouded in the darkness. He felt that he was looking through a screen of centuries back to the dim outlines of other campfires, and feathered heads and painted faces gathered around it, listening to the words of the tale teller.

But he was forgotten. The interest of that circle dwelt with an almost painful concentration upon the words of the narrator.

And Porfirio Vega, forgetting all things—forgetting even the shame of his brother and his own hatred of Estaban, lost himself in his tale which he carried forward with an emotion which became rhythmic as the tale progressed. Sometimes his very body swayed with the words which came readily out of his heart, without any preliminary searching of his mind to find them. His eyes burned or grew dim by turns, and his voice rang to a piercingly shrill pitch or dropped again to a heavy drone.

So he began in the following manner:

I come, my dear friends, from that country which lies between Las Viegas and the Sierra Tigre. Men were never meant for that country. Only mountain sheep and goats lived there in the old days, for the wolves and the lions had killed all the cattle which browzed in the valleys. To be a trapper in that country was to risk one's life greatly—to set snares on the edges of precipices, to toil up cliffs and down from morning to sunset. And there were no other people who ever crossed that wild region until the coming of the Estaban!

No, do not think that it was this Cristobal. It was another Cristobal Estaban, who was the grandfather of him whom I hate, and whom my brother Gonzales hates.

Well, the old Estaban was a grand man. He had had wide estates once, in the best portion of the plains on the highlands. His cattle ran on those plains by the thousands and the tens of thousands. He was so rich that he could build—as church, do you see?—as easily as I snap my fingers. Well, he was like a king. And then a politician came to envy him. He said to the president, why should we not have all these fine lands of Estaban? For did he help us when we wished to start the revolution? No, let us take his lands from him and all his horses, and all his cattle, and let us make him a beggar while we become very rich. Let us hang him.

Because, do you see, that was the best way and the gentle way, they felt, for it was better to hang him first and then rob him, since he would suffer more to see his property taken from him and live, than he would to die and have his lands taken from him afterward.

That was a very wrong thing, as I shall agree with you. But this great gentleman, the Estaban, when he learned that they envied him, woke up out of a happy life and showed that he was a lion. When they came for him, he killed many of them, and he took a few men who wished to die with him, and he fought his way through a thousand miles of men, and he came with only three servants to our mountains.

They were worse than a desert. Men could ride after him into a desert, but men would rather die than be forced to ride through our mountains. For who could ride there except a few with fine horses whose feet were like the feet of cats—men, besides, who knew all of the trails and where it was possible for a horse to go and where it was not.

So the Estaban came. And he was, as I tell you, a lion. So are they all. All the Estabans are lions, like this man. Men were not men when they faced the Estaban. They became like sheep. So!

For a while the president sent men to hunt the Estaban, but when they came, the Estaban and his men killed the hunters—oh, many of them were killed!

At last they came no more. Señor Estaban was let alone. After that, he began to do strange things. He had with him a box of jewels. He sold them one by one. With them he bought cattle and plows and axes and men on the plains. He brought them up into our terrible mountains. With his many men he plowed the narrow bottoms of the box cañons and made them grow wheat. Such wheat! That soil had never been worked. Wheat grew as tall as a man's head! I have seen from one acre two thousand pounds of the best wheat!

It was harvested and drawn up out of the cañon hearts by pulleys. Then it was carried over the mountains by trails which the Estaban built—mule trails, because wagon roads would have cost too much. No, do not think that it was the wheat that he carried away. He harnessed some of the power of the rivers and made them turn wheels in the valleys. He made flour. It was flour which the mules carried. And there was a great cost in carrying it. But still the Estaban began to grow rich. For he was luck itself.

If he sent men to cut away at the fence of a rocky hill to make a trail, those men laid open a vein of good ore. That was the way!

He raised fine horses and mares in the rich bottom lands of the cañons. And on the hillsides, where a sheep could hardly stand, he raised mules. If they were wise of head and sure of foot, they lived. If they were foolish and slow, they lost their footing and rolled to death down the side of the mountain. But they learned. As you know, a mule will learn anything in the world. They learned how to live and to run like mountain sheep on those cliffs.

They were not very large, but they could carry a heavy man all day. They were as strong as horses and as wise as wild goats. And other people heard of them. The price of a mule from Señor Estaban became the price of a fine horse.

So still he made money and more money, and cut more trails through the living rock, and plowed more valleys. He cut timber. And it was the finest wood, and sawed in his own mills. He raised the best wheat and ground it to make the finest flour. He found mines, and they were all rich. He turned our terrible mountains into a river of gold. That was the Señor Estaban.

He built a palace on the flat top of a mountain that looked over the entire world. A king would have lived in it. It was so high on the mountain that the clouds rolled beneath it. The eagles did not fly so high. The sun shone there forever.

That was the Señor Estaban! He became rich again. And once more the president heard of his wealth and came to steal his money with an army. And Señor Estaban gathered all his men. There were hundreds and there were thousands and they all rode on the little mules that could walk up the face of a cliff as a fly walks up the side of a room.

They came behind the soldiers of the president and

killed them by night. When the soldiers of the president were tired in the hot middle of the day, these men came on them, riding their mules as if they were flying with wings, and they killed the men of the president.

So the president prepared to send a greater army. But then there was a revolution and the army did not come.

But you are weary of this story?

CHAPTER XVI

The Son of Lions

"No," said Ramirez. "Continue. Because the blood of these men flows in the veins of this Estaban whom we have seen."

"A little of his blood," said Vega, "but I shall tell you of that in time."

And he continued:

When Estaban would have a wife, he left the mountains and crossed the sea and came again with a pale woman, and she bore him a son with red hair and blue eyes. The Señor Estaban was then an old man. Men said that he could no longer have children, but at what other men say all of the Estabans laugh and will always laugh. It is their way!

A little later the Estaban died. He left a widow and a little child.

"We will now make the wealth of the cañons and the mills and the mines our own wealth!" said the people of the mountains.

And they tried to take these things. Why, they asked—and they were very right in asking—why should a man with red hair, who calls himself an Estaban, take such wealth in Mexico?

The Estabans are lions. This widow was a lioness. She raised many men. She fought the rest. She killed many of them. She nailed their bodies while they were still living to the limbs of trees and built fires under their feet.

And it is some of her blood that runs in the veins of this Cristobal Estaban whom you know! She was a terrible woman, very small, and very white, and with blue eyes. She was a smiling woman. I myself have seen her when she was very old. I was then a strong man, but I trembled—because I knew that she was a lioness.

Well, aimigos, this son of hers was a man almost before he was no longer a child. He had a man's knowing and man's way of doing. When he was fifteen years old men said: "This is not the Estaban again. This is a greater Estaban. This is two lions in one man!"

And they were right. He was very great. There was nothing that he feared. There was nothing that he did not dare.

He was less lucky, however. When he hewed a trail through the living rock, he did not find a gold mine. When he plowed the valleys, the wheat no longer grew as high as a man's head. But still he was very rich—oh, very rich! And every year he grew richer, until he said: "I must have a wife!"

He did not go through Mexico to find one—through Mexico, where the women are the loveliest in the world, as all men know, but he crossed the seas and found a pale woman with blue eyes. And he brought her home and a son was born to them—but his eyes and his hair were black. That is the Cristobal Estaban whom you know.

But only his eyes and his hair were like his country. For the rest, he was a stranger. When he was only a little boy he would not drink pulque and spat it out. He would not ride a mule, but asked for a horse. He was a stranger. And people said it was sad that the mountains should come into the hands of a stranger who wore the name of Estaban.

But when he was a boy, like his father he was a man also. But he was greater. When he was twelve a thief, a strong man, came into his room and tried to kill him and rob him of the treasures which were in that room. But Cristobal took him by the throat, and when the people of the house came they found the man almost dead.

I remember that time, and how old men talked. They said that the strength of a man was in the hands of that boy. They said that if his grandfather was one lion and his father was two, there were four lions in the blood of this Cristobal, the third of that name.

For, consider that while he held the thief by the throat, the thief got a knife out and cut him many times, but still his hands kept to their hold! This was like a man, and a strong man, and not like a boy.

Therefore, while he was still a child, people feared him, but they did not love him. And to this day, where is there the man that loves the Estaban?

So the time came when he was to go away to school, and his mother took him away across the seas. And while he was away across the seas—for she was a foolish woman, and not like the wife of the first Estaban—she gave all the keeping and the care of the lands of Estaban into the hands of one man.

That man was a lazy, jolly fellow. She had said to him: "Send me so many pesos each year and I shall not ask any questions! But my son must not want while he is away learning how to be a man!"

As if an Estaban needed teaching in order to be a man!

Ah, amigos, it would have made your heart bleed to see what was done with the estates of the Estaban. Or, if you are like me and the mountain men, it would have made you laugh!

This lazy, jolly man, he said to himself: "I shall send to the widow all that she asks for every year. It is much, the estate will pay us twice as much! Yes, three times!"

So he went to the great city, to Mexico, and there he lived as kings live. He spent two thirds and he left a third for the lady, but even in the very first year things did not go well. For those mountain men are sharp, hard men, and they need a master's watching. They began to steal and cheat the master who was absent. They began to live easily. They began to put the rent in their own pockets. And they would pay the secretary of the jolly man ten dollars and keep the rest of a hundred.

So in the second year there was not enough money to give to the widow of Estaban and her son, the third Estaban, and also for the jolly man to keep living in Mexico as he had begun to live. But he would not change his ways, because he dreaded to come back into the hard mountains to live again.

Yes, he would not do that, and therefore he said to himself: "I shall gamble and make much money and then I shall have enough for everything."

So he cut his own throat, for he gambled and lost so much that every one in the city knew of it, and every one in the land knew of it. But the news did not reach to the widow Estaban, because she was far across the seas. There she was, while the jolly, fat man said: "I have lost at gambling this time, and I need much money—hundreds of thousands of pesos!"

So he sold many of the mines and got money enough to keep on living like a king and to send plenty to Madame Estaban, also.

Now, in the next year, it was also like this. For now he gambled to get enough money for himself and for Madame Estaban, but also he gambled hugely to get enough money to buy back the mines. And he said: "My luck is bad, but if I keep doubling, I shall be sure to win!"

But he did not win, and at the end of the year he had to sell all the rest of the mines and a part of the rich timber lands to have enough to pay his gambling

losses and to send the money to Madame Estaban
—and to keep on living in the style of a king in Mexico!

Well, my friends, you see the end!

The Widow Estaban asked for money and for more
money, because, she said, her son was becoming a
man, and his needs were great. When the jolly fat
man heard that the Estaban was becoming a man, he
shook in his boots. But he said: "Now I am sure to
die, because this is an Estaban. But I shall live happily until the end!"

And so he spent more money than ever, and if he
was like one king before, he was like two kings now!

Then Madame Estaban wrote to him: "I have heard
strange things—that you are selling parts of the estate!"

And he wrote to her: "That is all a lie! Send an
honest man to see the truth."

So she sent an honest man, but the jolly fellow had
much gold in his hands and he made the honest man
see what he wished the honest man to see, and the
honest man went back to Madame Estaban and said:
"All that has been said is a lie. The estate is richer
than ever."

So, after that, Madame Estaban closed her ears
when she heard stories.

But all this while, mark you, the Estaban was growing to be more and more of a man, and the jolly fat
fellow shook in his boots when he thought that an
Estaban would some day call him to an account.

But still, he could not stop living as he lived. For it
was very delightful, and he was treated like a king
—or like two kings, so long as he paid the way for
himself and for all of his friends. They told him what
a wise and clever and fine fellow he was. And he liked
to have the people in the street point to him and say:
"There he goes! He lost a hundred thousand pesos last
night, but he is smiling to-day!"

Well, the people of the mountains are not fools. They
are like Gonzales. They are like me, and we both have

eyes. We saw what was happening. We heard stories from Mexico. And every year we saw that more and more of the estate was being sold.

What would we do?

We would do what any wise man would do. We would help ourselves and keep something for ourselves when everything was going to ruin.

But, after all, the estate was very great. If we drove off a few sheep one day and said that they were our own—who cared and who watched? For a few dollars in the pocket of the secretary of the jolly little fat man closed the eyes of the jolly little fat man.

And if we drove off a few cows, the same thing was true.

Then we saw that the secretary did not like the honest men, because they paid him no money. And he gave bad reports of them, and the jolly little fat man began to send the honest men away.

So the rest of us who were honest said: "If we are honest, we will be sent away. Let us send a hundred dollars to the secretary."

But since we were forced to send a hundred dollars to the secretary, was it not right that we should take some of that money back again?

Yes, surely it was right. And when we drove off a few beeves, was it not in human nature to drive off just a few more and so to have a little profit over the money which we sent to the secretary?

But all this, in the end, was coming out of the pockets of the estate of Estaban.

And every year more was lost, and every year the Estaban was closer and closer to being a man, and all the men of the mountains trembled when they thought of what would happen when he came back as a man, if he had been such a boy as we knew him to have been.

Yet those were jolly days. And if you go through the mountains now, they will tell you that the finest man who ever lived was the jolly little fat man. And they were right. He wanted to be happy. But he wanted all other people to be happy, also. He did not care how much money they took. He wanted them to smile and to love him when they saw him.

And is not that a fine thing?

But, after all, the money that he spent made the estate shrink and shrink.

The mines were all sold, and then some of the great timber lands into which, at such a great price, the Estaban had built the roads through the living rock. And after that some of the grazing lands were sold, and then many of the fine mules. And then some of the blood horses were sold. And then some of the fine farming lands in the box cañons.

And every year the great estate shrank and shrank, until we began to see that a thing which had seemed to be endless did, after all, have an end, and that the end was sure to come before long.

The jolly little fat man saw it, too. He was no longer jolly, but always sad. He was no longer fat, but the skin of his face hung in great folds.

Then he came to see the mountains, and wherever he rode we went out and blessed him and smiled on him, but he looked at us and the tears ran down his face.

"Alas, my children!" said he. "The Estaban is coming!"

CHAPTER XVII

The Return

What he had said was true. We in the mountains knew that the jolly little fat man had gone to the coast to meet the Estaban when he arrived. We heard the story —how the little fat man, on his knees, told the story of all that he had done and begged Don Cristobal to forgive him and let him help to build up the fortunes which he had thrown away.

Don Cristobal laughed and walked out from the room.

That was a foolish thing that he did then. The little fat man *had* been a fool in spending money, but he was a wise man in making it.

However, the Estaban had a great idea of what was due to him. For he felt that, whatever had been done by the little fat man, the estates of the Estaban could not be taken away from him, any more than his kingdom can be taken away from a king. He was young, this Estaban. He was the youngest and the proudest and the strongest of all his proud, strong race. His mother and his father were dead. There was no one to guide him or to teach him, now.

The little fat man was heartbroken. He and his father before him had always served the Estabans. He sent to beg Don Cristobal to see him again. But the Estaban sent him a message and said that he had forgotten that there was such a person in the world as the little fat man.

Then the Estaban went up into the mountains where his father had built up a little kingdom on the great foundations that his grandfather had prepared there. Wherever he rode, the Estaban would say: "All of this valley is mine, is it not? And the forests on each side of the valley are mine. And those great mounds on the slopes yonder—they are the mines which belong to me, do they not? And all the cattle and the sheep and the horses and the mules that I see—they are mine also, are they not?"

Then the men who rode with him would say: "No. All these have been sold."

At this the Estaban would reply: "How can a thing be sold when the sale is not ordered by the owner? If a man without authority sells my land, is the sale good, or is the seller a thief?"

To these things the men around the Estaban could not make any answer. There was a sort of sense in what he said. And yet, after all, the lands had been sold, and some sort of money had been paid for it. There was no doubt of that.

Don Cristobal rode on and on and finally he came to the great house which stood upon the flat top of the mountain. And walking there through the garden and standing on the highest building like an eagle on its rock, Don Cristobal said: "All of those mountains are mine. We shall see what the laws have to say about these matters!"

He went to the law, and the law said two things: That the little fat man was a villain and that he should pay back some certain sums of money—millions and millions of pesos; also, the law said that the sales of the land were good sales, that he had been given a power of attorney.

Now, when the law had said this, and had declared that the Estaban could not take back his old lands peacefully, he went again to his house on the mountain and sat down in the ruined garden and looked over the mountains and the valleys that had once been his.

On the evening of this day there came riding two muleteers, one on each side of a third man who was also on a mule. All were of the breed of Estaban. These two helped the central rider down and carried him into the garden. It was the little jolly fat man. He was jolly no longer, and his hair was white. He fell on his knees before the Estaban again and he said: "Listen to me, my master! I have stolen the blood out of your veins. I am a villain and a dog. But still let me serve you! All these mountains and the valleys and the riches in them I have sold away from you. I have sold them here and I have sold them there, and those who rented lands now live on their own grounds and serve themselves.

"But all is not well with them, señor. All is not well with them. They have no one master to guide them and to direct them, and they are like children who need much teaching. The miller charges the farmer too much for the grinding of his wheat. The miner breaks down the great roads and will not repair them —and who is there to make him? And if one man repairs a road on his land, on the adjoining land the way is allowed to go to wreck. Wheels no longer roll along the roads in the mountains. There are only the pack mules. And what profit can the mines make when they must pack out their ore and can no longer truck it away? Only the richest veins can be worked. And so the mines are dying!

"And the farmers must pay high to the muleteers who carry the flour away from the valleys. And much of that flour is lost or spoiled or sold for poor prices when it is brought down into the lower country. And the name of Estaban is no longer stamped on everything. Men will not pay for a mule with a strange brand the same price that they were glad to pay for those wonderful little mules which were bred and owned by the Estaban and carried his stamp upon them. So the mines are dying, and the farms are dying. The mules are not bred with care and they grow worse with every year. And people begin to starve. They rob one another. They give up hope and stop working. And they cannot understand why it is that lands which were so rich a few years back are now worth nothing at all.

"Therefore, hear me, master," said the little fat man, "and in the name of Heaven let me undo the harm which I have worked upon you! Do you take this house and the lands which are left to you. They are enough to make a long, narrow strip through the mountains and down toward the coast on the one side and to the great plateau and the railroad that runs north and south on the other side. In a year, those men who are living on your lands will be prosperous again. They will be paying their rents to you. And the roads will be repaired, the crops will move forward, and the ores will be brought down from the mines cheaply over the good pavements. Wheels will roll through your lands again, and they will make your wealth grow.

"Then the other shepherds and the cattle-growers and the miners will all say to you: 'Take us back! Now we are starving. Once we were fat under your father's and your grandfather's care. Take us back. Repair the roads. We will deed the lands to you. We will become only your tenants. Punish the bad men by sending them out of the mountains; keep the good men and let them work for you and for themselves.'

"So in five years, señor, you will be the master of more than even your father before you possessed!"

This was the speech which the fat little man made to the Estaban. It was a wise speech and everything that he spoke was the truth. But the Estaban had the pride of a lion and the pride of a devil in him. He stood up and said: "If a dog bites me, I do not let him come again and lick my hand."

When he had said this he walked away. The little fat man remained sitting in the garden with his head in his hands, and when the muleteers came up and touched his shoulder, they found that he was dead.

The Estaban now said to those men who were around him: "Should I wait until the people offer as a favor to me the thing which is mine by right?"

Then he took all the strong armed men whom he could find and rode out. He would stop at a man's door and say: "Do you belong to yourself or to the Estaban?"

Of course, when he did this and when he began to ask for the rents, the people were afraid. I think that they would have done all that he asked, but he asked for the back rents of the lands. That was too much. The people all saw that he was wicked, and they began to band together and resist him. Some of them sent away to the government, too, and got the help of soldiers. But the Estaban came down from the mountains with not a hundred men and in the middle of night he rode through and through the camp of those soldiers. He killed many of them, he took all their rifles, their horses, their mules, and the little cannon which they dragged for the mountain battles.

This was all well, but in that battle with the soldiers he had lost many of his own men. And when we of the mountains saw what had happened, we said to one another: "This lion is about to leap on us, now, and tear us to pieces. Our backs are to the wall. Let every man stand shoulder to shoulder. We must fight for our lands and for our lives!"

This was the manner in which we spoke to one another. We gathered together in a great number, as fast as we could, and when the Estaban came near to us he had less than eighty men riding with him on the little mountain mules, and we had four hundred fighting men. That would stop him, such odds of men and of ground, you will say. But you do not know the Estaban!

He rode straight into the faces of our guns. We killed or wounded half of those who followed him, but the rest would not give back. They knew the Estaban, too, and they followed him right into our lines, cheering.

But we did not cheer. We had ten men to every one that followed the Estaban. But all of us felt that the devil was fighting with him, or else he would never have dared to ride up to our rifles with so few men.

So we gave back from him. Our bravest men grew weak. We began to run, and his mule riders could have killed us in heaps, but the Estaban rode everywhere, saying: "These are my children. Do not hurt them!"

That was very good of him, yes, and when we got safely away we sat down together and some of us said that we should go down and submit to this terrible man, because we could never beat him, but he would ride among us until he had destroyed us. But others of us said that he would treat us like his children—yes, but like the children of a poor man, who makes them work very hard and gives them no money! And we said: "Let us steal down on their camp while they are tired from riding and fighting, and surprise them this very night!"

That was the thing that we did. In the middle of the night a hundred of us came stealing down. There were hardly thirty of the men of Estaban left around him, and all of these were asleep. When we came in we either cut their throats or frightened them away. And some ten of us got to the Estaban himself and laid hands upon him!

It was a terrible moment to us! I thought that by that moonlight I should see the ropes with which we tied him shrivel and snap as though they were fastened around red-hot bars of steel. But there was no miracle. Only it would have made you shrink to see the rage and the shame that was in the face of this Estaban to think that he had been mastered by his own people!

When we had tied him we wondered what to do. We were frightened, of course. For we knew that we had laid hands on the very person of the devil himself.

Then it was that Gonzales said that we must make him swear not to hold a grudge against us. And we would promise to become his men again and work for him and all of us would pay him the rents which we owed him, if only he would be a father to us and swear to hold no grudge against us for the thing which we had done in taking him into our hands upon this night.

This was done. Gonzales and some of the older men went to him and begged him to give them an oath, after which they would all become his men again and his children. But he laughed and told them that he would make them sweat for this evening's work.

We were all very frightened, and then a devil put into Gonzales' mind that we should force him by pain. And some of them—all very hard men—took the Estaban. What they did we could not tell, because we only saw them bending over the spot where the Estaban was, crowded all together. And then we would hear them making a demand of him—then a silence and no answer.

At last, we could stand it no longer. We burst in upon them and there we saw the Estaban lying on the ground. They had been torturing him to make him give us his promise. But when we broke in on them, they were afraid of us and we were afraid of them, and all of us were terrified by the thing that had been done. So we turned and fled away and left the Estaban lying there in his pain.

But after that I never heard what had happened, and I thought that he was surely dead from what he had suffered on that night. I thought that he was dead and that he had been taken and buried by some of those who were true to him to the end. But I see that I was wrong. This evening I have seen his face again, and I tell you, friends, that I am very sick at heart. I see that he is saving himself and collecting his strength and very soon he will hurl himself like lightning fire upon those mountains and those mountain people! It will be a dreadful day. Heaven have mercy upon us!

CHAPTER XVIII

Three Tasks

Thus ended the narrative of Porfirio Vega. It was followed, properly, by a hush of respectful consideration such as men pay when they have heard some extraordinary matter.

Young Diego Ramirez was the first to stir.

He had sat like an Indian—like one of his own earlier ancestors—cross-legged on the ground during all of this recital, motionless, except for the slight wavering of his body to and fro as he grew more and more excited toward the end.

Now he leaped up and began to pace up and down, gesticulating and talking rapidly.

"Oh, what a stroke of ill luck that I should have had to make an enemy of such a man as this Estaban! What a stroke of luck—and what a tower of strength he would have been to me if I could have made him my ally! If I had won here, I could have given him the strength to go back as a king should among his people, and we, together, would have been of a strength——"

He broke off in the midst of these thoughts, and added: "Vega! Vega! What devil brought you and Gonzales into my camp?"

"It was good pay, señor."

"Good pay! Have you not the lands that were stolen from the Estaban? Were not they enough to keep you at home?"

"Ah, señor, not stolen, but bought fairly from him."

"Idiot! Have you no shame to say that they were bought fairly? Have you no shame?"

"Ah, señor, we did much wrong. But we would have made amends if he would have let us. But there is a need for a little time, surely!"

"I wish to Heaven that you had never left your native mountains!"

"Señor, if you were to see those mountains now, you would not say such a cruel thing. The pleasant homes are emptied now. The sheep and the goats come down from the hills and worry the little patches of grain which still grow here and there in the valleys. And the wild cattle stable themselves in the falling houses. It is very sad! To journey ten miles even on foot is a terrible day's work in those mountains. And the pack horses can hardly bear themselves along, to say nothing of the extra burdens of a pack. The roads are gone, and that country without roads is like a body without arteries. It is entirely useless and very weak and dying!"

Porfirio Vega ended again, and Diego Ramirez said: "Well, this is a bad fate. The Estaban has become an enemy. He will hover about my camp until, like a hawk, he has picked off my best men—unless you, Jim Gore, can go to him and make my peace with him. Tell him that a Ramirez sends a greeting to an Estaban. The Ramirez, also, is the last of his line, and like the Estaban he is attempting to regain a lost strength. Perhaps we can join hands and do great things together. In the meantime, I pray Señor Estaban for all our sakes to leave off all entrance into this town of mine. A time may come when I could be useful to him and he could be useful to me, but just now that time has not come. If he stays near the town, he troubles my men. He spoils the work that they must do. Do you understand me, Jim Gore?"

Gore understood him well enough. A hawk like The Doctor hanging around a lot of men was enough to make them all as timid as a tribe of chickens. He realized all of that. And whatever this work was that kept Ramirez and his men so thoroughly and so mysteriously employed in old San Filipo, it was plain that he could not be bothered by such serious outside interference.

So Jim said that he would carry that message back to Estaban.

"Tell the Estaban that I should like to meet him again and discuss terms of an agreement that may be pleasant for both of us. In the meantime, remember that I have made a proposal to you, Gore. I need steady and faithful men. You have heard the story of Porfirio Vega. I tell you, my friend, that I would give a great deal to have ten men as true to me as the very ones who tormented the Estaban!"

Even the slow mind of Jim Gore could understand this, as he turned it over and over in his mind while wandering slowly out from the town. For the men of that Estaban had tormented their master out of the very excess of their fear of him. It was to get his promise that he would let them come back to him!

Now this seemed to Jim Gore a tremendous background against which to see a man, and yet as he considered what he had seen and guessed of The Doctor, he decided that that artist with words, and weapons had a need of exactly such a stage as this to walk upon and find himself at home.

It was to Jim as one who finds a road companion turned into archangel or archdevil, he hardly knew which. But he felt that the Estaban would probably fit more easily into the second category. He continued pondering, in this fashion, and walking slowly ahead, until he reached the first upward pitch of the slope toward the mine, and then he heard a voice just before him.

There sat the Estaban on a stone, smoking a cigarette in the moonlight and enjoying the beauty of the valley. The strange tale out of old Mexico in which he had been clad died suddenly in the mind of Jim Gore and left before him only the reality of Chris, alias The Doctor, alias Colonel Dice.

What was The Doctor saying?

"Who was the blind man, Jim, who said that color died under the moon? Or perhaps he was right, if he was a poet and meant that color dies, but leaves a ghost of itself behind. Now if you will look at that scalped mountain head—but you are not interested in such stuff, of course. Tell me what happened. And what did that Ramirez want with you? Did he hire you to take my head to him? Did he offer you a price, Jim?"

"Well," said Jim, "there is only one thing that keeps me from pulling up my stakes and drifting away for parts unknown—and that's the promise that I've made to you. But I'm tired of the game, Chris, and I want to get out of here. I'm partly tired, and I'm partly scared."

"True!" said The Doctor. "Tired and scared—but honest. Oh, Jim, if I had half a dozen men as honest as you, I would put a girdle around the world and lock it up with a brass lock and put it into my pocket. That's how simple it would be. No, old-timer, you're not going to get away from that promise to me. I need you too much. Now tell me what Ramirez said."

The offer of Ramirez and the covert threat which it contained was repeated for the benefit of Estaban.

He heard it through with a good deal of interest, and toward the end Jim Gore felt with satisfaction that he was to prove a successful ambassador. However, just as he reached the close, The Doctor rose and began to walk back and forth with the long and soft step which was already becoming familiar to Gore.

"It is a pretty thought," said The Doctor. "I am to make terms with this upstart. He is the last Ramirez, does he say? And therefore he will treat on terms of equality with the Estaban? The fool forgets that there is a difference in positions. I am threatened, Jim, by this Ramirez. If I do not keep my hands off his precious town and his men in it, he will see to me——"

He broke into a loud laughter that rang far and wide through the night.

"He has not the slightest knowledge of me," said The Doctor, "or he would never make such a proposal. Neither would he send an emissary. He would come and present himself in all due humility. *Due* humility —do you mark me there?"

He had grown outrageous—this Estaban. His pride had taken him by the throat and transformed him into a veritable madman, it seemed to modest Jim Gore. This was the man of whom Porfirio Vega had spoken with trembling, and no wonder! This was the man who had charged a mountainside against quadruple odds. What had been hard for Jim Gore to imagine was simple now. The Estaban strode up and down like the very picture of a tyrant.

At length he paused and clapped a hand on the shoulder of the miner.

"It's an odd thing, Gore, isn't it?" said he. "A very unpleasant coincidence, as you might say, that just as we begin to get on the track of a first-class, hundred percent mystery, we are forced to take into our consideration this rascal Ramirez with *his* pretensions. Heaven only it is annoying! Damnably annoying!"

"Sure, it's annoying," answered Jim Gore. "And besides that, it means that we got to pack away from here and get to another section of the mountains. Or, if we stay here, we'll have to keep the white flag waving so that other folks ain't going to make any mistakes about our intentions."

"A white flag? As a ruse, but never as a fact, Jim. Never in this world! We are here, Jim, with a threefold mission, at the present moment!"

"Sure," said Jim Gore. "We have the threefold mission of saving your hide, saving my hide, and getting away from Ramirez and his hired gang. That makes three jobs, well enough."

The Doctor laughed merrily.

"You are actually a delightful jester, Jim," said he. "No, no! What we have to do is, first of all to find out a little more about the delightful girl who is making headquarters in the ruined church in San Filipo at the present moment."

"Delightful girl? Delightful Jee-rusalem!" groaned Gore. "I don't want no more familiar acquaintance with her than I have already. It will do me fine, Doctor."

"The second task," said the implacable Cristobal Estaban, "is to hunt down the trail of that same bar silver which the greaser was carrying over the mountaintops when you cleverly intercepted him. We must never lose the sight of such a fortune as is likely to be connected with that trail!"

"Mad once, and mad twice—that makes just plumb crazy," said Jim Gore. "Well, Doctor, go on and tell me what other little thing we have to do besides flirting with a ghost and mixing up with a buried treasure?"

"The third item," said The Doctor, "is happily a matter of this world only."

"I am glad of that," said Gore. "What is the third little thing?"

"It consists in teaching this Ramirez that he is an infernal upstart, and that as for dictating terms to the Estaban, he himself is in serious need of my protection. Consider these matters, Jim. Then tell me if we will not have a pleasant little game before us?"

Jim Gore peered closer. He made out that his companion was not jesting, but in deadly earnest.

CHAPTER XIX

The Challenge

So it was that Jim Gore said at last:

"Then I suppose that there is nothing for me except that I got to go back to tell this to Ramirez. And I hate to do it, somehow."

"And why, Jim?" asked the big man.

"Partly, Chris," answered Jim Gore, "because I got an idea that he might as soon as not put a knife in me if he found me disputing with him any and taking another side from him."

"My child," said The Doctor, "you are talking with a lot more sense than a man might credit you for, seeing how young you are. Young and innocent as the devil, Jim. But here you've hit the nail right in the middle of the nose. If you let Mr. Ramirez know that, far from going to work for him, you are going to hang out with his compatriot, Mr. Estaban, this swine is apt to string you up by the heels and leave you swinging like the pendulum on a clock. No, we won't do that. We'll send a messenger in to him."

"You are havin' your little joke again," said Jim Gore. "Go on, Doctor. Send in that rabbit with a message."

"We'll have to walk part way only," said The Doctor, "and then we'll let our messenger do the rest of the work."

Jim Gore was tired of guesswork, and therefore he turned without a word and fell in at the side of his long-stepping companion. They hurried back through the night toward the dim and ghostly outlines of San Filipo. The Doctor's way of announcing himself was to come to a halt and let off a pair of rapid shots from his revolver, and then utter a wild, wailing yell, that carried far and wide over the desert. Jim Gore, petrified, could only gape in his amazement. But the big man sat down and lighted a cigarette.

"What'll happen now?" breathed Jim Gore.

"The face it'll wear I can't guess," said Estaban, "except that the skin will probably be brown. Aye, and here it comes."

He added, "Two of it, at that!" as two horsemen came on through the night like two bits of wind-blown mist, and drew rein close to the pair of pedestrians. But they had no opportunity to ride in, for as they shouted: "Who is killed? Who cried?" The Doctor answered: "I, the Estaban, called, and two coyotes have answered me out of the desert. Go back to the wolf, your master, and tell him that Señor Gore does not wish to have dealings with him. He has chosen a different sort of a partner. He has chosen me, you dogs. And I, the Estaban, will take a day off from my more important work, when I feel moved to do so, and pay your master a visit, and break him up small and sweep him and the rest of San Filipo into a pile of junk. Do you understand what I wish you to report to your master, Ramirez?"

Those two rangers of the night Jim Gore expected to see fall instantly upon the injudicious Estaban, but instead, they merely bowed above their saddle horns.

"Si, señor," they answered in a soft-voiced chorus, and instantly they rode away toward the faintly glimmering walls of the town.

"Well," said The Doctor, "*that* is done. I hope that you approve, Jim. I hope that you feel right about it."

"Would you like to know just how I feel about it?" asked Gore.

"Yes, I'd really like to know."

"I feel," said Gore, "as though I'd planted half a dozen sticks of powder in the same room where I was hanging out, and then lighted a slow fuse to all of them, and locked the door, and then tied my hands and feet good and hard, so's I couldn't put out the fuses. That's about the way that I feel!"

"And why?" chuckled the other.

"You would never guess it," said Jim Gore, dryly. "But it's because I'm scared, man. This here Diego Ramirez, he may seem like small potatoes to you, but to me he's a lot like trouble with a capital T."

"Brother," said The Doctor, "you are right. He will make us trouble, and he's dangerous. And that is why this party is going to be pleasant. Very pleasant! There is no pleasure in hitting a man who is not looking. We have now touched the shoulder of Ramirez and we have told him that we expect to beat him if we can, and beat him thoroughly. He now knows that we desire nothing but a fair opportunity to sink a bullet through his head. And from this point on, we know that he will spare no pains to murder us if he can—and so, we have shown our hands to Ramirez and he has shown his hand to us—and let the best man win!"

Jim Gore threw up his hands.

"Does it look like a fair game to you?"

"Why not?"

"You—well, we'll call you a good man—good enough to beat any three of the men that that Ramirez has with him. And me, though I ain't much, say that I could account for one or even for two of them cutthroats, if I had a world of luck with me. But that is only counting for five of them. And he has five times five!"

"Pish!" laughed The Doctor. "This is all very well, but you must never forget that men cannot be added up like figures in a mathematical problem. Even a Napoleon could not do that. For he said to himself, I have so many men under me, of whom the enemy disposes of only so many. Therefore, when I meet him, I shall infallibly smash him to the smallest bits. But the trouble was that on a certain day he was not carving up an Austrian army. He was not grinding his heel upon a lot of Prussian automatoms. No, on that day he was face to face with the beefeaters for the first time, and the fellow at the head of the beefeaters was a stiff-necked chap whom the John Bulls liked to call the Iron Duke. And that made a lot of difference—a terrible lot of difference!"

"I dunno what you're talkin' about," said Jim Gore bluntly.

"Of course you don't," answered the tall man, taking the arm of his companion, and striding off toward the mine. "Of course you don't. But let me tell you that the chap called the Iron Duke was not just one man on that day of fighting. He was as good as ten thousand hard-fighting riflemen. He was as good as half a dozen cavalry brigades all lined up ready for charging. He was better than whole parks of artillery. And I'm telling you this just to show you what a difference one man can make, in certain games. War is one of them. And this is another!"

He flowed on with the cheerful vanity of a child.

"This Ramirez," said he, "is at the present time more than a little touched with doubt about you and me, because he has never run into anything exactly like this in his life before. He's wondering and doubting, and though he is sure that he has us in his hand, to squash us whenever he has a real mind to it—still there is a little doubt, you understand. He won't sleep quite as well to-night as he slept last night, and when he comes out to eat us alive, I hope that he finds me harder to digest than the Little Corporal found the Iron Duke. Do you understand me?"

"I got a general idea," said Jim Gore solemnly, "that you aim to be harder to lick than any ten thousand men, when this here Ramirez starts after our hides. But maybe this Ramirez ain't gunna be so easy to bluff out."

"Bluff?" echoed Estaban. "Bluff, my son, Are you in your right senses? Bluff? I shall dine on the liver of this Ramirez! But let us go on! I am sleepy!"

"Where shall we sleep," said Jim Gore. "Unless one

of us keeps watch all the night long, they'll have our throats cut before the morning, man!"

"Stuff!" said Estaban. "Stuff! They'll search for us to-night, but they'll never dream of searching at the mine. They'll know that *we* know that they're out for our scalps. And so they'll hunt every place except in the place where we'll be sleeping."

"Man! Man, could you really go back to the cabin and—and sleep there!"

"I could," grinned the Estaban, "and I shall. And you'll sleep, too, partner. And we'll be up in the morning, fresh as daisies, and the rising sun shall reveal us in the act of thumbing our noses at Ramirez. And so —heads up, Jim. This dance is just commencing."

"Sleep in a rattlesnakes' den to-night," groaned Jim Gore. "But where do we sleep to-morrow night?"

"If I knew," said Don Cristobal, "I should try to forget as soon as possible. That is the spice and the special beauty to the affair—that we can never plan more than a single day ahead."

They reached the little dark shanty on the side of the mountain, before the mine, and there they found all well just as they had left it. They dared not show a light, but, fumbling here and there, they found a few bits to eat. Then they rolled in blankets and slept. Even Jim Gore could not allow alarm to keep his eyes open very long, but presently he was spinning off to a land of wildest dreams, where Mexicans with knives and guns swarmed about him, but all the bullets and all of the knives that they threw at him were turned aside by a sweeping shadow that brushed in between—the hand of a specter riding beside him that wore the shape of Estaban.

When he wakened, he was hearing a harsh voice that said at his ear:

"Señor Gore! Señor Gore! The devil is loose!"

He looked up into the grinning face of the Estaban.

"What's up? Are they coming?" asked Jim Gore, leaping to his feet and reaching for a rifle.

The Estaban merely laughed.

"I have been standing here," said he, "watching you

ducking bullets in your sleep ever since the sun came up. Why, Jim, you are a sounder sleeper than a tired horse in a stall! But here's the day, man, and down there in San Filipo they're waiting for us."

Jim Gore rubbed the lingering sleep from the corners of his eyes.

"Are they waiting for us? But if you ain't fairly spry in stepping out of that doorway, Doctor, nobody but me will ever go out of this here cabin walkin' on his own feet!"

The Doctor glanced over his shoulder in time to see something stir among the rocks beneath the cabin door. He did not jump, but his step to the side would have opened the eye of a professional boxer.

And as he stepped a bullet whizzed into the cabin, and with a great clangor knocked a hole through a frying pan that hung on the wall. The noise of the report followed like the clapping of a great pair of hands with a coin held in either palm.

CHAPTER XX

Besieged

Jim Gore did the best thing for safety. He dropped for the floor and lay there, stretched out long and large, and gradually fetching himself, by means of snakelike wriggles, in the direction of the spot where his rifle leaned against the wall. But his companion, after the first side-step which had taken him a few inches away from the path of the first bullet, went about his business with very little concern—much as though he felt that there could be no further danger from the man beyond the house.

He got to his own rifle with a single stride and, tilting it high, he even took the time to squint down into the barrel, thus making doubly sure that it was clean.

In the meantime, he was talking, quietly, and without haste.

"Will you mind the rear of the house, Jim?"

"There's nothing there—nothing but a crack in the wall."

"That's what I want you to watch. You can lay to it that they're here in a troop. They won't come hunting us singly, or in pairs, either. And if there's one chap out yonder, doing a bit of sharpshooting at us to keep his hand in, there's more of them at the rear, trying to sneak up on us. Here's your gun!"

He stepped boldly across the cabin, and though, as he passed the field of the open door the gun beyond cracked again, and a bullet hummed wickedly through. The Doctor picked up a rifle of his companion and extended it toward the cowering form of Jim.

"Here you are, Jim, if it's your gun that you're hunting for."

Jim Gore stood up, dragging himself erect by little degrees, as though each movement cost him a separate effort of the will. But he made no attempt to cover the shame that he felt. He took the rifle, shook his head as though to clear his brain, and stepped to the rear wall of the shack, where a yawning crack an inch across gave him a chance to squint up the mountain. He had barely bent his head to it when a rifle clanged in the shack itself, and far down the hillside came a wailing cry. Gore turned, with the scent of the burnt powder in his nostrils and his eyes wide.

The Doctor was shaking his head.

"It was only an arm," said he. "And only a moving arm, at that. But I think it will teach them that we are not to be rushed rashly. I think they'll lie low after this. And down there among those boulders the sun will begin to do our work for us, before very long."

And he chuckled softly as he spoke. As for Jim Gore, he had been able to spot nothing but the innocent trees behind the cabin, and the big rocks which were strewn up to the edge of the pines.

"Shall I close the door?" he asked.

"No," said the other. "Let the door stay open. It will show them that we laugh at them. It's like an open, laughing mouth, to them. And it will make them wonder at us, and then worry. And men who worry don't shoot straight, Jim."

Three guns exploded down the hillside in rapid succession. The bullets, whirring through the doorway, sank with a pounding noise into the heavy logs. And The Doctor fired again. A wild, sobbing cry carried to them from the rocks.

"A little more trimming of them," said The Doctor. "But this time I am afraid that I cut a little deeper. I could see the shoulder of one of those rats. And a shoulder is a different matter."

The yell of pain changed to a furious chorus of denunciatory voices, and these in turn were lost in the roar of rifles. Most of these were excellent weapons, and through the great target of the open door big-calibered slugs whistled in groups of half a dozen at a time. But shooting, as they did, up the slope of the hill, the men of Ramirez could not fire at an effective level. They simply honeycombed the roof and the sides of the shack, sometimes biting straight through the logs, sometimes pounding deep and sticking in the wood. But when The Doctor and Jim Gore drew far back to the sides of the shack and got close to the floor, they were in no vital danger. Jim Gore lay prone, his heart in his mouth. But the Estaban sat like an Indian, cross-legged.

It was no new story to him. His eyes flamed and his lips smiled, and, puffing at his cigarette, he spoke in the pauses of the rifle fire, while the heavy bullets clanged on the stove and quickly battered it to a pile of wreckage.

"That time I reached some one of importance. A lieutenant of Ramirez, do you think? He yelled loud enough to have been a captain! And now they want our blood. *How* they want it! They even howl for it, Jim. However, it is perfectly snug in here. If only they don't rush us from behind while half of them pepper us from the front. Take a look, Jim, and see what's happening in the rear."

Jim Gore dragged himself to unwilling knees and peered out to the rear.

"There's nothing moving," he said at last, truthfully. And he flung himself back to the safety of the floor again.

"Nothing there?" echoed the Estaban. "That seems strange. Then why the devil are they laying down such a barrage from the front, if they don't want to prepare for an attack from behind?"

He stood carelessly beside the rear wall, as though he invited death, in the very field of the riflemen down the hill, but still he was untouched, and Jim Gore was too frozen with wonder to beg his companion to be discreet.

"Nothing here?" said the Estaban. "No—but was that bush yonder before? That one with the three stems—that little, low, broad one, Gore?"

Jim Gore was forced to rise and look again, and as he looked through the long crack between the logs, a whizzing bullet plumped into the wood beside his cheek.

He said with a gasp: "I ain't mapped out all the bushes out there. I can't say just where each of them was at first—and is now."

"Aye," answered the Estaban, "but I can! I can remember all of the bushes and all of the stones. And there is this matter of importance—that the little three-stemmed bush was not there before. And it cannot very well have grown up by magic, can it, Jim?"

And he smiled at Gore.

"We'll ask it if it is an honest shrub," said The Doctor, and instantly fired.

The bush dissolved. From behind it the Mexican who had been creeping gradually forward behind this meager screen, leaped to his feet. And with a shout he sprang for the shelter of the trees.

It was not far to go, but opposing him there was a

man with an unerring forefinger, and a revolver in which there were still five bullets. And as those bullets sped rapidly from the gun, The Doctor had a word for each.

"We'll tag him on one arm. Shall we, Gore?"

And as the gun spoke, the poor Mexican with a scream grasped at an arm—then let it dangle while he leaped forward once more.

"The other arm, then, for a memento."

And as he fired, the other arm of the fugitive fell helpless along his side, but still he ran on, shrieking with agony and with fear.

"But if he comes to pot-shot at us in this fashion, it's only fair that we should have a chance to pot-shot back again, isn't it, Gore? So let's stop him and have a little longer chat with him. What do you say?"

Gore, fascinated with horror, glanced to the side, as he saw that his companion was actually smiling as he spoke—a smile of the most infinitely cruel satisfaction—he thanked Heaven that he had this man for a friend and not for an enemy. It seemed to Jim Gore that all the powers of a nation of armed men would not be nearly so dreadful as to have this man for a real antagonist.

At that instant the revolver exploded for the third time, and the flying Mexican twitched halfway round under the terrible impact of the bullet—then pitched heavily upon his side and lay there wriggling and screeching in a way that reminded Gore of some inoffensive beetle, with half its legs plucked away by the cruel and random hands of some child.

And The Doctor smiled again, with his jaw thrusting forward.

"He will stay, as you see, Jim. And what a big fuss they are making about it!"

The attack on the fugitive had roused a perfect storm of fury from the other men of Ramirez who were gathered for the attack. Those on the downward slope of the hill could not, of course, see what was happening, but the yells of the unlucky man as the bullets whipped through his flesh told them fully as eloquently as their eyes could have done. And the Ramirez men toward the trees were already pouring in a hot fire. It seemed that a score of rifles—down the hill and up—were now concentrating a savage fire upon the little shanty. Two men from behind boulders and half a dozen more from the trees were making fire and lead spout from the muzzles of their guns.

To be sure, except for the shots that ranged through the open door of the shack, only one slug in five got through the walls, but still that cabin was the hottest place that Jim Gore had ever dreamed of being in. And the strange calmness of his companion only served to make him more and more uneasy. He wanted with all his heart to throw himself down on the floor of the cabin, and yet he was too fascinated to leave off gazing upon the spectacle outside.

Squinting through the shack at the fallen man, he wondered deeply whether or not Don Cristobal would kill the twisting, screaming wretch with the next shot.

But such a killing was not in the mind of Estaban. He balanced the revolver in his hand, then swiftly discarded it, and resting the muzzle of his rifle against the crack between the logs, he took his aim with care.

"Now, as matters stand, there is only one thing for it," he said. "Will they try to blow the shack off its feet, or will they simply see that one of their friends is in great trouble? Will they wish to buy him off?"

The wounded man turned on his face and made a convulsive effort to crawl away, but as he started to make headway, the rifle of Estaban spoke, and a leaden bullet turned to water on the face of the boulder just in front of the creeper. He winced down to the ground, then started again, and this time a shot whirred an inch from his ear.

He understood now. It was better to bleed to death slowly under the unmerciful rays of that sun than to get the next bullet through his brain. So he lay still, yelling continually:

"Comrades—oh, amigos—my brothers—it is I,

Miguel! I am not dead! I shall not die if you will give me help! For the sake of your souls! If I die abandoned here, I shall send the devils up from hell to haunt you. I shall be a witness against you hereafter. Do you hear—it is I—Miguel! Oh, agony! Oh, Carlos! Carlos! Oh, Diego—your brother calls to you——"

It seemed as though the shrieking voice of the hurt man was silencing the rifles one by one until the last one ceased. And the Estaban saw a white handkerchief waved from behind a tree.

He shouted instantly.

"Come forward, friend. I shall treat you like an honorable man, and not like the dog that you are. Come forward and let me hear how you will buy off the life of your Miguel!"

An elderly man who walked with a limp and who looked like an honest farmer, in spite of the vicious air which he strove to give himself by his twisted and pointed pair of mustaches, stepped forward from behind the tree and came slowly out into the open.

"Yes, Señor Estaban——"

The angry and sudden cry of Estaban made even Jim Gore start and shiver.

"Carlos Aberdona, you scoundrel and foresworn ingrate! Have I become 'Señor' Estaban? Am I not 'El' Estaban to you and to the rest of your rat-hearted thieves who have come up here from my own country to work for my enemy? Carlos Aberdona, go back to the trees and send out another man. I shall not talk with you!"

"Señor El Estaban," cried Aberdona, dragging his hat from his head with what seemed to be an instinctive dread and respect, "it is not my will alone that brings me here. There are wicked days in your land and your country, señor. We go out from it because we starve there. We are weak and helpless with hunger there. And so we go out to serve where we can —I and poor Miguel here, who bleeds to death among the rocks."

"Ha?" cried El Estaban. "Is he, also, one of my people?"

"He is one of your children, señor, as much as I myself."

"So! Idiots, pick him up at once and care for him —no, bring him to me. Quickly, Carlos. Bring him hither to me. You will kill him with your clumsy hands. Bring him here, two or three of you. Sacred devils, how could I know that he was not some common cut-throat? Quickly! Quickly!"

Three or four leaped out from cover and ran toward the fallen man.

And Jim Gore heard their voices as they called reassuringly to him: "Keep a high heart, Miguel, for El Estaban himself will heal you! El Estaban will take care of you and make you well, amigo!"

And the faint voice of the wounded man—drunk with relief—"Ah, may the blessing of Heaven fall upon him—el maestro—El Estaban!"

Jim Gore smiled for the marvel of it, and for the pity of it, too! That even such hardy fighting men as these should believe that a miracle was in the power of the Estaban! And yet they believed it—there was a smiling and a perfect surety in the men who carried the hurt one forward.

CHAPTER XXI

Master and Servants

They herded into the shack—three of them, carrying the hurt man, and Carlos Aberdona leading the way. His eyes widened at the thought of entering the presence of the man whom he had just been striving with all the force and wit at his disposal to destroy. He was not overawed because he had just been attempting to murder The Doctor, but because he was about to stop into the mortal presence of El Estaban himself. Like a serf about to appear before his highest feudal lord!

So it was with Carlos Aberdona. He ordered his underlings about in the sharpest of voices, so that by the veil of his authority he might shroud his own nervous apprehensions. And others were coming—stealing up among the rocks on the hillside, and swarming down from the trees above the house.

Jim Gore to The Doctor gasped: "They're comin' in a swarm——"

"Aberdona!" snapped the Estaban.

"Señor!" said the Mexican, in the voice of one addressing the wandering spirit from another world.

"I don't want a mob of strangers about me. Guard the door! Keep them back!"

Sublime impudence! To appoint one of his would-be assassins of the moment before to protect him while he worked! Jim Gore, listening, could not be sure whether his companion was inspired or insane. He rather inclined toward the second theory.

But Aberdona was swelled with the importance of this mission. He leaped into the doorway and shouted: "Stand back! Stand back from the house, or you are dead men! It is El Estaban who commands it!"

The terrible El Estaban, surrounded even by enemies who reverenced his power and his name, looked at Jim Gore and winked broadly.

And then he said in a voice whose sternness was quite melted away: "Unless some of them are my children, Aberdona. Let them come in to me. But quietly—the man is deeply hurt. There must be quiet and order——"

No need to caution them in that! They approached the battered shanty as though they were damned spirits entering the lofty doors of a cathedral. There was one who crossed himself—and instinctive gesture of the greatest reverence and fear which he knew how to show.

They stood along the wall, five or six of such men as the world rarely could have mated, except, perhaps, among the mongrel crews of ruffians who once sailed the Spanish Main.

All fighting tigers, with glaring eyes softened, and set jaws relaxed, they stood against the wall with their hats in their hands and beheld agape the tending of their stricken comrade.

The Doctor was not in the least aware of them. He had before him a hard task. For Miguel had bled much and was still bleeding, and fright had torn through his wretched soul a wound even more deadly than the bullets from the Estaban's revolver.

And now his clothes were cut away. The long, deft hands of The Doctor moved like lightning. A turniquet at the hip stopped one gush of blood. The wounds were washed and probed.

Once Miguel screamed in a sudden agony, recalled by pain out of his trance of weakness.

And the voice of The Doctor became as soft as the tones of a mother, soothing her child. The lines of anguish and the glaring fear of death faded from the face of Miguel. He looked up to the stern face above him and murmured:

"El Estaban! El Estaban! All is well!"

And then he smiled and all consciousness of pain and all the fear of death left him—a wonderful transformation to see. It sent a pricking chill down the back of Jim Gore. It was like witnessing a miracle, a thing which would never be believed by other men, if he first described the manner in which the three big-caliber bullets had torn through the body of the Mexican.

But, truth to tell, there was not another groan wrung from the throat of Miguel during the rest of the operation. And though he became grave, now and again, as the Estaban was forced to handle the wounds with a serious pressure, still his joyous belief in an assured life was a wonderful anaesthetic.

Time and again his savage-faced companions by the wall crouched and twisted their faces in attitudes of strained apprehension as they witnessed the treatment of their wounded comrade. But when they saw that he no longer cried out, then they turned to one another with incredulous, flashing smiles, and there was always the answering whisper:

"It is El Estaban!"

It was as though in that single name was explanation enough for all of the miracles that the mind of man might be able to conceive.

At last the bandages were complete—and if it had been a painful job to witness, there was no doubt at all that it was a thorough one. For the wounds had been well searched and cleansed, and the bandages were applied with perfect firmness and skill.

And now the wounded man was dressed again, but not in his own, slashed and tattered clothes. A pair of Gore's trousers were borrowed from the wall. And then The Doctor's own coat was drawn deftly about the shoulders of Miguel.

After that the hand of The Doctor rested for a moment upon the brow of his victim, while the fingers of his other hand touched the pulse in Miguel's wrist.

He began to nod in thoughtful satisfaction.

"This is all very well, and he is fast growing stronger. However, he must not be moved from this place—not to-day, nor to-morrow, nor in the next day.

"But on the third day, if he has a good appetite and begs for much food on that day, and if he would have a cigarette rolled for him—then you may make for him a stretcher and carry the stretcher with four men—not, you dogs, with a pair of horses. So you may take him softly down to San Filipo, stopping very often on the way, and taking water for him to drink.

"Furthermore, if you feed him a single meal of peppers and beans, he will die. And if he dies, his soul will come back to haunt you, Carlos Aberdona! Do you mark me?"

"Señor El Estaban—Señor El Estaban! In the name of Heaven, do not make me responsible for his life. For he is very nearly a dead man now. It is only by the strength of El Estaban that he keeps his life, even now!"

"Mark me now, Aberdona!" thundered El Estaban,

raising his finger and extending his terrible long right arm. "If he is not fed only on milk and stale bread softened in the milk, if he is not fed on this, and on this only—and in small meals, three times a day—if he is not cared for in this fashion, he will die and his soul will return from hell to hound you. And furthermore, when it is brought to my attention that this man is dead, then I will come after you, Carlos, and I shall find you, and I shall kill you, Carlos, and give the broken parts of you to the coyotes to gnaw—and you will be forgotten!"

Carlos Aberdona was transformed with terror.

"But," said El Estaban, "if you care for him gently, and never leave his side, and if you keep cold fresh water near him, and if you bathe him and keep him clean—if these things are done smilingly, for his sake and because I, El Estaban, command it, then I tell you that he will be healed. I, El Estaban, give you my promise. Do you understand me?"

Carlos Aberdona bowed almost to the ground and responded in a trembling voice, "It shall be done, señor!"

"Because," said El Estaban, "he is one of my children and the life of each one among my children is precious to me and must be guarded, because I will have it so."

He turned upon the half dozen brutal-faced pirates who were ranged along the wall.

"You, too, belong to me. You have run away from me, and you have been driven away. But some day I shall return. I shall make the land so that there shall be no law in it except the word of the Estaban. I shall come there and drive out the thieves and the robbers, except such as I choose to let live. The rest, I shall hang them up at the crossroads as a warning, except for a certain chosen few whom I shall put into my bodyguard!"

"Ah, señor!" breathed the brigands.

"Furthermore, every man's land which has been stolen from me shall be restored to me. And after it is restored to me, he shall continue to live upon it, and pay me a rental for it. I shall take care of him in trouble, and when I need him, he shall come to work for me. The sluggards shall starve, and the working men shall have full barns and fat children and their wives shall always have corn in the bins and pigs in the pasture. In all things it shall be as it was before, in the days of my father."

Now, in saying these words, which were not remarkable, except for a certain archaic note which was in them, El Estaban assumed a profundity of manner which Jim Gore had never observed in him before. The effect of the speech upon the men was extraordinary, for they of one accord threw themselves upon their knees before him. And the Estaban stretched his long, cultured hand above their heads.

"The Almighty bless you," said he, "and strengthen you, and give happiness in your houses and beauty to your children."

"Alas, señor, where there are no houses, and where the children are scattered——"

"I shall come, and gather you——"

"Señor, señor, let it be soon!"

"And in the meantime, tell the dogs yonder, who serve Ramirez because they have never known a better master—tell them that I choose to leave the place in quiet, and that I will not be disturbed and forced to turn from my way to punish some rash fool who dares to lift his hand against me. Jim, we are going!"

He said the last tersely to Gore, and Jim Gore mechanically gripped his rifle and stepped forth at the side of the tall man. Stepped forth, as he felt, into the instant presence of death!

CHAPTER XXII

Back to San Filipo

But there was no actual danger whatever. Out from the shack ran before them Carlos and his companions, crying out: "Be careful, amigos. El maestro wishes to leave in peace. He will not harm you if you do not touch your guns. Be warned. Do not stir in your places!"

And, to the astonishment of Jim Gore, not one of the gallants outside the house dared to raise revolver or rifle against them. They stood at gaze like very cattle, while Don Cristobal moved out among them and through them and across the mountain, until the welcomed shadows of the forest fell across the pair. Then, in their rear, a sudden clamor broke out. A gun exploded, and a bullet rattled among the boughs above their heads. Gore broke into a run, but the voice of Estaban stopped him shorter than a shot.

"But if they follow?" cried Jim Gore. "Ain't they comin' now? Ain't they comin' on the run?"

It was as though the eye of the tall man had hypnotized them. But so soon as that eye was removed, and they could think for themselves once more, they seemed to remember that they were in the employ of Ramirez, and that he had offered them, no doubt, a fat reward if they could bring in word that Estaban was dead.

However, Estaban himself, turning slowly around, scanned the trees behind him and then shook his head.

"They won't follow us past the edge of the wood," said he. "They've shed a little of their courage already to-day, and when they get in the dimness of the woods, they'll lose another section of it, you may be

125

sure. Have so doubt about our safety, Jim. But if we ran, now, they would sense it, and that would turn them all into heroes——"

"But if they *do* break through at us?" gasped Gore.

"Then we're dead men, of course. I've paralyzed the simple fools only for a moment, and now they are wishing that they had my scalp. However, it's better to walk on, and take the chance. A man has to sacrifice something for an effect of dignity, now and then."

"I'd rather a lot be an undignified living man than the proudest corpse that ever waited for a gravedigger," said Jim Gore. "And I reckon that you would, too, partner! Unless you've got out of your wits— hey! There they come!"

And Jim Gore leaped for covert.

Don Cristobal turned in leisurely fashion again and surveyed the woods behind him.

"It was only the breaking of a twig," said he, "that sounded a little louder than the rest, but nobody is coming after us. Listen to that pig, Carlos Aberdona, however!"

For the loud voice of Carlos could be heard at the edge of the trees urging his companions to break bravely into the woods, like true Mexicans and heroes. He would see that the leaders were rewarded, and that Señor Ramirez should pay a handsome sum.

"But he doesn't try the leading himself!" chuckled The Doctor. "And Aberdona ought to remember that when it comes to fighting, an ounce of leadership is worth a pound of language at any time! No, they'll give us a berth that will be wide enough! And after they settle down, they'll have something to think about. But let's march on, partner. There's no harm in putting a little distance behind us, if they don't feel that we're hurrying about it."

And so they strode on, Jim Gore for the nonce leading the way and setting the pace, while his tall companion ever and anon paused and turned back, as though his heart were really burning to be back among the men at the edge of the forest.

They kept on in this fashion for a full hour, before Gore, growing a little tired with the heat and the effort which he had been making, came to a pause.

"There's one thing," said he.

"Come out with it, Jim."

"What the devil happened, I dunno. But yonder we were, all copped up in that shanty, with twenty men around us—and all of them fighting men, too, judging from the straightness of their shooting, and all of them armed with good, modern repeaters. Why, *two* of them just to lie low and watch the front and the back of the house had ought to of been enough to keep us blocked up there till the night, anyways. But here we are, walkin' safe and sound out through the middle of 'em—and leaving three wounded men, one of 'em like to die. And neither of us got so much as a scratch! I'm damned if I understand how it could have happened!"

"A miracle!" grinned The Doctor.

"Aye," said Jim Gore soberly, "and maybe it was, for all that!"

He added: "What stopped them? What shut them up and made them stand around like a lot of fools while we got away—but the minute that your back was turned, then they busted loose again?"

"I'll tell you," said Estaban. "It was the effect of three generations. Those fellows were used to El Estaban so long that the name was like a charm on them. The same as the name of a saint charms the old hermit who lives off by himself."

"Maybe," muttered Gore. "That's a name for what happened, but it ain't an explanation."

"And then, when they saw the trees close behind me, they felt that I wasn't so queer, after all, but just a man. And so they came boiling out after us to eat us alive—until they saw the shadows of the trees before them, and began to remember that any one of those trees that they were looking at were broad enough to hide a man—and a big man, at that. So they stopped—and there you are!"

Gore sighed and mopped his brow.

"You've told about it; but still it's queer—danged queer. And I wouldn't like to go through it. And I wouldn't have got through with it, if I had had any other man in the world with me except just you. But those gents—they seemed like they pretty near loved you—but now they're hunting for you again!"

"They do love me," said The Doctor calmly. "But they hate me, too. They love El Estaban, because my fathers were wise enough to keep their tenants fat and contented and rule them with a rod of iron, you understand? And they hated my fathers for the very same reason."

"Hated 'em and loved 'em for the same reason? Is that good sense, old-timer?"

"Of course it is. Every child knows that he hates his father and loves him. Hates him because his father is a wall that keeps him from running out loose and amuck in the world, and loves him because his father is a wall that shelters him from the rest of the world. Do you understand?"

Jim Gore nodded.

"But the main thing," said Gore, "is that if they were under your thumb for a minute, now they hanker to get their claws in you again, like wildcats!"

"Not a bit! The main thing is that we walked out from that damned shack safe and sound. The second matter of importance is that they came back to me, if only for a moment. And having come back to me once, they may come back to me again. And if they come back again—why, Jim, with even a handful like that to follow me, I shall go off to conquer my kingdom again! Will you ride along with us if that time ever comes?"

Jim Gore threw up his hands.

"Not if you was to offer me a thousand dollars a day! But what're we gunna do next, doctor? Shall we head straight back across the mountains or——"

"We'll pick out a place to spend the day and have a good sleep. And when the dark comes again, we'll go down to the valley again—back to San Filipo."

The miner groaned. But he felt like a man afloat on a dismasted ship, with a hurricane blowing and a fiend at the helm. He dared not leave the ship, and yet he could expect nothing but death before him.

They did that day as The Doctor had directed. They found a shady cove among the trees, through the scattered outposts of which they could look down upon the valley of San Filipo. And there, because he was very far spent, Jim Gore presently went sound asleep.

When he wakened, he found that Estaban was sitting cross-legged, and on the ground before him he was dealing specimen poker hands—face up.

What hands were those that his too-well-trained fingers plucked from the deck! Jim Gore beheld three of a kind and a straight and a flush and four deuces fall upon the ground in one single set of hands. And the winning hand lay always in front of The Doctor!

He watched this for some time, until Estaban, without looking up, said:

"It's nearly sundown, Jim. Are you ready for the start?"

"Back?" said Jim.

"To San Filipo."

"Go where you want," said Jim Gore. "I ain't got the courage to leave you. And I ain't fool enough to enjoy being with you. Lead when you're ready!"

Before the dusk had settled over the valley they had started. They wound down the long slope, and as they walked the pit of the valley turned to purple, with the yellow San Filipo flowing through its midst, fringed with meager green. And from the town lights began to shine toward them with single, solid rays of gold.

There was little air—just enough stirring to keep constantly in their nostrils the acrid scent of the alkali dust. The air was thick with it, stifling with it, and the heat was like midday.

"How shall we enter?" asked Estaban.

"We can hike down along the river and get into the town that way, maybe!"

"Look yonder where that firelight throws a flush on the river! No, they are keeping a strict lookout on the river. We'll come in on the far side, and take the chance of the flying outposts which this Ramirez keeps circling through the night. You, Jim, are Hernandez. I am Guadalupe. We have been out for a walk after supper. And that is all that there is to it! Keep steady —and in a pinch let me do the talking!"

CHAPTER XXIII

Through the Line

So Jim Gore swallowed his fears, and they went on slowly together until they had circled toward the farther side of San Filipo. And the walls of the town seemed to grow greater and more black and ominous as they walked. Even The Doctor seemed to feel some touch of awe, and twice he paused on the way and looked about him.

But Estaban was not able to foresee the danger when it appeared. Two men rose out of the blackness of the ground just before them.

"Halt! Who are you?"

"Why, pigs," answered Estaban in a ringing voice, "do we have to tell who we are to *you?*"

"Are you too good to talk to us? We have guns that are not too good to talk to *you,* however. Put up your hands!"

And two rifles glimmered at Gore and The Doctor through the starlight.

"Put up our hands!" roared The Doctor. And then he broke into a great laughter, so unfeigned and hearty that even Jim Gore found himself smiling in sympathy, in spite of all of his fears. "We are to put up our hands! The señor's men rob one another and hold one another up!"

His voice changed to sharp anger.

"Who are you, fools?"

"Who are you?" growled the others sullenly. "And why do you stand there and talk, if there is nothing wrong with you? Come, let me know your names."

"I'll tell you," said Estaban. "Only because you have those rifles and you are really idiots enough to shoot. I am Guadalupe, of course. And this is Hernandez."

"Guadalupe?"

"Bah! Are there two Guadalupes in the town of a size with me?"

"What Guadalupe? I know of no Guadalupe——"

"Come, Hernandez. Pay no more attention to them. They dare not shoot. If they do, the señor will hang them up in the morning to teach them to kill his oldest servants. Oh! Oh, is it any wonder that that devil, that Estaban, should get away from thick heads like these two?"

And he walked straight on past the two sentinels, with Jim Gore striding hastily at his side, heart in mouth.

"Stop there—or we fire."

"You dare not fire. I invite you!" sneered Estaban. "Am I to explain myself to my own army? Do you kill your own kind, you murderer? When Señor Ramirez sees this, he will give you your pay and have done with you. He will send you back to starve in Mexico!"

One of the two sentinels grounded his rifle with a tremendous oath.

"Come back and say those things again, you dog!" he howled after Estaban.

"I shall say them in the day to you, when there is a chance for me to see the face that I shall step upon. Adios!"

He walked on, and Jim Gore at his side.

"That there is a fine beginning!" said Jim Gore. "A

sort of a good first page. On the second page we get ate up by cannibals!"

"Steady, Jim. We're through the crust, now, and the rest may be easy. We are going straight through. And if I find her again to-night, Heaven help me if I don't speak to her; and if she does not answer me, she'll have to dodge my hands! I've made up my mind to that!"

There was no answer from Gore. He plodded on with his head down, like one who has given up all his hope, and so they came hastily under the very shadow of the first crumbling walls. The Doctor plucked the sleeve of his friend.

"And here's another pair, Jim. Different stuff, this time, and riding as though they meant mischief. Get in among the rubbish with me."

They flattened themselves among the tumbling masses of weather-molded adobe bricks, but at that place there was not sufficient shelter except from the dark which would blend them with the ruins.

The two riders came rushing out of the night until their silhouettes rose gigantic against the stars. One swept on, but the other reined in his horse and called sharply to his companion.

"They went this way!"

The voice of the second man came from the distance, as he stopped his horse: "Around to the left. This way!"

"No, here. I think they went in here."

"Are you going to ride over those bricks?"

"We can walk."

"We'll find a needle in a junk heap sooner than we'll fine them there."

"We can try. What's that?"

He rode a little to the right. A dozen feet from the nose of his horse the two fugitives lay motionless, listening to their hearts.

"There's nothing here. But if they were two of us, why can't we find them now? Why have they hidden?"

"They haven't hidden. They've just walked on in. Besides, would even El Estaban dare to come into San Filipo after what he has done to-day?"

"He will dare anything. But we'll try farther down the wall and see what's there."

They made off with a sudden pounding of hoofbeats. And after they had been gone for a moment, the two crept to their feet, and still crouching, stole down to the inside of the heap of bricks.

"A lucky night!" chuckled Estaban.

"We've used our luck up for a month," muttered Gore. "The next time we get into trouble, it will be the finish of us. Dog-gone me, doctor, I figger that this is a good time for us to start right straight back the way that we came."

"Why, man," said Estaban, "it's as dangerous to leave the town, now, as it is to stay in it. More dangerous. No, now that we're safely in, we'll do what we can. Steady Jim! We've only begun."

"Where away now, then?"

"The church, Jim. The church, of course."

Jim Gore drew in a long breath and felt for his revolver with a trembling hand. Then he marched on beside the tall man. They wound among the broken forms of houses and finally cleared that quarter of the town and found themselves on the edge of the plaza in the center of San Filipo. There they paused, crouched in a shadow, and looked out upon the center of the square, where a tall bonfire was wagging its hot, yellow head high in the night, and half a dozen figures were gathered around it.

"How many men has he?" murmured Estaban. "Enough to keep a handy lot here in the middle of the town. And enough to stand guard outside, and enough to ride on patrol. And besides that, he must have fresh workers to go on with his search of the town—whatever it is that he's searching for. How, if he is searching for the same trail that we're on? The hidden silver, Jim? And what if we find it before him, and scoop it out from beneath his very nose? What would you say to that? Ah, there he begins!"

Somewhere beyond the plaza, and in the direction of the old Ramirez house, the fine voice of Diego rose in song above the twangling accompaniment on his guitar. And the shadowy watchers around the fire swayed their bodies in rhythm with the music.

"A happy man," said Estaban. "But perhaps he will be sadder before the morning. Even this bright fellow cannot sing and work at the same time. Let's go on."

They rose. And sneaking back into the deeper shadows of the night, they circled around toward the massive wreckage of the church. Once more they paused to take stock of all that was passing near them. But all the living sounds of San Filipo sounded faint and far away, except, now and then, some high-pitched burst of laughter, which made Jim Gore feel that their presence there was perfectly known, and that the men of Ramirez were laughing in glee. They had set a trap, and now the trap had made its catch. It only remained for them to close in and hunt down the quarry within the narrow confines of the town.

They left the shadows. They crossed the open space with the nunnery on the one side and the ponderous church remains on the other.

Far in the east, a moon was beginning to show itself, but though it lighted the upper sky, its slant rays still left the face of the earth as black as ever.

They came to the entrance to the under part of the old structure so terribly familiar in the mind of poor Jim Gore.

"Now, Jim," said his companion, "you remain here and keep your eyes opened. Look sharp, and get your gun ready. Hide here, behind this old pillar. In another minute, you'll be getting a little more moonlight here, and when that comes it will make your work a lot easier. You understand?"

"And what am I to do?"

"Wait until you see something come out of the church. If it's a man, let him pass. But if the nun in the black robe tries to come this way—why, up with your gun and tell her to stop. And if she won't stop—and if

she tries the silly dumb act which she tried before—
put a bullet a foot from her ear, and then I think that
you will get words enough out of her. If it *is* a woman
at all!"

"Even you got to admit," said Jim Gore, stammering,
"that it *might* be a ghost?"

"No, you blockhead! But it might be a man togged
out to look the part of a ghost, for all that I know. You
understand me? And with his face painted up, and the
rest, he might walk in the part of a dead nun as well as
any living girl that ever stepped. So that's why I tell
you to watch like a hawk. If the nun comes out, and
won't speak—and you fire near her—then watch yourself, for I'll be greatly surprised if a revolver doesn't
jump out from those robes and explode at your head!"

"And while I'm here holdin' down the gate to the
ghost yard—what'll *you* be doing, doctor?"

"I'll be in the graveyard itself!"

CHAPTER XXIV

A Discovery

Crouched in the shadow near the entrance to the cellarage, The Doctor removed his hat and smoothed back
his hair. He took his loaded Colt in the one hand and
his little electric torch in the other, and began his advance at once, so that Jim Gore, watching and listening
intently, heard not a sound. So very snakelike was the
ease of this progress that it made Jim even feel that his
senses must be deceiving him. It could not be an actual
man in flesh and blood, but it must be a mere shadow
—an hallucination!

The Doctor, in the meantime, moved steadily forward. Stealing along with infrequent flashes of the
light to read the state of the floor over which he was
passing, he soon gained the farther corner of the cellar

and turned down it toward the angle from which, the other night, the nun had been seen to appear.

But there was no sign of her as he approached the same spot again. He waited, sinking upon one knee to rest himself and to steady his nerves; and while he waited he listened to the far-off sound of the voice of Diego Ramirez, singing to the guitar.

It was not a cheerful sound to The Doctor, but still he did not flinch from the work which lay before him. He stood up again, and going forward still more slowly, he came to the spot where the miracle had happened, and the body of the girl had stepped out from the solid face of the bricks.

He flashed the light of the electric torch over them. But never did stone wall seem stouter, and never did stone wall seem more undisturbed by the hand of man.

Not only did the light tapping of a bit of stone against the wall give back no hollow sound, but the little blows of the rock scarred the skin of thinnest moss which grew across the wall.

However, it had certainly seemed that from this very spot she had issued, and The Doctor was not a man to believe in mysteries. Therefore, he took from the pocket a little bar such as a professional burglar would have recognized at a glance. With this he began to chip busily at the mortar which held two courses of the stones together. But though he persisted until, in half a dozen places, he had driven holes five and six inches deep, he could not find a spot which gave any promise that the wall was a false front.

But he was not impatient. Having made up his mind to investigate this matter thoroughly, he was willing to devote hours, days, and weeks to the task. And what was more to him than the hope of money to be found here, was the mystery of the nun.

Besides, he had the challenge of the fear which he had showed to spur him on. He felt that for a single instant on that other night he had showed something like the white feather, and he would not rest until he had removed the disgrace under which he felt that he had fallen.

So he labored on patiently at the unsolvable mystery of the stone wall which confronted him, when his left knee, on which his weight was resting, slipped a trifle——

He was on his feet instantly, frowning down at the floor and turning the flash of his light upon it. Because it had seemed to Estaban that the solid stone pavement of the church, covered thick with dust, had given way and suddenly moved a trifle to the side. He studied it gravely. It could not have happened. And when he tried the pavement again, and even stamped heavily upon it, there was not a sign of a movement beneath him.

He tried sounding the rock with sharp blows of the bar with which he had been working, but no hollow sound came back to him. It seemed, certainly, that the pavement of the church cellar was bedded in the bedrock itself, or else on the hard ground.

He went to work, therefore, to replace himself exactly in the position which he had occupied before, resting his weight on his left knee as exactly as he could in the same identical location where it had been before.

But still, swing his weight as he might from side to side, he could not produce the slightest motion in the stone on which he was resting his weight.

Then, at the last, he remembered that the bar with which he had been digging at the wall had pressed, at that moment, into a deeper crevice from which the mortar had been sifted out by long time.

He plunged the bar back into this place and, pressing with all his might, he felt something give with a slight grating noise—and at the same moment the ponderous stone on which he was kneeling shifted with a slow and gradually increasing swing to the left.

When the pressure of the bar ceased, the stone stopped moving; and when the bar was pressed, but the weight of his body removed from the stone, it stopped sliding again. The two things were necessary in combination, and when the stone at last ceased stirring, there was a gap a foot and a half in width at one edge of it.

Down this El Estaban peered as far as he could into the shadows. But he found nothing save a wall of darkness before him, and when he extended the light of the torch, all that he saw before him was a narrow passage, surely at its widest not above three feet, and with the whole coming to an abrupt stop some half dozen of feet beneath him.

El Estaban considered the matter long and seriously, his flash light turned out, and his chin resting upon his clenched fist, but all that he could see in the trench beneath the table stone was without any hint of a solution for his problem.

He determined, finally, that there was only one thing for him to do, and that was to lower himself to the bottom of the crevice and there make sure if the bottom were indeed bare of all information.

So, flash light in hand, he gave one sweeping view to the cellarage of the church around him, and then lowered himself down to the bottom of the crevice. And what he found was, at the bottom, a gap of two feet, invisible from above, owing to the roughness and obliquity of the stone, which shut off the view. And through that gap, he saw a passageway which sloped rapidly down into the earth—a narrow passage, in which the air was distinctly foul and choking.

He turned back, a little dizzy, and a little sick at heart, at the thought of what might happen to him in this obscure dungeon if the massive rock above him, closing the entrance to the tunnel, were to be closed above him.

For it was of a solid thickness great enough to drown any uproar which he might make to call for help. And if the stone were closed, perhaps it would not be many hours before the lack of oxygen would destroy him.

However, his brain cleared at once, and he turned

resolutely back for his work of exploration. Pushing the hand which held the flash light before him, he advanced steadily on his hands and his knees, and so came to a sharp bend of the tunnel, and to a point where it widened suddenly to four feet, and almost a sufficient height for him to stand upright in it.

CHAPTER XXV

The Pit

He straightened, therefore, and had just stepped forward with confidence when his foot passed through thin air instead of striking on the hard ground, and he lunged forward and down into emptiness. The flash light fell from his hand and rolled on the ground before him, while Estaban found himself hanging from the lip of the broken passageway over an abyss of unknown depth—but deep enough, as he could judge by the rattle of the pebbles which he had dislodged, falling to a great distance beneath him.

He tried to draw himself up, but a great fragment of rock broke away beneath his straining hands; and as it hurtled downward, he was barely able, in falling, to take a fresh grip on another and lower ledge.

Swinging there, quaking with horror, he heard the dislodged mass of stone bounding from side to side of the narrow chasm until it struck beneath him against metal, and enormous waves of sound boomed suddenly up to him, pounding his ears, making his very soul tremble with their immensity.

And he knew, while the long notes hung thick about him, that he was listening to the voices of the Bells of San Filipo in very fact!

Yet that made the mystery hardly less strange than it had been before. He swung himself lightly up now, caught up the fallen flash light, and turned its stream downward upon the pitch below. What he saw was a descent of fully fifty feet beneath him, and in the bottom of that gulf he could distinguish the broad, battered lip of a giant bell—the biggest of those famous bells of San Filipo, here fallen, here to lie and become a legend.

He did not allow himself more than a moment to make this observation and to switch off the spreading cone of light again. Then it seemed, in the intense blackness that covered him again, that he heard behind him a whisper as of a stealthy foot that trailed the rock. It was the merest ghost of a sound, but what Estaban had just been through had been enough to bring his nerves into most acute focus.

He dropped to hands and knees and thrust his revolver before him. And then he whistled a soft, soft bar of a song, and waited. That bit of a noise, he hoped, would encourage the one who had made that whispering noise to creep forward to the attack, expecting to find a man off his guard. And in the meantime Estaban was worming his way forward with the most infinite caution. He saw nothing before him. The blackness was so absolute that he could not see his own hand if he raised it within an inch of his eyes. But in another instant it seemed to Estaban that he heard just before him the sound of a taken breath.

Victory comes to him who can act as the tiger acts. Estaban leaped from all fours and struck with the clubbed revolver. The heavy weapon landed on flesh. And it landed with such sickening force that there was only a choked moan, and the sound of a falling body.

Then Estaban turned the white current of the electric light on the fallen man and saw a barefooted Mexican lying sprawled on his face.

The knife, on which he had depended too much, was close beside one of his limp hands. With the point of this knife Estaban pricked the other—not cruelly deep, but enough to rouse him with a start, and find the mighty hand of the conqueror upon his neck and the stern eyes of Estaban glaring into his.

"Now," said Estaban, "I have you on the edge of a ready prepared grave. I have only to slide this knife between your ribs, amigo, and then to toss you over the edge of the pit, there. And there's the end to you!"

A wave of apprehension passed over the face of the other like a wave of wind over a hillside covered with sensitive green grass. The very whiteness of his fear made Estaban smile.

"But," said he, "if you will be true to me and forget the others, I shall not hurt you. Do you hear? I shall not so much as lay the weight of a finger upon you!"

The other dropped to his knees, almost slipping through the hands of Estaban in the profundity of his relief.

"I am only a poor dog," he whined, "but I shall be a faithful dog to you, señor. Heaven witness me that I shall be true. Only—I am not worth the time of killing. But you have given me your promise. I see in your eye that your promise is sacred to you, señor. I trust you so much that I would walk before you with my back turned, and I would have no fear—no real fear, señor!"

"You lie," Don Cristobal. "But now you shall do that very same thing. You shall walk first and show me the way."

"To what, señor?"

To what, indeed? There was nothing for Don Cristobal but sheerest bluff, but he decided that he would try it. And lodged in his mind was the memory of another barefooted Mexican, who had carried a heavy load of silver on his back, up the steep mountain, and from the direction of San Filipo.

"Why, you idiot," said Estaban, "why should I be here except to find the treasure? Why *should* I be here, pray?"

The eyes of the peon flashed to one side and to another, and his face took on a dazed look.

"Carramba!" whispered he. "And do you know that, also?"

"Of course I know it. Or why else should I be working the underground passages here like an infernal mole. Will you tell me that?"

"It is not for me to think. It is not for me to speak. It is for me only to do what the señor would have me to do. And Heaven forgive those who told me that no other man could know this thing! What they lose, may it be upon their own heads."

So he struck out a compact with his conscience, and bowed his head again. At last: "I am ready, señor!"

But even though he was convinced that Estaban already knew a vast deal about the treasure, and even although there was the fear of death and the potent hope of life before him, still he went forward slowly. And after he had led the way for a considerable distance down the passage, which twisted and turned from side to side, apparently in the effort of those who had dug it to avoid the hardest strata of rocks, the peon paused again and leaned one hand against the wall.

"Is this the end?" asked Estaban.

"Alas, señor!" said the poor fellow.

"Come," said Don Cristobal, "do not tell me that I am about to find a miracle—a faithful servant!"

"Señor," said the Mexican, "if you could know the goodness of their hearts as I know it, you would not wonder that I wish to be faithful to them. And it is a worse thing than dying, to destroy them, as I shall have to destroy them."

"Then why must they be destroyed?" asked Estaban.

The peon looked at him with a sad but knowing smile.

"I have seen you, and I have felt your hand, señor. And I know that when you see the treasure, all the goodness will leave you and you will want it for yourself only—and the first thing is that the others must die! And what can we do? Not against a tiger!"

He threw up his hands in a gesture of abandonment.

"Come," said Don Cristobal sternly, "I have listened to you long enough. Now open the way to me."

"I do as you command. San Juan forgive me and intercede for my sin! Because if I owe my life to you, I owe to them my life, also. Alas, what a poor dog am I to owe a life twice!"

He went slowly forward again, and as Estaban followed, they came to a sharp double turn—and just beyond it to a heavy, clumsily made door. The peon drew back and whispered:

"All is in darkness on the farther side of the door. They have heard the bells of San Filipo, and they know that there is danger walking in the tunnel. What will you do, if you walk through into the blackness?"

"Trust that to me."

"There is a signal, first, which tells them that it is I who am returning. I shall make that signal, señor. And then do you open the door and walk through!"

"What is your name?"

"Garcia."

"Garcia, swear to me."

"I swear to you, señor."

"That you will speak the truth only."

"Heaven sees and hears me, and knows that I have received mercy from you."

"That is true. Now tell me, Garcia, how many persons are there in the dark beyond that door?"

"There are four, señor."

"Four!" muttered Estaban.

For that made the odds high, even to him, who rarely blanched from numbers. But he well knew that in a harumscarum fight in the darkness anything might happen. The hand of a child, if luck were with it, might do far more than the hand of a man. And he considered this matter thoughtfully.

"Four!" he repeated.

"But as the señor knows, I cannot lie to him. And two of them can do him no harm."

"Two can do me no harm?"

"It is as I have said."

Estaban paused. There was a note of honesty in the voice of the peon which urged him toward belief. And yet why any but strong men should be engaged in such a matter as this, which had to do with treasure underground, was past the comprehension of El Estaban.

But suddenly he decided that he must act without any further delay. All his fiery instinct urged him to pass through that door and cast himself among the people who were there. And he obeyed that impulse.

At his whispered command, the peon knocked rapidly four times against the door, and then Estaban found it pressed open, and stepped in. And as he stepped in, he brushed against the clothes of some one standing beside the door—some one in the act of holding it wide for his entrance.

"So, Garcia, there was nothing?" asked one who spoke Spanish with a strongly Anglo-Saxon touch to his accent. "Nothing has happened—but another of those infernal rocks fell in on the bells, I suppose?"

There was no chance for Estaban to answer, for suddenly the moral strength of Garcia, beyond the door, must have given way. The door was wrenched open, and into the pit of blackness Garcia was screaming: "Save yourselves. It is a stranger and a devil that I have brought back. It is not Garcia! Save yourselves—Antonio, José—it is a tiger and not a man—and he comes for the treasure. I shall be one of you to fight him!"

And there was the heavy footfall of Garcia as he leaped into the place.

But Estaban flattened himself against the wall, and waited. Once before, not many minutes ago, he had had to fight in the black of the night, and this was another strain of the same sort following very rapidly thereafter.

Not a breath stirred. Not a voice whispered. Not a foot sounded. But El Estaban knew that forms were stealing here and there, fumbling for him through the darkness. And he crouched, with a revolver in either hand, ready to shoot.

And he thought of Jim Gore—slow and stupid through he was, still he was an honest man who would have guarded the life of a friend in utmost need. To have had even Jim Gore at his back in this crisis!

But Jim Gore was far away and above the ground, crouching in the shadow of the church's portal, and perhaps dealing with dangers of his own, which may well have been drawn upon him by the ringing of the buried bells of San Filipo. All the town must have heard. And no wonder it was to Estaban that he and Gore, on the lip of the valley far away from where the mine stood, had been able to hear a whisper of a similiar noise.

He shut Gore from his mind. There was enough for him to do now without wishing for help where no help was to be had.

And just as he was nerving himself, he saw a vision before him that turned his blood to ice water.

Out of the terrible blackness of the dark before him, there appeared suddenly the face of the nun—the ghostly creature which had passed him on that other night in the ruined cellarage of the church.

All the black hood, and even the coarse grain of the cheap cloth, and the white cloth which framed her face whithin, and the deadly pallor of the face itself, and the fixed and staring, unearthly eyes, and the rosary hanging from about the throat of the vision—all these appeared clearly defined before Estaban, as though an inward light were shining from the woman and the ornaments which she wore.

And so dreadful was the sudden appearance of her that a groan of anguish broke from one of the other men in the room.

Estaban leveled his revolver—and then he lowered the gun with an inward oath. For if his reason were right, and if this were actually a living and breathing woman, what a sin would be his if he should destroy her!

Instead of firing, he raised himself and leaped suddenly straight at her.

His reaching left hand touched cloth—not any film

of the imagination, but honest, coarse, heavy cloth, and as he plunged close to the face, he clutched the body of a woman against him, and the odor of phosphorus, poisonous and sickening, filled his nostrils.

CHAPTER XXVI

A Proposal

If he needed another proof that this was flesh and blood, he had it in the sudden scream of the girl and then a man's voice shouting in broken Spanish; "Garcia—José—Antonio—in the name of Heaven—to her help!"

There was the sound of a rush toward him. He swung a revolver before him and the heavy butt clicked against a man's skull and felled him heavily, cursing in a stifled voice.

"Keep back!" said Estaban. "If you value her safety, keep back from me!"

Not that he meant it, but he was a desperate man, grasping at straws to save himself. He succeeded instantly.

"Aye," gasped the man's voice who had ordered the three against him the instant before, "keep back from him. Señor, in the name of Heaven, be gentle with her. We are at your mercy. Do her no harm!"

Even in the excitement of that moment, Estaban had time to wonder at her. For she was calm enough to attempt no struggle. The shock of his coming had wrung the first scream from her, but after that, she was quiet and made no outcry, made no move to escape.

"Yes," said the voice of Garcia. "It is better so. We could not handle him."

The fallen man groaned on the floor and scrambled heavily toward his feet.

"Make a light," said he who controlled the Mexicans.

"This infernal darkness stifles me. Make a light, and let us see where we are and who we have here. Have I your permission, señor?"

"I'll furnish the light," said Estaban.

He flashed on the electric torch and swung its broad ray around him.

He found that he was in a low, narrow chamber of a considerable length. At one side a white-haired man sat upon a great stone, with a crutch leaning against the wall behind him—token enough of the reason which had kept him from running in person to the help of the girl.

Of the three Mexicans, one of them was still reeling, with both hands clapped to his bleeding forehead, where the stroke had fallen, and the other two were plainly paralyzed with fright and with bewilderment, for the weapons hung down from their nerveless hands, and they made no attempt to raise them when the light flashed in their faces.

"Now," said Estaban, "we'll have every gun on the ground. Do you hear me! I have six lives in the chambers of this revolver, and a very active forefinger, amigos. Therefore, act swiftly, in Heaven's name."

He was seconded by the white-haired man.

"Drop your weapons. Do as he directs us. We are in his hands. Anne, you are not harmed?"

"I am not hurt, father," said the girl. "I am only shamed. What a fool, what a fool I was!"

"Good!" said Estaban as a knife and two guns clattered on the stones of the floor. "Now we can sit and talk together freely, and like friends. And who can tell? We may become friends, indeed, before the end of this matter. Is there any other light, to save my battery?"

A lantern was lighted at once; and more at ease under its broader glow, Don Cristobal looked around him.

He met, first of all, the gloomy eyes of the girl.

"You were in no danger from me," said he. "Less than you were on the first night, when you were the ghost!"

"It was you, then, on that night, also?" she murmured.

And she turned toward her father. He had started and nodded again.

"She said that you were not like the others, and that we were apt to have trouble with you again! Anne, you are a witch to have guessed it. And yet," he added, as he leaned forward and scanned the stranger, "I think that even I might have guessed as much. Señor, will you tell us how you came here?"

"By the stone at the end of the passage," admitted Estaban.

"I knew that. But how did you find the stone?"

"I saw your daughter come from that place on the night when she was a ghost of a nun." He turned and smiled at the girl. "And it seemed to me at that time that she had walked right out from the solid stone. I was working at that when by luck I happened to touch the right spring or balance."

"A balance," said the white-haired man. "A spring would have rusted away a century ago. It's a balance that moves that stone, and a very neatly poised balance at that!"

"And so I came on down the passage, except that I very nearly dropped into the pit and rang the bells of San Filipo with my own head, but I managed to send down a rock to do the ringing for me! And so, as you see, I met Garcia. You will see by the lump on his head that I took him at a slight disadvantage. And he came on and was for a time a sort of unwilling escort to me!"

Garcia turned upon him great eyes that seemed to beg him to say no more, and Estaban ended with a bow.

"Now," said he, "I presume that it is your turn to speak. Except that I should add that I am Cristobal José Rodrigo Orthez Estaban."

He continued: "And I speak English, also, if that will make it any easier for you."

"My name," said the other, "is John Warwick. And this is my daughter, Anne."

Estaban bowed deeply to her, and she bowed to him. But her face was blank. There was no sign of the social grace of a welcoming smile upon it.

"I have been for a long time an interested hunter in the southwest. And so, Señor Estaban, I have found in San Filipo something which, it seems, interests other people than myself. Is there anything more that I should say to you?"

"Nothing," said Don Cristobal. "Except that you might tell me how you are to pass your treasure through the lines of this fellow Ramirez."

"As for that young scoundrel," said the other, "his patience will give out after a time. There is no doubt that his patience will have an end and that he will move his men away. Because his pocketbook is not great enough to endure such an expense except through a very limited period."

"I don't know," murmured Don Cristobal. "I shall be surprised if his search doesn't make him begin to do a little mining among the foundations of the church of San Filipo. And then he might find—however, here you are, it seems, with your treasure."

"I have said nothing about a treasure," said John Warwick coldly.

"I have only guessed," smiled Estaban, "but I am in a position to guess that there is a great treasure of silver buried near by——"

An eloquent glance of relief flashed between the man and his daughter, and Estaban added smoothly enough:

"And gold, Mr. Warwick."

"Gold!" exclaimed the other. "Who could have put such nonsense into your head? There was never any gold mined in this valley—not for centuries! Not for a hundred years before the silver mines were worked!"

Estaban shrugged his shoulders.

"Now, Mr. Warwick," said he, "I am about to become sentimental for the first time in my life. I am about to be generous, sir!"

"You astonish me," said John Warwick.

"You have made your discovery. How, I don't ask, because it is no business of mine. You have broached your mine of gold and of silver, and now you wish to keep your treasure for yourself. Well, sir, I am the last man in the world to investigate the proper claims of a gentleman and his daughter to such a property as this, and at your request I shall merely withdraw from this tunnel, replace the stone at the farther end of the passage, and then leave you and your men to salvage your money as well as you can."

John Warwick stared at a speech which was, assuredly, quite the opposite of what he had expected.

"But," said Estaban, "you are a sensible man, and even a fool would see that you need more strength than these can give you. Your time is limited even more than the time of young Ramirez. You may run out of food. And of that he has plenty. And you cannot trust to such clumsy fingers as those of the three fellows who are here with you, or even to the invisible hands of the ghost of a dead nun. But, Mr. Warwick, being a sensible man, you are going to send a man down the passageway to reclose the tunnel, after he has brought my friend Gore back, and then you are going to sit down and invite me to become your partner in this work."

CHAPTER XXVII

A Bargain

"Blackmail!" breathed Anne Warwick savagely.

Her father raised a gravely reproving hand.

Then he said to Don Cristobal.

"Otherwise, if you are not made a partner, you will

go to Ramirez and tell him what he may find and where he may find it?"

Don Cristobal smiled.

"Say the word to me, sir," said he, "and I shall turn and leave you and take myself definitely away from this place and this town—unless one of Ramirez's bullets stops me on the way! But in the meantime think the matter over. No one can get something for nothing. I have tried it for a good many years, and failed dismally. On the one hand, you offer to me—and to my partner, Gore—one half of the treasure which you have found. On the other hand, I offer you my services to remove that treasure."

Thought clouded the eyes of Warwick, but his daughter exclaimed in a passion:

"You make an offer of yourself to people who already have three devoted men working for them. Are you not ashamed, Señor Estaban?"

He turned upon her. She had thrown back her hood and he could see more of her face and the excitement in her eyes. But he answered as impersonally as though she had been an image worked in wood.

"You are a cripple, a woman—and three ciphers!"

She caught her breath, speechless with indignation.

But he went on: "So far as this treasure is concerned, you are worthless—the five of you are completely worthless! I smile when I think that you began the task of removing a bulky treasure in silver by carrying it on the backs of men up the side of the valley and over the mountains to another hiding place, where it will probably be found and looted—and perhaps the back trail will be followed again to the starting point, as I have followed it!"

"Do you think——" the girl began, but her father interrupted.

"Let me talk to Señor Estaban. I think that we may find a reasonable basis for an exchange of ideas, may we not, señor?"

"That is my hope," said Don Cristobal.

"Very well. You begin by telling me that my three

men who are with me are worthless in the task of removing the treasure?"

"I do."

"Then give me the reason for it."

"Look in their blank faces. That is your answer, I feel—and a very complete answer."

"Why cannot my daughter and I do their thinking for them?"

"Set them out in the open and tell them how they will be able to escape from this town, for instance. Then you will see that your thinking can do them no good."

"It is true," murmured Warwick. "Of that, I had not thought."

"In the meantime you face starvation."

"And will you find us food?"

"I shall either steal food for you from the camp of the enemy, or else I shall devise a means of removing the treasure in completest safety."

"And for this work you would claim a half of the spoils?"

"For this work I would claim a half of the spoils."

"A high rate of wages," said Warwick.

"No, a fair partnership. Besides, I am aiming at a great goal of my own, and I cannot afford to play for small stakes."

"And if you fail?"

"I shall be a dead man before I fail."

"It is not hard to *say* such a thing, Señor Estaban."

"Neither is it hard to do it, if you have before you a hope as great as my hope. I tell you, Mr. Warwick, that I am trying for the possession of what is really a small kingdom that I can make my own if I have the sinews of war for the fighting that must come first. And therefore I cannot let down my demands. Either I play for half of the total, or else I don't play at all. Am I clear?"

"Very clear—very clear."

"I shall wait for your decision, Mr. Warwick."

"If I want you, I pay you a half?"

"Exactly."

"If I don't want you, you are willing to leave this place and forget that you have ever seen me here?"

"That is it."

"And I must trust to your word?"

"You must."

Warwick turned to his daughter in a fashion that showed he was accustomed to leaning on her.

"What shall I do, Anne?"

"Can you ask me, seriously? Why, refuse, of course, and we'll fight it out as we began—by ourselves!"

"Will you tell me your reasons, Anne?"

Now, by that fluttering lantern light, in the dampness of that underground chamber, with the trickle of water faint in the distance, and the smell of the earth in the nostrils, the ordinary courtesies disappeared, and the eyes of Anne Warwick were hard and impersonal as the eyes of a fighting man when she turned to survey Señor Estaban again.

"I don't trust him," said she. "And he comes at the last minute to get his share of the harvest, when he did no sowing of the crop. I don't like it. It's a sort of cheating!"

Don Cristobal did not allow his expression to alter so much as by the flicker of an eyelid. He bowed a little to her and turned with an air of gravely detached attention to listen to the judgment of Warwick himself.

And John Warwick began by canting his head to one side and nodding in agreement with his daughter. He even went so far as to part his lips to speak, but when he looked up to the tall, muscular body of Don Cristobal, and the dark, lean, ugly face, his words died unuttered upon his lips.

He said slowly. "We are in the hands of Estaban. But there is honor in him. And where there is honor there is a strength of mind, also. As for the other matters, his coming was a shock. But we must forget that and consider things as we find them. We have found

the treasure and started to remove it—but at a rate
that might have required years, Anne. You know that
we computed that time. And all the while we were in
danger of a discovery, as Estaban says, that would
rob us of our accumulated labors. Furthermore, it is
true that we have very few provisions left; and you
know yourself that Ramirez keeps an eye like a hawk
above San Filipo, and it is impossible for any of us to
stir about there—impossible for any man, unless he
has the nature of a panther in him!"

And he paused, and ran a calculating eye over the
tall, sinewy frame of the stranger.

"Estaban!" said he suddenly.

"Yes?" said Don Cristobal.

"Give me your hand."

Señor Estaban took in his own powerful fingers a
hand as chill as death.

"I shall give you an implicit trust, Estaban."

"I shall be worthy of it," said Don Cristobal.

"Father!" cried Anne Warwick.

Señor Estaban turned slowly toward her.

"I have to tell you, in the first place, Miss Warwick,"
said he, "that the partnership has been definitely con-
cluded. Your opinions were foolish from the first, and
now they are not wanted or asked for."

"Señor Estaban," cried the girl, "what manner of
breeding may be——"

"Hush!" said Estaban. "This is an affair for men
only. Your father is here to work in your interest. I
am here to work in my own. Neither of us can be
bothered by your nonsense and your foolish outbreaks.
You make an excellent ghost of a dead nun, señorita.
Why do you not keep in that congenial role?"

"By Heaven, Estaban!" breathed Warwick, "you
must not speak to her in this fashion!"

"Don't encourage her," said Don Cristobal, "or you
will have her in a tantrum directly. Let her swallow
her rage. It will be good for her. In the meantime,
we have business to talk over."

"Dad," said the girl, with soft fierceness, "will you allow a man to insult me?"

Don Cristobal broke in with a smooth voice.

"There are no insults without passion," said he. "I am not in a passion. I am prepared to work my hardest with your father to bring out the money which must eventually go to you. But in the meantime, I tell you the truth as I see it about yourself. We cannot be troubled with a child's wishes. They are not of a sufficient importance. Am I clear? You do not enter into my mind enough to anger me, child. I merely warn you now, that we cannot be hampered by your talk and your objections. And as we wish to talk alone, you had better leave us at once."

Miss Anne Warwick stared at him with eyes so great and so filled with fire that they were wonderful to behold. And then she answered with a fierce breath:

"You are contemptible! You are——"

She paused for breath, and Don Cristobal, bowing to her, suggested:

"Continue! There are many more things that you may say. I am an ugly villain. I have the manners of a pirate. I am a despicable brute. I take advantage of a superior physical strength in order to tyrannize over the helpless women. You may say all of these things. And if I have not thought of enough points, continue from the point where I left off, if you please. Continue, Miss Warwick. But having said your piece, then be quiet hereafter."

She looked wildly at her father, but John Warwick, as one in a trance, stared at her, and then at the tall figure and the calm face of Don Cristobal, and he said not a word to either.

"Dad! Dad!" cried the girl. "You agree with him —and you hate me as much as he does! Oh, I want to die!"

And she turned and ran from the room, and burst open the heavy door, and rushed away into the darkness of the passage.

"Garcia—Antonio—go after her and find her—

bring her back. Take the lantern—heavens above, what will she do?"

Garcia's hand lunged out for the lantern, but a grip like iron took him by the shoulder and stopped him. The quiet voice of Don Cristobal said:

"Let her go. This is the first lesson that she has ever had, it seems. Let us make it a thorough one. One that she will never be able to forget."

"Estaban," said the bewildered father, "you have spoken a great deal of truth. I couldn't help feeling the truth of what you said—but so cruelly—and when she is half angel, as you cannot know. I must have her back. Let Garcia go——"

"Let them go or stay, as you please. You are an older man than I, Mr. Warwick. But if I were you, I should wish to let her see the other side of herself for a time. She has thought of herself as an angel all her life. Now that there is a chance for her to dwell on the devil that's in her, are you going to interrupt? Why, man, her heart is swelling now. She thinks of suicide, but she won't harm herself. She thinks of blowing up the tunnel and all who are in it. But she won't do that. And most of all, she is waiting to have us pursue her and beg her to come back, and beg her to forgive us. Tush, man, if you treat her as a woman and not as a heavenly baby, you will see at once what a change will come! She will be what she is intended to be—a charming person—a woman."

Mr. Warwick struggled for a moment with his first thought, but the words of young Señor Estaban sank deeper and deeper into his mind.

And at last he lifted his white head and smiled faintly at Don Cristobal.

"I begin to see the light!" said he. "I think that even if we fail to bring the treasure away with us, you will have been worth a full partnership, Estaban! Garcia, stay where you are. Antonio, do not stir a foot after her."

CHAPTER XXVIII

The Legend Hunter

Mr. Warwick, having keyed himself up to this dramatic point, obviously needed a moment to relax, and as he relaxed he smiled at first and then chuckled to himself.

"My poor, dear Anne!" said he. "In all the world the very finest girl! And yet——"

"And yet——" Don Cristobal echoed.

And they smiled at one another.

Mr. Warwick roused himself.

"Antonio, go through the passage. Above, you will find—where is your partner, señor?"

"In the shadow near the entrance to the church, keeping a sharp lookout. Come to him carefully. He is in a nervous frame of mind and may be tempted to speak with a gun instead of his voice. But tell him that The Doctor is sending for him. He will understand and he will go with you. Adios, Antonio. And go quickly, because every moment is rasping the nerves of poor Jim Gore raw."

Antonio saluted like a good soldier, and then was gone.

"And now," said Warwick, "since we have become partners you must see the cause of our partnership."

"I want nothing better."

"Then come with me."

The cripple stood up and, supporting himself with the crutch and with a cane on his right side, he led the way down the chamber where Jose, the third of the peons, pushed open a rickety door. But Don Cristobal had time to pause.

"Jose," said he, "I notice that you still walk with a limp. I thought, in fact, that before I was through with you I might not see you walking for a year, let alone a day, but my friend Gore interceded for you. Otherwise, my friend, you might *never* have walked again. For, Mr. Warwick, he was a stubborn devil, and kept his tongue quiet for your sake as though it were for himself!"

Jose rewarded this encomium with a silent baring of his teeth which he doubtless intended to serve as a smile, but which was actually a grimace that might have done credit to a death's head. His malice shriveled his eyes small and bright, and they bored like knives at the very soul of the tall man.

"It was a cruel thing, Estaban," said Warwick gravely.

"As cruel as the devil," said Estaban freely. "But just a minute before, he had been taking pot shots at a friend of mine—or a fellow who was on the very edge of becoming my friend. And there you are! I was impatient. And for a while I was tempted to break him in two and make into crows' meat. However, that's all past. I am your friend now, Jose, so long as you want me for a friend. But for the sake of your good health, remember that I have my eye upon you constantly and that I shall be ready to guard myself in case you become absent-minded. You understand, Jose?"

Jose understood, but with a scowl as black as the darkest night.

And Señor Estaban stepped on behind his slow-moving guide, while Jose hurried ahead to carry the lantern.

They twisted down a narrow passage and came to another crazily built door, where Mr. Warwick paused once more.

"Aye!" said he. "The first time that I faced this door, my heart was in my mouth, Señor Estaban! And that was not so very many, many days ago—but time travels slowly, slowly when all your hours are underground!"

"Very slowly," agreed Don Cristobal. "Or in a

prison. I have been in a prison for a spell, and therefore I can understand!"

"Shall I tell you the whole story, briefly?"

"Do so by all means."

"Before we look, then, I'll tell you. You must understand that I was once a good deal more active than I am at the present time. The rougher the country, the better I enjoyed it, and the harder the hunting, the keener I was for it. And that, naturally, finally took me west, after the grizzlies and the mountain sheep.

"My third trip, while I was trying to swarm up the side of a rock as straight as the wall of a house, I missed a hand hold and fell. And this was the result!"

He pointed to the crutch with a shrug of his shoulders and a faintly deprecatory smile.

"One grows used to such things in time, but at first I felt like an eagle with its wings clipped. I could not understand and I could not be quiet for a long time. But lying in the door of an adobe hut, watching the shadows crawl across the face of a cañon day after day, and sleeping out at night and watching the whiteness of the stars and the depth of the mountain-desert sky—why, those things, Señor Estaban, gradually ate into my soul, as you might say. And suddenly one day I realized that I was having a better time listening to the subdued chatter of a couple of Mexican women in the kitchen—they were doing the cooking and the nursing—than I had ever had when I was out freely wandering around and studying wild life—after it was dead!

"Because there was something in the half-breeds, the Indians and the Mexicans that was a great deal more exotic and romantic and strange than the habits and the looks of any grizzly or mountain sheep. And a charging tiger never looked a bit more terrible than an Indian with the devil in his eyes—either from too much whisky or from anger.

"But I didn't have to climb boulders to study these people. I could do better by lying still and recuperating. That was a great discovery to me. They did not think a great deal of me. A cripple is a total blank to a Mexican. They talked in front of me as freely as they would talk in front of an old woman with one foot in her grave, you see?

"And the greatest pleasure of all was when they began to spin their yarns. Legends grow old quickly in the West. A fact to-day gets the velvet trimmings of an old tradition in five years. And in half a lifetime it will become a myth. That's the way, as you know better than I do, perhaps.

"Very well, I stopped hunting with a gun and by climbing mountains. I began to hunt with a camera, and walking slowly about on my crutches, sitting half a day at a time where the shade was the coolest and the talk was freest. They took no notice of me. And after a time I had some of those romantic yarns running in my blood. There was a good deal of repetition, of course, an immense lot of primitive childishness that was really charming, and above all, there were the stories of places and people who were more than half real. And among the rest of the lot I found the stories about San Filipo.

"You know, of course, that the story of San Filipo is popular, but I don't think that you realize just *how* popular it is, or how the old folks are never tired of talking about the bit of desert that was turned into a garden and back into a desert again—and how the dam broke and the bells rang as they fell—and how the bells, now and again, were said to have been heard again. And finally I met a hard-headed youngster who had sharpened his wits stealing horses, and I heard him swear, when he was sober, and in the middle of the day, tersely and bluntly like a man telling the most naked truth, that he himself, during an earthquake in the San Filipo valley, had actually heard the bells of San Filipo ring!

"It was odd enough to give me a shock, you may imagine. You meet such things with a smile in a tale of the Middle Ages. But in twentieth century daylight it is a different matter. That man's vow stuck in my mind, and brought me two years later down to San Filipo itself to listen to the stories on the home ground. And what I heard brought me back here on two successive summers. I was willing to take the heat and the dust of the days for the sake of the stars, the coolness, and the stories of the nights. And finally I came here with my daughter, and she and I, señor, were in the town when the earthquake happened a short time ago—not many weeks—and the bells were heard again. And we heard them with our own ears!

"Now, with the first rumors, years ago, about the audible ringing of those bells, I had guessed that the bells, when they fell from the burning church tower, had simply crashed into an underground cavity and remained there—simply because their great weight carried them a long distance down, and because no one ever had the courage and the sense to search the ruins thoroughly to find them.

"So I started to find those bells, but I started out in a very thoroughgoing manner, and learned all that I could, in the first place, about the houses which had once been about the church. Among the rest, I learned that the one which used to stand above the site of the place where we now are, had been the home of a rich citizen—a man named Ramirez—a cruel devil of a man who had been said to wring money out of silver ores which other miners gave up working as not paying. But this Ramirez made the ores pay. And this interested me a great deal—I mean to say, the name interested me a great deal—and the reason was one that I can tell you now.

"About seven years ago, when I was first beginning my explorations in the southwest, in this very valley of San Filipo, I came across a family of fallen gentry —and in the family I found a boy with a naturally beautiful tenor voice——"

"Diego Ramirez, of course?"

"Diego Ramirez, naturally. And now you are beginning to guess at all of the story which is to follow?"

"I never guess," said Don Cristobal, "unless I'm forced to it, you understand? I detest guesswork when it's possible to get at the truth in any other way!"

So the older man nodded at him with his rather pathetic, twisted smile, and continued: "So I managed to take the boy under my wing and carried him away to New York with me—and then off to Europe. And I saw to it that he had a thoroughly good education grafted onto the rough foundation which had been given him before. And, of course, I saw that particular attention was given to his voice, which is really fine enough for concert work if the lazy rascal would work with it a bit more!

"But this brings me closer to the point. When I heard about the rich Ramirez who had once lived in this house, I had a thrill of queer hope that perhaps I was going to get back some of the wealth which I had recently lost—a good part of it in the extravagant education which I gave to young Diego. But before I can tell you how those hopes first grew up in my mind, I must make you understand all that I heard about that strange Ramirez, the mine worker, the slave driver, the man-eater."

CHAPTER XXIX

A Fortune in the Earth

Mr. Warwick had paused a moment to collect his thoughts, and then went on:

"There is no use in giving all the details. What I knew was that this Ramirez had managed by the use of the most unscrupulous means to amass a large sum of money. Silver by the wagonload was carted from the mines to his house here in San Filipo and it was said that he shipped it out again and got back gold in exchange for it. However that may be, the important fact is that he spent his entire life in collecting precious metals—because that was the form of wealth that appealed to his imagination, you see. But after this life of labor it was found on his death that there was practically no estate to leave to his children except the mines, which he had pretty thoroughly worked out.

"People said, in part, that if he was a keen fellow to take wealth out of the ground, he must have been an idiot in his manner of investing it in other properties. And other people said that it was simply the will of Heaven, punishing this rascal by turning the gold and silver for which he had committed so many crimes, into dead leaves and dust in the end.

"At any rate, San Filipo didn't bother its precious head for very long about the matter. It decided that Providence was great and mysterious in its ways—and with that it turned on the other side and went to sleep again.

"But I, Estaban, when I thought this matter over, decided simply that it was the highest sort of folly to imagine that a man clever enough to have piled up a fortune should have thrown it away in foolish investments so that not a real trace of it remained. There was no *proof*, you understand, that the money was thrown away—except its absence from the estate. The old codger left no will—too mean for that. And he had no confidential secretaries, et cetera. So a sort of a dream idea came to me that if I searched for the bells of San Filipo I might as well search the foundations of the house of this same Ramirez.

"And that is what I started to do. But first I told young Ramirez my purpose. I thought that, since he was the nominal heir to the old family, he ought to have a chance to share in the loot, if there was any.

"He was away in Europe, and I wrote to him my purpose and my double goal, and invited him to come back and join me in the hunt. In the meantime, I did not wait for him, but came straight to San Filipo where I started the search with as much secrecy as possible.

"In my hunting expeditions, I had always taken along with me the three peons whom you have seen, and after I was crippled I still kept them as servants whenever I went to the West. I knew that I could trust them, for when a Mexican becomes your man, he becomes it with heart and soul, you know. Therefore, I used them for the task. We secretly brought food and drink into the sub-basement of the old Ramirez house. And then we began our digging.

"But we got nothing here. Finally we changed our operations to the basement of the old church, and then, at once—in the very first night of our work—Garcia touched the combination which budges the big stone —the same one through which you found an entrance to the tunnel.

"And following down the winding way from the church, we finally came to this place, though we were nearly stifled by the foul air and had to spend three evenings in the exploration. But finally we came to the door which you see here, and pushing it open we saw this!"

As he spoke he set his crutch against the door and pushed it wide. As the lantern was raised Señor Estaban saw before him a dark, low room, roughly chopped out of the solid rock, and in that chamber there was a huge pile of blackened bars, piled up like cordwood.

He did not have to be told what it was. He recognized these bars by their similarity to those of which the pack on the back of Jose had been composed on that other day when Jim Gore had his first sight of the mystery.

Don Cristobal took off his hat with an instinctive gesture of respect, and as he stood there, drinking in the significance of the scene, Warwick looked thoughtfully upon him.

"Of what does it make you think, Estaban?" he asked.

"I see the horses and the riders who will go with me to win back my own estates," said he. "I can even see the mountains and smell the dust boiling up along the trail, Mr. Warwick. How much of this stuff is there here?"

"I've made a fairly accurate reckoning, and I make it out to be about a million and three hundred thousand dollars in value, besides this."

With that, he hobbled to a corner of the room and dragged a tarpaulin from a smaller heap. But underneath the tarpaulin there shone forth to Don Cristobal a dull yellow luster.

He snatched up the tarpaulin and flung it back over the pile.

"And that?" he asked.

"Not such a big heap," said Warwick, with a glitter even in his more philosophic eye. "But it's more precious stuff. I shifted that heap and took the trouble to weigh every one of those heavy little bars."

"A labor of love!" grinned Don Cristobal.

"A labor of love!" nodded the other. "And altogether it works out at seventeen hundred thousand dollars, my friend! Mr. Ramirez in the old days was not such a bad business man, after all. He even knew how to dispose of his treasure in a place where no one could find it at his death!"

Don Cristobal shook his head, filled with wonder.

"But tell me this—how was it possible for him to conceal such a mass of stuff, such an actual tonnage of treasure? How could he have done that? Somebody must have known!"

"I've pondered on that," admitted Warwick, "and my idea is that all of this stuff was brought first into some other chamber—probably an upper one, you understand, because we are very far beneath the ground at this lowest point of the excavations. And old Ramirez, I believe, chose his times for working with his own hands in the cellarage of his house until he was able to dig a small passage down through the stone, and then he enlarged the passage until he excavated this chamber. He did it so cunningly that, work as I may, I cannot find the spot at which he sank the shaft down from above.

"However, it may be that he actually began from beneath the church, and worked out the passageway to this point, fairly secure that no one would ever have dreamed of hunting in the cellarage of the church in the hope of finding a treasure there. But in the end there is a simpler explanation of all this. He may have set his men to work and drilled out two tunnels —one from beneath his house, and one leading up to the church—and after they had nearly completed the task, with his own hand he cut the link which connected the two, and thereby remained the only man with the key to the mystery. I'll show you later the spot where the tunnel came to an end in what apparently a solid wall of rock. But we finally found that it was only a blind—a great slab of stone fitted so that it would roll to the side into a deep niche—and it has remained rolled back there since we first moved it.

"At any rate, no matter what he may have planned, we got to the treasure chamber through more than fifty feet of bedrock underneath the foundations of his house. And if luck had not brought us here, I'm sure that the treasure would never have been located at all.

"But now that we have it, Estaban, I want you to let me understand how we can possibly budge it!"

Don Cristobal nodded.

"I'll start thinking about that later on. First, I'd like to know about this younger Ramirez and how he happens to be of the opposite party at the present time?"

Warwick flushed.

"It's a nasty story," said he. "You must know that a year ago he astonished me by suggesting that it would be a good thing, perhaps, if I were to arrange his marriage with my daughter. Well, sir, I knew that Ramirez was well-bred, and had plenty of the old Castilian blood in his veins, than which nothing is better, but I knew also that there was a liberal sprinkling of the Indian blood in the same veins. And much as I like certain qualities of the Indian, I cannot say that I want him in my family as the husband of my daughter. However, I did not say so to Ramirez. I went to Anne and told her what Diego had suggested. She was astonished and disgusted, and she even went to Diego and told him point-blank that this was nonsense.

"He seemed a great deal upset. He even flew into a rage and talked a great deal of rot about the importance of his position by birth—to the general effect that he would be actually stepping down to marry a girl like Anne. After his passion, however, he seemed so down-hearted that I packed him off to Europe for a rest and some fun. That was why he happened to be in France when I wrote to him about what I intended to try in San Filipo.

"Now, Estaban, here comes the rub. I had told him in the first place what I hoped to get. But after I made the discovery, I was so excited that I wrote another letter which would reach his boat when it arrived in New York, and I said in that letter that he would be wise to hurry, because I had found a great treasure —a treasure in gold and silver so enormous that I hardly knew how to move it and would wait until his coming, to give me his advice and his help!"

He paused and leaned a hand against the rough wall of the room, filled with gloomy thought.

"He came," said Estaban, "and when he came, he created a suspicion in your mind by his actions?"

"There was a wolf in his eyes!" said the older man. "There was actually a conscienceless wolf in his eyes, I tell you. And in my first interview with him he had the effrontery to compliment me on the skill which I had shown in recovering his inheritance. He just blandly assumed at once that the whole quantity of stuff belonged to him, you see?"

Warwick paused again, breathing hard with anger. Then he resumed: "I brought him to his senses a little with a reprimand. I did not tell him that he was assuming an ungrateful attitude. I did not talk about what I had done for him. I merely pointed out that though this property may once have been in the Ramirez estate, it was no longer owned by them. And although one might assume that this was the buried treasure of the old don, there was no one who could be able to give his testimony to that effect in a court. And the treasure would certainly have remained untouched if I had not come across it by using my wits, my patience, and my money.

"This brought him up on a hard rein, of course, and he began to protest that he had never for a moment forgotten all that I had done for him, and that his only interest here was to see that the Ramirez treasure actually was turned over to me for my use. However, his talk and his attitude was a little too patent. I finally cut him short and told him bluntly that I did not like his attitude and that I was afraid that I could not trust him. He replied with a tigerish outburst in which he told me that he was tired of cringing to me and that he would maintain himself in his own way from this point on. I told him not to speak like a fool, and asked him what resources he had, and he brazenly reminded me of some of the gifts which I had made to him.

"In the first place, he had saved a great part of the spending money which I had always showered upon him. In the second place, since I always gave him whatever he asked for, he had soon made a point of asking for a good deal more than he used, and so he accumulated a secret bank account of reasonable proportions. Besides, when he listened to the talk in my house and heard chatter about speculations, he picked up enough hints and tips to work on, and he actually had the effrontery to use that information to play the market. How much he made I don't know, but he vowed to me that he was already wealthy enough to live comfortably on his income. He then gave me my choice in a fashion as cool as you can conceive. He would allow me to admit him into partnership, when he would be entirely at my service in the removal of the property, or else he would promptly set himself to work to tear the whole treasure out of my hands!"

CHAPTER XXX

Bad News

Warwick lighted a cigarette and began to smoke it in the greatest excitement and trouble.

"I laughed in his face when I heard such talk," he continued. "But still I was very worried. And then I told him that he could do what he wished. I hoped that I should never see him again! That was the manner in which we parted. But at the time I really did not see in what manner he could do me any harm worth mentioning.

"I went on planning a manner in which we could start that treasure out of the ground without getting the attention of other people. In the meantime, young Ramirez lounged around the town and twanged his infernal guitar and sang his songs. But his wits were working. He accomplished two things: One was to buy out, for a song, every one who had any possessions in the town of San Filipo. The other was to bring up a store of wild-riding vagabonds out of old Mexico. And they are to be the tools with which he will rescue the treasure from the ground.

"He found that he had one great trouble. He could guard the town with ruffians like these, but he could not mine in it, because they scorned such manual labor. Guns were their favorite tools. They were above hammers and drills.

"So he cannot get at me, buried underground as I am. And I, on the other hand, cannot get out. He keeps much too close a guard! And his money will last longer to pay wages than our food supplies will last here, underground. He has his hand at our throats. And before long we'll be forced up out of the ground and into his hands—and money and all will come to him, because he would never hesitate to use torture to make the Mexicans talk to him everything that they know! So there you have a fairly accurate picture of just what has happened. I have sent about eight hundred pounds of bar silver out of the valley on the backs of my three men while I tried to figure out a way to move the whole mass. But I dared not send the gold in that fashion. Frankly, I knew that I could trust them with silver, but gold is a different matter. There is a sort of a poison in that, you understand!"

Don Cristobal smiled.

"Eight hundred pounds!" said he.

"A good deal—to be taken out by man power, eh?"

"Eight hundred pounds of silver is sixteen thousand dollars. Could you tell me where it is hidden in the mountains?"

"Of course, but what of that?"

"It is a lever, and a fairly strong one. And I think that if it is used in the right way, I may be able to manage things to that Diego will be pried away from his ancestral heritage in a very rude fashion. However, all is dim in my mind, at present. All I know is that sixteen thousand dollars is a fat sum—a very fat sum, Mr. Warwick, when it is turned into—nitroglycerin, say—or into certain types of fighting men!"

"I don't understand you," murmured Warwick.

"Don't try to, sir. Because you are not a lawbreaker by nature. But no matter how you may argue yourself out of it, and no matter how perfect your abstract title to this treasure may be, you haven't a single foot, legally, to stand upon. Not one! This Ramirez—the cunning dog!—has in justice no claim to the money. But in the law, he has a double right in that he is the heir of the man who got the money together, and in that he now owns every inch of the ground in which this treasure is now hid! You see?"

"I see," nodded Warwick. "You are not very hopeful, I know."

"Hopeful?" muttered Estaban absently. "Let me see. How far is it from San Filipo to the sea?"

"Two hundred and fifty miles or so."

"Ah! So far as that?"

"I know, Estaban, because I planned on sailing up the old river to San Filipo in a flat-bottomed boat last year. But I gave up the job, because I discovered that the course is simply checked off on every hand with sand bars that would make even navigation with a shallow boat a hard thing against the current."

"Two hundred and fifty miles!" sighed Estaban. "It is a great deal—at ten miles an hour, twenty-five hours—and then, these are the days of telegraph and telephone! Ah, Warwick, it will be a great gamble!"

Warwick shook his head.

"I don't know what you're talking about," said he.

"Aye, of course you don't. And I don't dare tell you, because it's too great a chance. However, what I propose to do is to leave this place, break through the lines of this Ramirez, and then head for that spot in the mountains where the silver is hidden. I shall need four or five animals to pack that quanitity of the stuff at the rate of speed with which I intend to travel. And then—however, I must not burden you with details. I can only say that I hope that I shall be able to turn the trick for the sake of all of us. Will you trust in me? I can do the thing in three weeks, perhaps, if everything goes well. If you go on short rations, can you last that long here?"

Warwick closed his eyes with a groan.

"Three more weeks of this damned darkness and gloom! I cannot chance it, man—not with the girl!"

"Send for her and ask her."

"Would you leave it to her discretion and judgment in a time like this, when she is hating us with all of her might, and particularly hating you?"

"Send for her by all means. There is more strength in her brains than in the brains of half a dozen ordinary men. Go out, Jose, and bring the señorita here!"

Jose turned without a word, and disappeared through the door, while the two men found their way back to the other room where they sat in a profound silence. For behind their backs there was a heaped treasure of three millions—a force to change the current of a thousand lives—a sort of silent music that made a tremor in the soul of big Estaban and sent his thoughts flying far to the south, to his own land.

A stir of air as a door opened, a light crunching of sand underfoot, and yonder was the girl herself, with her steady eyes fixed upon them.

She did not speak. She merely waited.

"Anne," said her father, "we're sorry that what——"

She raised her hand.

"You were rude to me, but I acted like a fool. Let's not talk about it."

"Well," said her father, "Estaban—in short, he wants to find out where the silver is in the mountains, get to it, and use it as a lever, as he expresses it, to pry Ramirez away from San Filipo. And he needs three weeks to do the job. Do you think that you could stand that long a wait here underground—on shortened rations?"

She nodded instantly.

"And you'll trust this to Señor Estaban?"

She flushed a little but she made herself look straight into the face of the big man.

"I'll trust him," said she. "And—I think he'll do what he says."

"Then," said Warwick, "we'll take the chance. Heaven knows whether we'll be dead or forced by famine into the hands of this Ramirez by the time that you come back, but I think that this chance is worth the taking. And if you want to work for the cause in that way—then start now, friend, and work fast. We shall be counting the actual minutes until you come back."

There was a subdued muttering of voices in the passage beyond the door, and the door itself was suddenly cast open, and before them stood Antonio, gasping for breath.

"The holy saints protect us!" stammered Antonio. "All is lost!"

"They have found the tunnel," cried Warwick. "And then everything *is* lost. They can burn the air out of this place and stifle us to death in no time at all!"

"Tell me, man—have they found the way to us?" demanded big Estaban.

"I cannot tell—but I think they will soon be here——"

"Speak only what you saw, heard, and did. Begin with the moment you left us."

"I went down the tunnel, señor. And I came to the open end of the passage. And there I waited a little time, because it is an awful thing to be in a holy church in the dark of the night as the señor understands. Then, at the last, I put out my head and looked around me. I started creeping down the shadows of the church, and all around me, outside of the walls of the church, I can hear the voices of men. And they are talking loudly of one thing only—of how loudly the bells of the blessed San Fiipo had rung upon this night, and how they wish to Heaven that the dawn would come!"

"And Jim Gore?" broke in Estaban harshly. "What of him—and the devil take the rest of your news. Why have you not brought my partner back with you?"

"I should have done it, señor, with a great happiness. But it was not to be. I weep, señor, that it was not to be. For when I sneaked like a snake out from the shadows and into the light of the moon which lay outside of the walls—there, as I lay, I heard men talk and saw them leading away a man whose arms were tied behind his back.

"The señor—the Ramirez—he was with him, talking and asking a great deal of questions. But this

Señor Gore, he would not speak a word in answer to him——"

"He's a heart of oak!" declared Estaban. "He knows nothing, but even if he did he would not talk. They could not tear a confession out of him. But was he in danger with them?"

"I saw one of them strike him in the face."

"I shall skin half a dozen of them alive for that!" vowed Estaban. I shall roast and toast a few of them for that, the dogs! Tell me, man, how he bore it?"

"I heard the hand strike on his face. I did not hear him speak afterward!"

"What coward and brutes!" groaned Estaban. "And what fools, too—if they knew that I was the friend of that man. And then what happened?"

"I was about to start back softly when my foot slipped and made a noise. I heard a shout behind me. I fled like a madman. Guns were fired. Bullets leaped around me. I reached the mouth of the tunnel. I leaped past the entrance. I pressed the lever. I saw the great rock slide across the entrance gap. But their voices were right above me, and surely, surely, they must have seen the stone move!"

CHAPTER XXXI

Escape

The men stood agape, staring heavily at one another. And as they stared, even tall Estaban lost some of the luster from his eye, while Warwick muttered:

"Then we have lost everything! They are stealing on us now! They will be here at once! By Heaven, Estaban, I should almost like to have blown up the passage and kill all of us, only to keep them from getting the treasure which we have found!"

"Aye," said Estaban, with equal gloom. "I understand."

But Anne Warwick pushed open the battered old door and listened.

"Antonio was wrong. They have not come!" said she.

"They are probably stealing like so many cats down the passage, even now," said her father, and the three peons shrank away against the wall.

"They would not steal down the passage," said the girl. "They would want lights. And they would want noise, too, of their own voices, to help them along such a black place. There is nothing to fear. They are not coming. Antonio was too frightened to be sure, and we are still safe!"

Estaban and her father looked at one another in shame and relief, equally. And then Warwick smiled shamefacedly.

"I think that she's right," said he. "But now at least they know that there is a secret passage somewhere in the shadows of the cellarage of the church. They will keep on searching until they have found it."

"Do you think so?" smiled Anne Warwick. "I have frightened them with a dead nun's face—poor thing! —and besides, it is the church itself where they are searching, and these fellows are too superstitious to search well in such a place. Even Señor Estaban did not have all of his wits about him in the church of San Filipo!"

She smiled still as she glanced at him, and Estaban flushed to the temples as he acknowledged the hit.

"Turn and turn about is fair play!" said Anne Warwick.

"You are right," said Don Cristobal. "Turn and turn about is fair play, and you have hit me back! I hope that there may be a truce, now. Still—there is only one way that we know out of this dungeon, and Ramirez holds the key to the gate. It will make a bad business of it all!"

"A bad business—a business that cannot be accomplished," said Warwick. "And the best way, my friend Estaban, is simply to cut the agony short and give ourselves up."

"What share would this young Ramirez give you of the treasure, do you think?" asked Estaban, suddenly.

"I think that he would give me any share that I asked—if Anne would marry him."

"Bah!" breathed Estaban in great disgust. "And if she did not?"

"We would get not a penny for our discovery. That is plain!"

"Very well, then," said Don Cristobal. "I shall wait one day. In one day these people are apt to grow tired of probing at the stones under the church. Superstition will frighten them at night. And if they searched a hundred years, they are not very apt to find the key to the mystery! To-morrow night I shall attempt to get out and away. And now, this is an excellent time for sleeping!"

All the rest of that night and all of the following day the men of Ramirez labored in the cellar of the church of old San Filipo, so moldered with time. They trenched away the soil and dug among the stones, but still they could not find the exact spot where the fugitive had so mysteriously disappeared.

And finally, as hands grew weary and mind uneasy, men were heard to say to one another:

"Is it so strange, after all? There are things known to have happened in this place—spirits without bodies, bodies without spirits. Ghosts walk in this church; and does a ghost need have a passage? It will melt into the solidest stone!"

This talk came to the ear of Ramirez.

"Does a ghost yelp like a frightened puppy?" he asked in much anger.

"Let the master talk," murmured his men. "He will have his own thoughts and we will have ours. If it had not been a ghost, how could it have disappeared?"

And they tapped the stones with their picks to prove their arguments.

In such a spirit little is ever accomplished. Such unwilling workers were not, ten of them, equal to a single miner with undivided mind, and young Ramirez shrugged his shoulders and sighed. Had he been a lesser man he would have raved and cursed, but he was a philosopher and he knew these people by simply looking a little deeper than ordinarily into his own mind. Therefore he retired on the next evening to the patio of his house and there, as usual, the sound of the guitar rose, and his voice swelled genially upon the cooling air. The watchers at the church of San Filipo listened and smiled at one another.

"The master is no longer so sad," said they. "Hang up the lantern, Roderigo. Why should we not play with this pack of cards. Because they will never know what we are doing, and as for a ghost, it will not bother us. Man or woman, it will not come our way!"

Roderigo, having crossed himself, sat down cross-legged, and in an instant the pasteboards were whispering against one another as he shuffled them with most expert touch.

If there were a slight grating noise among the most distant shadows in the cellarage of the church, it merely caused Roderigo to lift his head for a moment. Then, since it was not repeated, he decided simply that he had heard nothing at all, and in the blandest humor he set about continuing the card game, while a stealthy form glided out from the darkness behind him and lurked behind a broken pillar to watch the game.

After that, it moved on again, with a step as soft as the step of a cat. It reached the moon-whitened courtyard and, slipping around the shadows at the edge, it passed across behind the house of Ramirez.

There that shadow coiled up behind a shed and watched the forms of half a dozen horses which moved in the inclosed ground that served as a corral and pasture. He watched them until he could guess, for their form and their movements, which were the best of the lot, and when he had made his selection, he turned boldly into the shed itself.

A squat figure sat on the floor with a lantern swinging beside his head from a peg on the wall, and in his lap was the bridle which he was repairing.

"Hello—amigo?" said he carelessly, without turning his head.

"Aye," said the stalking shadow; "amigo!" and took the squatting man by the throat.

There was only a brief, fumbling sound. Then, his head swathed in a sack and a gag between his teeth, the watcher was rolled into a corner, hands and feet securely tied. And Estaban went on into the corral.

This was slower work, for they were wild, strong, fleet creatures, these horses, and the smell of the underground was strong upon him. Yet he caught one by one the horses which he wanted and took the saddles from the shed. When all was ready, he lowered the bars and led them out and carefully put up those same bars again to keep the remaining pair from breaking away and then turned up the back alley.

But the back alley was blocked with an enormous mass of fallen rubbish. He had to turn back and ride toward the house itself. And as he passed the shed once more, he heard a muffled scuffling and beating, where the bound man was trying to attract attention by making a great noise, and succeeding very poorly.

And now Estaban turned with his little cavalcade into the main street and went straight past the house of young Ramirez himself. That youth stood with three of his best lieutenants at the gate to his ruined patio.

"By Heaven!" said he. "That near horse has a carriage like my own red devil of a bay. Hello, fellow! What are those horses and what is your business with them?"

Well did the Estaban know that voice! But he turned in the saddle and answered with an oath: "I do the business of your master, fool. Is that business enough to please you?"

The lieutenants of Ramirez would have run out to take him, but young Ramirez merely laughed. "He does not know me!" said he. "Let it go, but find out where those horses are being taken?"

As a man moved forward to ask the question, Don Cristobal sent the horse beside him into a lunging gallop with an adroitly placed kick. And then all of the quartet raced forward.

"Hold them up, there!"

The voice of Estaban was heard cursing and raving.

"They are devils—not horses! I shall halt them at once, señor! Oh, that so many fiends should have been wrapped up in the honest hides of good horses!"

And, in the meantime, with heel and quirt he was maddening the four so that they shot down the street and turned the broad bend of it, and when they reached the mouth of the street, where the three guards were standing, Estaban yelled at the top of his voice: "Stop them—in the name of Heaven and of mercy—stop them! They are running away! They will destroy me! Brothers—amigos—help! Help!"

The three guards ran out to stop the four; and stop them they would have done, had not the whip and the foot of Estaban been so busy that he sent them on in a plunging fury.

The three guards saved themselves by leaping to the side.

"Who has sent a boy and a fool to handle four such horses?" said one.

"Let them run until they have run themselves down!" said another. "It is no business of ours."

And the quartet fled like a chariot team under the scourge, running head to head, with a beautiful precision that swept them at once far away into the night.

Once out of earshot of the town, Don Cristobal turned well to the left, and before long he was up the slope and on the crest of the rise beyond. There he paused to look back for a moment. And as he watched, he saw an increasing flicker of lights in San Filipo.

Men were being roused. And he laughed when he

thought of the cause of the excitement. There was only one regret in the mind of big Don Cristobal, and this was that he should have had to abandon behind him his old comrade, Jim Gore. He thought soberly of that for a moment, and then he put his face northward to the next task which lay before him.

Before the dawn it was completed. For the directions were most explicit. He could have felt his way blindfolded to the spot, and before the gray of the next day began, the four horses were loaded. Eight hundred weight in silver bars had been put on their backs, and he was off again, to the south and to the east.

He pushed those horses hard.

He knew well enough that the trail of four horses could not be covered for very long. And therefore his time was not his own, even if it had not been that he wished to make all haste for the sake of the friends who waited for his return—waiting underground in San Filipo.

He doubled like a hunted fox, and taking a distance only far enough to insure himself against observance from the town itself, he had crossed the valley of the San Filipo again and was off toward the southern hills before the sun was its own width above the horizon. Crossing them, he was still driving straight south. But the way was dusty and soft with sand, the sun was hot, and he had with him four horses, heavily loaded. For two hundred pounds of dead burden is twice that of living flesh. So, by noon of this day, Don Cristobal was beginning to turn in his saddle and look anxiously behind him up the trail down which he had come.

CHAPTER XXXII

A Trade

He came to a country as filled with ragged mountains as the sea was ever filled with storm-sharpened waves, where the view was rarely clear for a quarter of a mile at a time, as the trail dipped arduously up and down among the defiles. And here, as he climbed with the four horses to a rough height, he looked back over the uneven face of the country and saw, far behind him, a stream of half a dozen riders who poured over the crest and were instantly gone.

Don Cristobal rode on, and as he rode his swift fingers opened and examined the mechanism of his repeating rifle. But most of his attention was for the horses. They were of the toughest mustang stock, crossed, not far back, upon true thoroughbred blood, and they had been given the sort of upbringing on the mountain-desert which creates strength of heart and limb, and bigness of wind. Still, they had done gigantic work since they left the town of San Filipo, and the dead weight of their packs told keenly on them.

"If I could tell you that it was silver that you are carrying," murmured Don Cristobal.

And then he glanced back over his shoulder once more.

He saw a wooded slope not half a mile away, and there, he determined, he would make his stand. He still could escape easily by cutting the silver-laden animals adrift and spurring on with his lone mount, but if he discarded the treasure the purpose of his mission was lost, and he might better be back in the underground passages beneath the old house of the dead Ramirez with Warwick and his daughter and his men.

He had no thought of such a mild surrender. Yonder in the wood he would fight and, with a few well-placed bullets, bring down as many of them as he could. And if, after that, they chose to pursue him through the forest, they would be brave men indeed! And though the odds were six to one—well, he had faced such odds before this time, and come off scatheless!

So he rode on, his heart like steel. But, for that matter, he did not have to harden his spirit for this work, for he knew that young Ramirez had gathered for his crusade a band of chosen cutthroats, as little worthy of mercy as they were incapable of extending any.

Down the slope he went, with the tired horses laboring in their stride, their heads bobbing with the effort of the gallop, and so he came to the edge of the woods, where the trail split and divided into two ravines. Which was the way of the true trail he could not tell, for the bottom of each ravine was covered with black, broken rocks, great and small, where the hoofs of a thousand shod horses would hardly have left marks worth following.

He did not have to wait for a guide. A brown, round face of a ten-year-old boy appeared from behind the trees and the youngster came slowly toward him. Don Cristobal met him with a smile and a wave of the hand. And the child's eyes sparkled with pleasure.

Don Cristobal pointed up the trail behind him.

"Look, amigo, and tell me if you see men riding there behind me—six of them!"

"There is nothing, señor."

"Heaven be praised."

"They are not friends, señor?"

"They have murdered and robbed many others as they, now wish to murder and rob me!" said Don Cristobal. "On which side is the true trail?"

"To the left! May your horses have new strength, señor!"

And he shook his head at the heaving flanks of the horses of Estaban.

"There is no hope for that. But you, amigo, may do more for me than strength."

"I?"

Don Cristobal felt in his pocket for money, and then changed his mind. It was not through money that the heart of a boy could be utterly won. He thought of another thing, and drew out a hunting knife. It was the brightest and the keenest steel, with a handle of stout brown horn, all mounted and chased with heavy silver which served it as a balance and a weight in case that knife was to be used for throwing.

"Here!" said he. "This is for you—to help you remember that I rode with my four horses by the right-hand ravine. Do you hear?"

"I hear you, senor. Yes, and I shall remember! There is no boy in the village will have such a knife as this! Heaven bless you, señor!"

Don Cristobal spurred his tired horse on. And the lead ropes came taut one by one, and the quartet lurched with trembling knees down the right-hand ravine. And it seemed to Don Cristobal, as they entered the mouth of the narrow valley, that he could see the leaders of the pursuit winding in view behind him, riding lightly, unweariedly!

He pushed his own tired quartet hurriedly along, but it seemed nightmare ages before they dipped around the first bend.

Then he dismounted and walked slowly on, carrying his rifle in the hollow of his arm, and leading the four. The sweat rained from their bellies as they struggled along with dead eyes and stretching necks, pulled unwilling by the lead ropes. There was no cause for hurry now. If the brown-faced boy at the forking of the ways told the necessary lie, the six men of Ramirez would go lurching off on the false trail. And he was saved—for the time being. But if they went on the true trail behind him, then no haste on his part could be of any avail. Better to stand his ground among the boulders at the edge of the trees and let the horses and their silver be shot down around him!

So thought Don Cristobal, and walked calmly on, waiting for the best or for the worst.

When he gained the top of the next rise, the sound of running water made his horses prick their ears. Still there was no sound of horses on the rocks of the defile behind him, so he turned aside and found a little vagrant stream wandering down into a tiny pool. He brought the horses up one by one and gave each a swallow. Then he took water in his hat and sluiced it over them, after he had removed the saddles with their ponderous saddlebags. There is nothing better than such a cooling bath to raise the spirits of horses, and during a whole hour he worked over them until the life was back in their eyes and they were busily reaching for herbage.

At that sign of revived spirits, he resaddled them, and presently he was once more on the trail. Now let the pursuit find him if it could—he had four horses which were ready to gallop fast and far!

But there was no sign behind him all during the rest of that day. He made an early camp and there he let his horses graze. He himself slept in lieu of eating, and in the small hours of the morning, long before the beginning of the dawnlight, he was on his way again.

Straight south through the mountains he held until he came on the sight which he had expected—a little town pitched on the crossing of two roads—dim white streaks across the brown countryside. By noon his horses were tethered outside the doors of the bank. And half an hour later he had carried the heavy saddlebags into the office of the president.

"As sure as my name is Stephen Fanwick!" said the shrewd president, "this is stolen silver, my friend!"

"As sure as your name is Stephen Fanwick," said Don Cristobal, "you are very wrong. This is not stolen silver. But it is silver that is being hunted for by six hard riders with six straight-shooting rifles. Now Mr. Fanwick, there is sixteen thousand dollars' worth of good metal there—and I am willing to take a thousand dollar loss on it for spot cash!"

"So?" said Mr. Fanwick. "Fifteen thousand dollars is a great deal of money! A great deal! And if some one comes along and claims stolen goods——"

At the same time he was busy shifting the bags one by one onto the scales and weighing their contents. And he was busy cutting open the bars with a tap of the cold chisel.

"Look," said Don Cristobal. "Is this a sign of any modern mint—this crest that you see on the bars? And does that look like treasure that has been current——"

"It looks as though it had spent a hundred years underground!" said the president.

"It has spent longer than that. Now, Mr. Fanwick, who can produce a legitimate claim that stretches back as far as that? I can go on to the next town. It is only eight miles farther. But I'm in a desperate hurry, and I've told you the reason for my haste. I want the money, but I want it now—at once. You understand me? And so, sir, I shall make a big discount. I shall offer you this money for twelve thousand dollars. For every three dollars that I take in, I shall be losing one. You make a net profit of four thousand dollars—four thousand dollars that you do not have to show to your bank, four thousand dollars for your own private pocket. Now, Mr. Fanwick, do I get the cash?"

Mr. Fanwick was a man who made quick decisions. It was that power which had enabled him to build up his bank until he was a power in the cattle country. He looked Don Cristobal fairly in the eye.

He rose from his chair, left the room, and came back in five minutes. He counted out twelve thousand dollars in bills and placed the pile in the hands of Don Cristobal.

"One more matter," said Don Cristobal. "Out yonder in the street there are four horses with tired legs and Mexican brands on them. I'll trade the four of them for one good horse. Can you get it for me?"

"Come with me!" said the banker. Since even the heart of that little town was country, he led the tall man through a side door and into an empty lot where three animals were cropping the sun-dried grass. "Take your pick," said he.

"The gray," said Don Cristobal without hesitation.

"An ugly brute—and I give you my word that it's fifteen years old if it's a day. Look at its teeth and its temples, if you doubt me. I want you to see that I don't intend to rob you, my friend."

Don Cristobal smiled, and his white teeth flashed in the sunlight.

"I don't want to use him for another fifteen years," said he. "I want a horse that will be able to carry me through thick and thin on one long ride. And this is the nag for me."

"You will have your own way," smiled Mr. Fanwick. And there was a flash of admiration in his eyes as he added: "I'd almost sooner part with a leg than with that horse. He's the toughest and the wisest thing that ever wore a saddle. I wish you joy of him."

But Don Cristobal did not pause to hear the last of this. He had hurried to the street, and came back carrying over his arm one of the saddles which he had stripped from the back of one of the four. This he threw upon the old gray. As he pulled up the cinches, Mr. Fanwick still stood by, smiling and nodding.

"You have saddled a horse before," said he, "when speed meant something to you. And I should like to know, between you and me, how many men have died in order to give you all of that silver. Tell me, my friend—were there not three other men in those three saddles when you started on the trail?"

Estaban smiled, and then he chuckled softly.

"I have not killed a single man for it—as yet!" said he. "Now, how far is it to the railroad line?"

"Eighty-five miles, if it's a mile. A good two days of riding."

"One day for a horse like this gray."

"You may get with him to the railroad before to-morrow morning, but you'll leave a dead horse behind you."

"Mr. Fanwick, he's not a flesh-and-blood horse to me—he's my hope, running on four legs. And eighty-five miles he must do. And if six men should come through the town—you might point out that I have turned up the north trail, and that I intend to keep along it!"

"Good," said Mr. Fanwick, "and I have an idea, stranger, that if you stopped—collecting old silver—you might have the making of a banker in you!"

CHAPTER XXXIII

The Return

Straight south from the town rode Don Cristobal, his head and his heart aching with an exquisite numbness of absolute fatigue. Before he was a mile away he turned a bend and saw, not a hundred yards off, six tired horsemen upon six tired horses, whitened with dust, and streaked with black where the sweat had freshly formed and washed little rivulets through the accumulations of dust and of salt.

They were the hunters of Ramirez, who had thus ridden so far south upon his trail. And there was still life enough in them to make them utter a wild yell of excitement.

What unlucky misfortune had made them decide that the northern trail was the wrong one and had started them to the south again, Don Cristobal could not guess. But he knew that six men came storming at him down the narrow trail, yelling and sending a small storm of lead before them.

He twitched the old gray over the fence beside the

road, and put him down the steep pitch of the slope beyond. So he dipped out of view of the six hunters, and when they came again within the sight of him, he was far below, ducking the gray out of sight still a second time around the shoulder of the hill.

They should have known, having failed in their first attempt, that it was worse than folly to chase a freshly mounted fugitive with their leg-worn steeds. But they were like so many hounds when a fresh fox is scented, no matter how weary they may be. They stormed down that slope in their pursuit, each screaming encouragement to his comrade.

As they rounded the same shoulder of the hill past which Don Cristobal had just gone, they could see him far away, gaining at every stride of the gray, but still they had not sense enough to stop!

For he was within range, they told themselves, of any lucky rifle shot. And happy the man who won the eternal gratitude of Ramirez by bringing down the arch foe.

Moreover, he remained temptingly no farther away than this. If their own horses were tired, surely his seemed to be no less so. And they spurred and cursed and raged and raved in the hope of catching up with him. Now and again they would fire a shot at him, but the distance was really great, and since they did not stop, and dismount, and fire from a rest, they did no harm to Don Cristobal.

All through the rest of that day he led them across the mountains until one of their horses staggered and dropped, and another came to a halt with hanging head and stiffly-braced legs that trembled at the knees. Then, in the softer coolness of the evening, they came to a stretch of gently rolling ground, and they had the misery of seeing Señor Estaban touch his gray horse to a gallop and canter swingingly away across the swells, leaving them hopelessly far behind him.

Then they turned savagely to one another, sick at heart, starved, weary, and with all the strength run out from their souls. For they saw that they had been wretchedly tricked by the fugitive, and drawn on and on until, in the midst of a hopeless desert, they were left with utterly spent horses, with all water at a frightful distance, and with no shelter from the cold of the mountain night, which was gathering rapidly above them. So they drew into a huddling cluster and stared bitterly after the gray horse, as it twinkled out of view in the twilight.

But Don Cristobal rode on, now at a steady trot which ate up the miles swiftly. And he stuck with his task while the gray horse weakened and weakened through the night, and the ragged miles strung out behind him like a thing of dread.

He was long without sleep. Exhaustion was hammering at the base of his brain. But still he would not pause, and drove the gray relentlessly. Time was precious—precious. For when the tidings that his men had failed got to the ears of young Ramirez, the tidings would at the same instant be that the fugitive had headed for the railroad. And unless Ramirez were a perfect fool—which he was certainly not—he would be able to deduce that Señor Estaban was prepared to dip south toward his own land, in the hope of bringing back assistance to the party which was eking out a miserable existence underground in San Filipo—eating hope from day to day!

And in the hands of Ramirez there was money, and the telegraph through which he could reach other friends in Mexico, no doubt, and bid them take care that they find Don Cristobal on that same railroad line!

All of these things were present, therefore, in the mind of Estaban as he dismounted from the staggering gray, stripped the gridle and saddle mercifully from its head and body, and with a slap on its dripping rump headed it slowly toward a glimmer of starlit water, far to the left and down the slope. That would mean life to the gelding. But for Don Cristobal the way still led straight ahead toward the railroad.

He got to it over the next rise, three miles away,

and every step of that distance he covered at a slow run, like a tireless Indian. And crouching by the tracks, in a knot of shrubbery, he pulled the belt tighter about his empty stomach and listened to the murmuring of the engine in the distance, and the humming of the tracks, as it drew nearer.

He had gone up the line to a steep grade, and as the train hit the incline, its speed slowed and slowed, and he saw the headlight of the engine rocking to and fro as it labored over the rough track.

The first cars went by with a noise like a falling city, for it was a string of empties. But as the rear of the train approached it slowed greatly, and he was able to get a grip on the rearmost platform of the caboose. A moment later he was on top of the train, and when the freight stopped at the next station, Crisobal Estaban was safely ensconced in a box car, and there he fell fast asleep.

He wakened with a hand on his shoulder and a great shaft of blinding daylight falling upon his face. The train had stopped, and a Mexican was bending over him, with a face shining with excitement and varnished with sweat.

"You are Señor Estaban?" he stated.

"I? echoed Don Cristobal. "*I* am Señor Estaban? Who the devil says that?"

"Hey—Enriquito! Approach here and read the description!"

Enriquito approached, therefore, and staring in, with one hand shading his eyes, looked curiously at Don Cristobal. Then he read aloud:

"A very tall man who looks like a fighter, with a narrow, ugly face and who——"

"It is you, señor!" said the gendarme. "You will come with me!"

He took out a revolver and tapped with the muzzle of it gently upon the stomach of Don Cristobal.

"Ah, well," said that worthy. "You are too sharp for me. There is no getting around one of you smart fellows! So give me your hand and help me up, will you? I'm half sick and more than half helpless."

"Very well," said the gendarme. "No tricks—and there is my hand—ah——"

The last cry was stifled almost as soon as it was uttered. There was a brief gagging sound, the noise of a head bumping against the loose boards of the box car, and then Enriquito raised a yell that sent an electric quiver down the spine of every one within hearing, and made men instinctively reach for guns and knives.

And Enriquito turned to flee toward a whole group of gendarmes standing in the distance—whose presence, in fact, had made the first officer so confident in his approach to Estaban. But before good Enriquito had taken two strides, a pantherlike form leaped from the open door of the box car and two high, sharp heels were planted in the small of his back. He bent like a bow and pitched upon his face.

And Estaban fled past him, running like a deer.

He perceived that he was in a little Mexican town. By the range of white-capped mountains around the spot he realized that he had slept a prodigious length of time. As the group of gendarmes, which had obviously been sent to this point to stop trains and to search for him, turned in his direction and greeted him with a chorus of "Stop, or die!" Don Cristobal got to the first knot of horses.

There was a tall youth, and a brave one, standing by the horses, and he snatched a gun from his holster and tried a snapshot at Estaban. It had the fate of most snapshots. It cut through the empty air, and the next instant the bony fist of Don Cristobzl landed on the jaw of the youth, and the latter crumpled into the dust and lay like a fallen scarecrow, weakly limp.

The next leap of the Estaban brought him into a saddle. A single jerk on the reins spun the horse around, and he was away like a shot with the dust boiling up behind.

And the gendarmes came full tilt behind him. They had horses as good as his. They rode as well, or nearly as well, and there was not one of the lot who was such a burden of poundage to his mount. But they lacked one thing, and that was the concentration and the cold-mindedness of a desperate man. For Don Cristobal saw all that was about him with a calm deliberation that was just a little swifter than the movement of a lightning flash. And when he decided to begin shooting, though he whirled in the saddle and appeared to fire instantly, it was in reality an aimed shot that struck the leading horseman somewhere below the hip and toppled him screeching out of the saddle.

Two of the others drew up to look after their fallen comrade. The other three galloped on with much shouting, but not a bit of spurring. And presently they dismounted and fell on their bellies to shoot down the fugitive at long range.

And Don Cristobal rode blandly on, and let the rein on the little brown mare beneath him fall slack. He knew that the instant pressure of this danger had been, for the moment, removed.

And now he had before him his own country. There were still hot leagues of journeying, still hot leagues of climbing and thirst before him, but beyond, hanging in the central sky, brown and purple and capped with white, were the mountains of the country of which he was the exiled king.

Well might the hand of the law be stretched out, at a hint from Ramirez, to intercept him. They did not want him back there in his own land. For they knew what his strength might become there. Once he gained enough strength to make a rallying point, once he was able to make a unit for a start—then woe to the established authorities! His power might spread as fire runs in a field of dead grass!

All of these things drifted slowly through the head of Don Cristobal as he worked his way up the slope and toward the distant heights. And there was much unsolved in his mind. He could not tell, for instance, what root of affection for the Estabans might remain in the hearts of the country folk. It might be that they

regarded them simply as a fallen power of evil—
great ugly giant forms in the midst of the past. Or it
might be that there was a real yearning for the return
of the semifeudal power of the Estabans, and the peace,
the order and the prosperity which that house had established through those same mountains.

In the meantime, here was the law pressing fast
behind him. A hundred, two hundred soldiery would
be dispatched at once to follow his trail, capture
him, and hang him to the nearest tree. And Don Cristobal knew, and smiled.

In the middle of the afternoon he entered the first
defile. He could remember that when he fled from his
own land and from his own people, it was through that
same defile; and now, as he rode toward it, the hills on
either side seemed to Don Cristobal like forbidding
giants.

He took off his sombrero and waved it to them, to
the right and to the left, and so he entered the cool
shadow of the gorge, and rode out, an hour later, into
his first view of the interior country of the mountians.
It was too much for any short glance. So he paid no
attention at all to it, but, hiding his trail behind him
as well as he could, he made into the covert of a wood,
and there pitched his camp for the evening.

CHAPTER XXXIV

Recognition

His rifle won the dispossessed lord of the land his supper. And as he crouched on his heels, Indian style, and
ate rabbit— half raw and half roasted—he peered
out through a gap in the pines and beheld his lost domain.

It seemed, for the most part, a mere sea of mountains, so very rugged, so broken, so covered with gigan-

tic cliffs and split across by cañons, that Don Cristobal
Jose Roderigo Orthez Estaban, smiling to himself, drew
in a great breath and nodded in reverence to his grandfather's memory—he who had first come to these
lands, an exile, and had yet seen their hidden possibilities, and where only mountain sheep had found
broken pasture, had made a happy home for thousands of prosperous men!

He thought of that, and of "the jolly little fat man"
through whose mingled folly and rascality the mountains had been made into a desert once more. And
then he gritted his teeth and raised both of his long,
powerful hands toward the heavens, in a mute vow
that whatever strength of body and mind were his,
should be spent to the last scruple until he had re-
claimed the wilderness, or the wilderness had devoured
him!

So thought Don Cristobal. And having finished his
meal, he went forth to the brow of the slope and lolled
to smoke a cigarette on the verge of a fifteen-hundred-
foot plunge to a little valley beneath. The bottom of
that valley, at that distance seemed not much larger
than the open hand at arm's length. Yet once this had
been a valuable little corner of the great domain of
the Estabans. There were fifty acres in the bottom of
that valley. And once it had yielded crops of wheat and
of barley that would have staggered the very imagination of a lowlander. And once the very sides of the
hills had been cultivated. With a fond eye of anguish,
Don Cristobal sketched in the remaining marks which
showed where the terraces had run.

But all was burned and brown, now. Where there
had once been richest and deepest verdure, there was
nothing except what the spring rains would nourish in
this unlucky place. And yonder he saw the tall skeleton
of the mill, where once all the wheat had been
ground to the finest flour before that flour was carted
from the valley, so that there might be as little wasted
effort as possible. There was the house, too—or all that

was left of its blackened foundations, for fire had consumed it and gnawed at it's bones.

Where the water came from that had once been sluiced into the little valley to make it green and prosperous, Don Cristobal could not guess. That had been the work of one of his forefathers. Cattle had swarmed these hillsides. The wheat had grown tall, below. Little orchards had surrounded the houses. And men had grown wide of shoulder, and women gay, and children blithe and brown. He thought of these things, and he set his teeth again.

Once more the former picture should be repainted, if Heaven would be his help!

This was only the outer fringe of his kingdom—yet a sign of what was everywhere. Here there was not a living creature, however. Not so much as a single steer browsed on the dead grass in the valley. Yonder he should find some traces of the former grandeur—some scatterings of life!

He rode on through the evening light with a rested horse, and still, when the stars came out, they saw him climbing through the next pass, raising echoes from the cliffs on either side with the sound of his horse's hoofs —long, lonely echoes, that leaped from rock face to rock face.

He crossed the pass and descended beyond, where a second valley floor widened beneath him, and there he saw the gleaming of a handful of lights. Here were his people, at last!

But what would he mean to them? What significance would he have in their minds? An unwelcome master returned? A hated stranger? One whose capture and surrender to the law would let them reap a reward of blood money?

However, he rode on, and when he came to the first house, by the side of a dry ditch that had once been a brimming irrigation canal, he found the family gathered around the door of the hut—a fierce-faced man of early middle age, and two huge boys of eighteen or nineteen.

They rose to meet him, stepping past the women. And each bore a rifle in his hands—sure sign of the only law which was observed in that wilderness. And Don Cristobal regarded them with a savage satisfaction.

Such were the men by whom the wilderness had been peopled. To such a size they grew. Such were their hands and their shoulders, and such were their steady, brave eyes. Even in their ruin they showed the blood from which they came. They were dressed in rags, but they carried themselves like a king and two princes.

"I have come," said Don Cristobal, "for a bed, food, and fodder for my horse."

"Are you from Teodoro?" asked the father of the family. "Or who has sent you?"

"I have sent myself, señor."

There was an instant of pause, and then the man replied, gloomily: "Pepillo! Take the horse and feed it and hobble it. Ignacio, go up the trail and see what you can see. You—get him food!"

One son, putting down his rifle, led the horse away. The other instantly swung off up the trail with a great-striding gait like a trained runner. The wife stood up and bundled herself inside, and her daughter slipped in at her side.

The householder remained in the starlight with the stranger.

"And who are you?" asked Don Cristobal.

"I am Valentin Oñate."

"I have heard of you," said Don Cristobal.

And, indeed, he had. For was not this one of the valiant troop which had ridden at his side in the fighting of the last great battles when he strove to win back his little kingdom by force? Was not this one of the brave troopers? Younger then, but resolute and fearless. Now grown dogged and savage.

"You have heard of me?" said he sulkily. "Aye, and much good you have heard!"

"I have heard that you shoot straight and ride well," said Don Cristobal.

"My friends are my friends, and my enemies are my enemies!" said the other suspiciously. "And who are you?"

"One who has not seen this country for many years."

"That is no answer," said Oñate, with a growl rising in his throat.

"It is answer enough, however," said the Estaban coldly. "There was a time, Oñate, when you were a man who kept his family well. Now I see that you live like a pig in a sty. Are you not ashamed?"

The big mountaineer gasped. "Stranger, your horse has tasted my corn—but you have not!"

The threat which this remark implied seemed not to be understood by Cristobal. He went on:

"There was a time when you kept a *mozo* to help you in the fields!"

"I have two sons, now," said Oñate, breathing hard. "What need have I of any other help?"

"At what do they work?" asked Don Cristobal. "They once were happy boys. They went to the school. They were kept clean. They had shoes on their feet. What, Oñate! can they not even be clothed like men, now? At what do they work, then?"

"Señor," said the householder through his teeth, "to me it is not as to some others in these mountains. A stranger who asks for food and shelter may take my last crust and sleep in my own bed even if I have to lie on the ground. I shall take from my own mouth to give even to his horse. But I tell you, beware of such talk as this! I am not a patient man, and I have borne much already!"

"Good!" said Don Cristobal. "I shall go inside the house and see your wife. I remember that she was a pretty woman. She was proud of her mantillas in the old days. And she had a slim little foot on which she liked to wear crimson shoes. I shall see her now!"

Oñate, stifled with rage, stepped with clenched fists behind the stranger, who now loomed against the fire-light and the lantern light of the inside of the hovel.

"Whatever you see, señor," he said, "if you speak of it to her, I shall strangle you!"

Don Cristobal returned no reply. He stood in the doorway, and called: "Are you ready for me, señora?"

"You must wait for your time," she snapped back at him, without turning from the fire. "I am no witch. I cannot make something out of nothing before you have time to turn around."

The pretty girl, in the act of carrying in a bucket of water from the well, cast a side glance at the tall stranger, and then she stood petrified with wonder and with awe. And Don Cristobal, staring sternly back at her, knew that she understood. She must have been the veriest child before he left the country, but still she knew the face which the men of the blood of Estaban wore.

Suddenly she breathed: "Madre—madre—madre mia—it is a ghost, and not a man. It is the devil come to us!"

And she fell upon her knees, cowering against the wall, and the tide of water from the overturned pail washed across the feet of Don Cristobal and through the door behind him.

Her mother turned, at that, angrily, with the spit raised and ready in her hand. But it fell with a thud upon the hard-packed dirt of the floor.

"El Estaban!" gasped she.

A sort of strangled scream came from the throat of Oñate. He leaped into the hut and faced the big stranger.

"Sacros santos!" breathed Oñate. "Señor, señor, how have I spoken to my father!"

And he fell upon his knees before Don Cristobal.

A moisture dimmed the eyes of Estaban. He took Oñate by the hands and raised him to his feet. And the girl rose in the corner, trembling and white. But she was not too frightened to smile, wonderfully and suddenly, at Don Cristobal, as a child might have smiled at her king.

CHAPTER XXXV

The Night Watch

Look in upon Estaban half an hour later.

He sits at the table in the best chair which the house can afford to him. Yonder is the señorita, working softly and hard to prepare a little delicacy in the shape of a roasted duck, whose neck has been hastily wrung for the occasion. Here is her daughter, fleeting backwards and forwards, trembling with excitement, undoing with one hand what she does with the other, but frantically eager to please. Here is tall Pepillo on one side of the door, leaning upon his rifle, his eyes on fire as he stares at Don Cristobal. He has carried a message through the dark to his brother and given the golden tidings that El Estaban himself is in their hut this night. But most of all, here is the elder Oñate, swelled with pride and shaken with joy.

No one will sit down. The flash of Oñate's eye would blast wife or child who dared to sit in the presence of the master. For such, Don Cristobal discovers, is still his position in the heart of this Oñate. He is a man of sense, is Oñate, and Don Cristobal asks him crisp questions, one right after the other.

"If I stay in this country, what will happen to me, Valentin?"

"I, señor, and perhaps a dozen others, will die for you. Lastly, you will die for yourself. And there is an end!"

"And if I come here with a small troop of armed men—say, a score of riders, Valentin?"

"There are fifty soldiers always camped near the edge of the mountains. They will be hunting for you now, I have no doubt!"

"When I come with my twenty men, I ride down the fifty in the night. Or I strike them in midday and scatter them as wolves will scatter dogs."

"Señor," said Oñate, "that will be only a little beginning. There are others. Fifty more are here, fifty are there, and in the very center of the mountains there is an entrenched camp where a hundred soldiers are constantly kept—all savage men and good fighters. They pick the bare bones of the people. They pick the bare bones of your men, señor!"

"If I come with fifty men, Oñate?"

"Fifty men! Ah, but that is an army! Fifty men? But that would be five hundred, in a single day. When the news went out that El Estaban had returned and that he carried with him fifty fighting men, all the mountains would rise. Half of them would hate and fear your coming. But half of them would run to you and beg you to own them and rule them again as in the old days. And in a day you would have five hundred men behind you. Their hearts would grow big, too. Ha! there would be fighting then! We would take the soldiers and break them in pieces."

"But after that was done, what if the government interfered? Would not the president be very angry, Oñate? Would he not gather a great army and march against the mountains?"

"Señor," said Oñate, laughing, "I cannot tell. But I can tell that already they must be sick—those people in Mexico City—of the money which they have to spend to keep these mountains quiet! They must be sick of their work, and if you told them that you had come for the sake of making the mountains pay taxes once more—why, they would forget the dead soldiers, and the price of El Estaban's head would disappear."

"Do you think this, my friend?"

"I think it! Because, in a month, you would have more than a thousand men here ready to fight for you, and to beat a thousand of us they would have to send five thousand soldiers. We would shoot them down like rabbits from behind every rock, and they know it. There was Pedro Comas. He ran into the mountains with a dozen men last year. They hunted him with twenty. Five of the twenty came back! They hunted him with fifty. The fifty could do nothing. They sent two hundred men through the mountains, and even then Pedro Comas escaped away from all of them. No, the soldiers of the president do not like to ride or to fight in this country of ours, señor! If you come with fifty men, the country is once again yours! I, Valentin Oñate, will swear it. Or else, I shall die for you first, and my two boys shall die after me!"

"Aye!" said the deep, young voice of Pepillo at the door.

Estaban dropped his chin upon his fist and forgot the food which the good wife put before him.

"Fifty men?" said he. "Yes, and I may come with more than fifty. But in the meantime, I need a dozen good fellows like yourself, Oñate. Men with steady nerves—men who know me—men whom I have led into battle. Men, also, who are willing to die. Do you know twelve such men?"

"Here, señor, are three to begin with!"

"I do not mean that. Only one man from every house. None except him who leaves a son to take his place in the household. I want steady men, my friend —men who are between forty and fifty years of age. If they have not quite the spring in their legs that they once had, it makes no difference! They are old enough to have known the better days in these mountains and they will be willing to fight to bring them back again. Can you find twelve such men and bring them back to me here by the morning?"

"Aye, señor! I can find them."

Don Cristobal took money from his wallet and counted it out.

"Here is a thousand dollars in American money, Valentin. Take it with you. Tell each man that he will be gone for a month. Tell him to bring his best rifle, ammunition, and two good horses. If he has not a horse, take some of this money and buy him one. And each man shall have fifty dollars——"

"Señor, señor, we will not do this thing—whatever it may be—for money, but for El Estaban!"

"Do I not know that? The money is not hire. It is to keep their families when they are away with me, and that is all. There is no price to be paid for blood, Valentin. There is more money if this gives out. No, take another thousand with you, now!"

He pushed the bills across the table, and Oñate took them with trembling fingers. And Señora Oñate stood straighter and swelled her chest and fire flashed from her eyes to think she had a husband who could be trusted by other men—by another man so great as El Estaban himself!

Only Pepillo, by the door, looked on with eyes that went dark with greed. For he saw two thousand dollars —a fortune—passed carelessly across the table. And there was more behind—there was five or six times as much—an incredible amassment of wealth!

There was a shed behind the little house, and there the women removed for the night. Oñate rode far away up the valley and over the hills to carry his message and leave a trail of money behind him. And up the valley in the opposite direction. Ignacio waited with the ceaseless patience of a hawk to take the first tidings to approaching danger. But back and forth before the door of the hut moved Pepillo with a long and soundless stride.

Now and again he paused and, stepping to the door, he looked in at the unmoving form on the goatskins in the corner of the house. That was El Estaban, and how soundly he seemed to sleep!

As for that money, with his own eyes Pepillo had seen the tall man place it in a breast pocket. Would it not be a simple thing to steal a hand into that pocket and take the money softly forth, then to glide away to the corral and take a fast horse—that little roan with the tiny, wicked eye—and ride across the mountains? They could never overtake him. And if this deed meant that thereby he was sacrificing all ties that bound him to his kin, what man would not venture such a loss for the sake of money that would make him a rich man in another country?

Ten or twelve thousand dollars—or even more! Why, with such a sum a great farm could be bought!

Such were the thoughts of Pepillo. And finally, he turned in through the door, moved across the floor, and leaned noiselessly above Estaban, a knife in one hand while the other probed deftly for the money—and found it and drew it gently, gently forth!

There was no warning of what was to come, but fingers like hot steel shrunk suddenly around the wrist of that hand which held the knife. And that hand went numb, and the knife slipped from the powerless fingers.

He did not cry out, but he leaped up and away like a startled wolf. His backward lunge merely drew the panther after him. He was caught, dexterously gripped, and a moment later he lay on his face, helpless, his arms twisted cruelly behind his back.

"Now, Pepillo," said Estaban, "do you beg for mercy and forgiveness? Do you beg, Pepillo?"

"No," said Pepillo. "My knife is in your reach. Take it and drive it into my back. I am worthy to die."

"Ah?" said Estaban. "I thought that you were only a foolish boy, but I see that you are a man. Stand up!"

The arms of Pepillo were released, and he raised himself slowly to his feet. His right hand coiled about the butt of his revolver, but the gun was not drawn. In the blackness before him, there was no shape of a man, only a voice, which said:

"Now, tell me. Was the money worth this?"

"No," said Pepillo bitterly. "All the money in the world is not worth such shame!"

"Hush," said Estaban. "Not a soul shall know of it. It was a sin, but it was a sin against your father, and the father of your father. I shall not betray you. For in shaming yourself you would shame me, my son."

Pepillo was stunned. He loosed the revolver, and laid his hand upon his forehead, for surely he had not heard aright.

"Señor, a devil came up in me," said he.

"I have myself heard the voice of that same devil. You will never hear it again. All is forgotten. But keep good guard through the rest of the night. I have great work before me, and I must sleep undisturbed."

Pepillo dropped to his knees.

"Padre mio," he sobbed, "teach me how to serve you—teach me how to die for you!"

"The time may come when I may ask even that of you. But now you can do nothing except to take the money—here—and guard it for me until the morning."

Estaban laid down again on the goatskins, and Pepillo remained on his knees, pressing the bundle of bills against his breast. He heard deep, regular breathing—this time El Estaban slept indeed. And Pepillo rose closely to his feet and stole from the house.

The money he put inside his belt, and buckled the belt tight. And then he began once more to stride up and down through the night before the house.

It was a clear night. The stars were all burning low —low as the vague, vast tops of the mountains, it seemed, which held up the sky with their shapeless pillars here and there. And yet there was nothing that Pepillo looked upon that was so great as the emotion that swelled in his breast.

He felt himself magnified by the hugeness of it. He feet himself transformed and uplifted above the heights of these mountains. And as he walked he breathed deep and held his head high.

It was no longer money which was buckled inside his belt. It was the trust of a man whom he had betrayed, and as he walked back and forth, tall Pepillo said over and over again: "The day shall come when I shall show him that I can die for him."

And he said again: "Valentin Oñate is my father. El Estaban is my father also. My truer father. God be kind to him and make him a king over us once more!"

To Pepillo this was a prayer, and his first prayer. It came out of his heart, from depths which he had never guessed were there before. And it seemed to him that he had been born again, and that he was now a new man. Which, after all, was true.

So that when Valentin Oñate rode back through the dawn light with fifteen men at his back, he hardly knew the stern and lighted face of his son who kept guard before the house.

CHAPTER XXXVI

The First Victory

There was a breakfast for all the troop in the house of Oñate. To furnish forth the feast, the good woman had to slaughter the last of her tribe of chickens. However, they were sacrificed, and such a fragrance of roasting meat filled the house as had never been known there before.

And there was such eating as had not been seen since the days of which the divine Homer sang. Estaban watched them eating. And he gnawed the leg bone of a rooster and studied their faces.

There was not a head which was not streaked with a bit of gray. There was not a single pair of shoulders which was not a trifle bent from the square. But their eyes were bright, and their seamed faces were resolute, and it could be seen in every man that he had lived past his illusions. Life was not a pretty game to him any longer. And he himself was no young god. Each had ceased yearning in his dreams for worlds of conquest. Each was able to fill his eye, now, with small things, and yet to fill it completely. And what obsessed them all was one great fact—El Estaban in person had come back to them.

They were not foolishly embarrassed. They accepted him gravely and reverently. And they eyed him with a certain amount of caution, as though they knew that they had before them no slight work, and wondered how effectual he might prove as a leader. What they saw in the lean face and the dark eye of Don Cristobal seemed to reassure them. And the more they studied him, and felt him studying them, a mutual confidence arose.

They had nearly ended their feast when three shots in rapid succession sounded up the valley, and Oñate with a shout leaped to his feet and warned them that it was the signal that the soldiers had been sighted by Ignacio, who had kept his post faithfully all this time.

But if they were soldiers who rode across the mountains, they had been traveling most of the night, and their horses could not compete with the fresh ones which the men of Don Cristobal bestrode.

They had not even a sight of the enemy, as they rode away through the morning; and through four days of steady traveling there was no sign of soldiery. But as they traveled Don Cristobal took careful note that there was crying poverty upon all sides of him.

Even in those places where the irrigation works had not been allowed to fall into ruin, there were few cattle, and the cultivated fields were hardly a tithe of their proper extent.

"Because," said Oñate, "how is it worth the time and the labor of a man to inclose new ground and put crops and water on it? When his cattle are fattened, the robbers come down off the higher lands and carry everything away. And what they do not take the tax gatherers collect, and he is left with all his labor spent, and poorer than before! That is why we raise enough to eat, and no more! Or even less, because it is better t go half starved than to fatten the robbers or the tax collectors. But it is this way through all the mountains. The good days are dead, Señor El Estaban!"

"We shall have them alive again," answered Don

Cristobal. "Have no fear of that. We shall have them alive again."

And he meant what he said. But these hardy men did not place too much confidence in his promise, and therefore he did not renew it. They had not so much as demanded of him what work he led them toward, and so they came out on the last headland of the mountains and looked across the narrow strip of lowlands to the great blue sea beyond.

"My friends," said Don Cristobal, "we are going to ride to the coast and leave our horses there."

They gaped at him as though he had suggested to winged creatures to proceed on foot.

"We are going to the coast, and take a boat, and travel north by sea," said Estaban.

Their faces grew blanker than ever, but not a word did they say. They had decided, to their own satisfaction, that there was sense in this man, El Estaban, and they were willing to let him do their thinking for them. However, it was a dull and solemn group that Estaban left behind him on this night where they camped in the brush, when he went forward toward the town alone.

It was a wretched little spot, with the masts of the fishing boats swinging slowly back and forth against the sea in the distance, and always a white sail drawing a triangle against ocean or horizon here and there. Into the huddle of houses, which leaned together as though for comfort in their poverty, Don Cristobal entered and found soon enough what he wanted.

There were half a dozen motor fishing boats of one kind or another, and Don Cristobal, when he let it be known what he was looking for, had them all shown to him eagerly enough, and outrageous prices asked. But his choice was a universal disappointment, for he picked the oldest and the slowest of the lot.

It was not even a round-bottomed boat! And as they confided to him seriously, it could never be taken to sea except in calm weather, and if the original owner had not been a madman, he would never have spent money foolishly in wasting a motor upon her!

She was a broad, shallow, bluff-bowed shapeless creation, which looked, as Don Cristobal himself said, like a raft with a wall built around it. However, it was the very thing that he wanted! For it drew wonderfully few inches, and the propeller, in case of need, could be angled up so that it churned only the mere surface of the water.

It was dreadfully slow, to be sure. In a dead calm, he was told that she could manage six miles an hour, but he had his doubts of that, and he was right. And when a wind arose and piled the waves before her, she could make no headway at all.

"Señor, señor!" said an aggrieved rival as he saw himself losing the sale, "if you buy her, you are buying an anchor, not a boat! She will not sail—she will sink if it blows a capful of wind!"

Don Cristobal heeded not. There was an ample space in her. There was more actual deck room than in any two of the other boats, and so he closed on the spot, and was frightfully robbed to the tune of eleven hundred dollars!

But back to the brush he went and led down his crusaders. In the village plaza he auctioned off their horses, and saw them go at ten and fifteen dollars a head. The mountaineers were stung to the heart by such prices. Still there was nothing for it but to accept. Only saddles and bridles were stripped from the horses before they were turned over to their new masters. And the procession started mournfully down for the boat at the same time that a telegraph instrument was ticking forth to the ear of a brown-faced operator in the town.

El Estaban and about fifteen men have headed for your town. Arm every man and boy capable of carrying arms and put them on horseback to hunt for the outlaw. A money reward if——

The frantic yell of the operator rang through the little adobe building. He began screaming his news at the top of his lungs, and in an instant all was excitement.

The sound of it swept on the wind to El Estaban and his men on the crazy old pier to which they were marching.

He paid the fisherman his named price for the boat and then sent him back to the village.

"They are about to make fools of themselves," said he. "They are about to attack me, but you are to let them know that I am not through with them yet. I want a month's provisions delivered to the boat, here. And I am coming back to order it, my men with me. If there is any resistance, I shall burn the town and shoot down the idiots as they run. I have been trifled with long enough. Remember, amigo. I am the lamb of peace, offering good money to those who will sell me what they want. I have paid you a robber's price, and I am willing to go above the market value for all the other things that I want. But in the meantime, I am about to come back, and what they will not sell for hard cash, they will have to sell for blood."

"Señor," said the fisherman, "will you tell me who you are?"

"I am El Estaban!"

It struck the fisherman dumb. Then he turned on his heel and made off at a skulking run.

They righted the boat. They baled out the water which seeped steadily into her through several cracks. And then they towed her back to the root of the pier, for the tide was in, and she swam with ease only a few steps from the beach.

All this was not accomplished without some disturbance. For a dropping fire had been opened from the outskirts of the town, and men could be seen forming and mustering in the main street. One bullet clipped Valentin Oñate across the shoulder—only a scratch, though it brought a bright stain to his shirt.

But he tied up his hurt without a word, and Don Cristobal looked around upon the faces of his men with satisfaction. It was what he had hoped for—it

was all his desire and in a large measure. Not an eye
went dim, not a cheek paled, not a hand grew unsteady,
not a single foot was hurried in this emergency.

He led them up to the top of the pier and formed
them in a column of fives, three deep, with an ample
interval between the gaps, so as to make his little
army seem as numerous as possible. And, like some
ancient commander, he made a little speech to them
before he led them on:

"Yonder," said Don Cristobal, "in San Marino. The
people have enough men to eat us—to swallow us
at a single volley. But they are not going to fire that
volley. They are thinking about my warning, and they
are feeling, amigos, that their town is a little too small
to digest El Estaban with any comfort. They are thinking of this; and, furthermore, they are beginning to
wonder if I shall not be able, after all, to set fire to
the houses? And if we march straight in, you will see
them fire one or two random bullets, and then dissolve
like a mist before us!"

And so the little troop strode on. Before them, more
than half a hundred men were gathered, shouting, yelling, loading rifles.

"Kill them!" "Charge them now!" "Ride them
down!" "Let them come closer first!"

Such were the enthusiastic bits of advice which
leaders in the crowd yelled to one another, but there
was a deep undertone of awe that spoke in answer to
them from scores of throats:

"What devil is in them, that they dare to walk into
our teeth in this manner? And is not that El Estaban
—the tall man walking in front with his hat in his
hand—and smiling? Ha! It is he!"

Such were the words or the thoughts in that undertone. And a little quaver of uneasiness ran through the
throng.

"One moment, comrades, I go to get my new rifle!"
shouted one. And another: "I go to fill my cartridge
belt. I shall come again at once——"

And another remembered that he had forgotten to

leave an important message with his wife—who was one among the shrill-voiced harpies who watched everything from the tops of the houses. However, all of these who remembered that they were needed elsewhere, were in the front line of the townsmen, and as they pressed back and through the rear, they disturbed the general order. And others began to move backward, until it was a disorderly mob indeed that confronted the men of the advancing Estaban.

And then, in the most cheerful of voice, Don Cristobal shouted: "Ah, my children, is it peace or war?"

"War!" yelled the women on the housetops. "If you capture him, the president will make you rich!"

"Peace!" shouted the men in the street with a sudden conviction. "Peace—and Heaven bless El Estaban!"

And they began to throw up their hats.

Such was the taking of San Marino.

CHAPTER XXXVII

The Approach

There was not very much in that, you will say—fifteen gray-headed veterans, with a stern-faced young man to lead them, marching upon the rabble of a town, and the town rabble greeting them with cheers rather than with bullets, as rabbles are most apt to do. And, indeed, such things had happened before in Mexico, times beyond counting. There was this difference here —the man who led the resolute fifteen was something more than a mere casual bandit. He was an outlaw with a past which extended back through three generations of history. And therefore his little deed was greeted with the more attention.

Across the breadth of the land the tidings swept to news editors, and with one accord they wired to Mexico

City to learn "what is the attitude of the administration."

The attitudes of the administration were wired back to them at once. Don Cristobal, the sole surviving Estaban, was a murderous cutthroat who had made himself notorious by butchering the population of an innocent town, and had left the streets of San Marino reeking with gore. And, in the meantime, fifty thousand pesos in gold would be paid to the lucky patriot who brought in the head of the outlaw, dead or alive!

So spoke the central government. It was not troubled by the fact that events at San Marino had been of a complexion quite other than that which they had represented. What was of importance to the administration was that it had been furnished with an ample excuse for putting its foot upon the rash intruder into national politics. And the order went forth also to double the guards through the armed camps of the Marino Mountains. For the chances were nine out of ten that the villain intended to reenter the country through which he had just made his first excursion. And excited gentlemen pointed out to one another that a single Estaban had entered the Marino Mountains and come out multiplied by fifteen. Suppose that the fifteen should enter and become multiplied by the same numeral? That would then begin to be a different matter!

In fact, the little exploit at San Marino ran like a quake across the country, but long before that tremor had reached the farthest extremities of Mexico, Don Cristobal had bought an ample supply all of the provisions which he could think of, and his boat was loaded with wine and ham and garlic and onions and beans, and half a hundred other good edibles. He had paid in full and a little more than full every claim for every article that he selected. And when he marched his men back to their boat, the population of San Marino followed him—man, woman, and child, and laughed, and cheered, and begged him not to sail too far out upon the sea, but to return soon. For they should not forget that he was their father and that they were his children!

He stood up in the stern of the boat before the motor was started.

"The day shall come," said he, "when San Marino shall be a city again. The mountains shall live once more. The sheep and the cattle, the hides and the wool and the flour shall come down to San Marino to be shipped. And the pier will be rebuilt, the houses made strong, the warehouses crammed—that time is not far off, my children!"

They were so overjoyed that they ran into the water up to their necks, stretching forth their arms and calling him their savior. But then the motor was started, and the boat swayed forth toward the sea.

He ran the old tub south, with a mildly following sea, until the low mist shut out all view from the shore. Then he swung her about. So doing, she proved her unseaworthiness. She gave her broadside to a roller, and instead of lifting to it, let it stagger across her, and for a moment she seemed on the point of wallowing to the bottom of the ocean.

There was one frozen moment of expectation. But then Don Cristobal, at the helm, got her pointed against the sweep of the waves, and she plugged slowly ahead. Yet even in that grisly moment he noted that the gray-headed mountaineers had not flinched. They stood stricken, but without a sound, and when the crazy old boat righted itself and began to slide quartering across the ridges of the waves, they set to work to bail her out without any command. And Don Cristobal smiled with set teeth.

What would happen when these grim old dogs fastened their teeth in the young gallants of Ramirez?

He kept on this course as long as the light of the day lasted. Then, in the clear starlight, he turned her prow in toward the shore. A land breeze was blowing, but under the lee of the shore they made good weather and *La Mariquita*, for that was her name, doubled her speed.

Five days the old hulk staggered northward, until a tide of gray-green water was seen entering the sea— the current of the San Filipo River—and here he turned the craft up the stream.

They lodged on a sand pit at the end of the first day. But all hands poled her off and they drove doggedly up the river once more.

Woe to the liar who had named the speed of *La Mariquita* six knots! For three days she struggled with the sluggish current of the river, and at last they saw the ruined crest of the church far before them in the light of the dawn.

Where the willows leaned far out across the water, they drew *La Mariquita* into the shore. Other willows were cut and laid across her. And two men were left in charge. With thirteen men at his back, Don Cristobal marched for the attack on the town.

During the heat of the midday, they quartered themselves in a patch of brush. They went on again in the evening, when the sun was almost westering to the horizon. By this time, the crew of *La Mariquita* would be urging the old boat up the river again, out of her place of concealment, to bring her close to the ruins of San Filipo. And there was need of swift action on the part of Don Cristobal.

In the meantime, what was the chance that he and his men could come close enough to the walls of San Filipo to deliver a charge, before they had been discovered by one of the wide-ranging scouts of Ramirez?

Small chance, indeed! For to their right and front they saw a horseman put his mount to a gallop and come directly toward them, swerving his steed to the side when he was twenty yards away, and remaining there with his rifle at the ready—a broad-shouldered, brown-faced, alert Arab of the mountain desert. Don Cristobal halted his men with a sign, and then to Valentin Oñate he said: "Go forward, Valentin. Tell that fellow that you are the leader of this party, and that we have come up the river hearing that there was a need of good fighting men in San Filipo. Say anything to keep him busy in talk while the rest of us steal closer to him and get him in our power."

Oñate nodded with a faintly ominous smile and went forward, shouldering his rifle and waving a hand in sign that he came peacefully. But he had not changed ten words with the stranger when there was a sudden shout, and the Estaban was amazed to see the follower of Ramirez leap from his horse and seize Oñate by both hands, while the pair of them began to talk at the same time, and laugh.

And then Oñate was calling:

"Come up, amigos. It is my brother's son! It is young Agustin Oñate himself! There is no danger from him!"

Don Cristobal and the rest were instantly on the spot, and the Estaban recognized one of the grim faces of those men whom he had seen before in the hut of Jim Gore, when he had taken care of the wounded man. He took off his hat and stood bare-headed before his former master.

"Now, Agustin," said Estaban sternly, "how is it that you have still been fighting against me?"

"Alas, señor," said poor Agustin, "a man takes money and orders and does what he is told. And he does not think, until there is a chance like this. I do not wish to think, Señor El Estaban. Ha! All these old comrades have followed you up from Sierra Marino —Julio, my cousin!—Lorenzo!"—he broke off to wave to two of the company who he seemed to recognize— "and they have let you do their thinking for them. I also wish to let you think for me, señor. Tell me what I am to do, and it is done, or else Agustin is a dog and has no honor!"

"How many men of Sierra Marino are in San Filipo?" asked Don Cristobal.

"There are only four besides myself, and one of these is sick."

"What? Only four?"

"The Ramirez found that all of us still loved El Estaban and he has discharged us one by one, with money, but with no kindness. He waits for more men to come to him—and then he will send the last of us away."

"Good! And how many men has he in San Filipo?"

"Almost forty, señor!"

"What? Forty men?" groaned the Estaban.

"Forty men," said Agustin Oñate. "The news has come up this way about the taking of San Marino, and that started Señor Ramirez into a great fear. He sent out messengers. They brought back fighting men every day. Every one has worked very hard. There is the guard to be kept around the church where Señor Warwick is—and around the town—and all the messengers to ride out and back—and to go——"

"Señor Warwick is in the church?"

"Beneath the church, señor."

"Ah, Ramirez knows that, does he?"

"Señor Warwick has tried to surrender."

"Impossible."

"But it is true, señor. He has no food."

Don Cristobal groaned again.

"I was there and I heard everything!" said young Agustin. "The voice of Señor Warwick was heard calling for Don Diego from beneath the church. Don Diego came, and a guard with him, and I was one of the guard.

" 'What terms will you give, Diego?' said Warwick.

" 'When I have beaten my enemy, what terms should I give?' said Don Diego.

" 'Am I only an enemy?'

" 'You have made me think so.'

" 'Diego, Diego, I have taken you up from the gutter.'

" 'I have paid for all that by accepting your insults.' "

Don Cristobal interrupted with a great oath.

"Did the dog dare to say that?"

"He did, señor."

"Be quiet a while. This is too much for me to stomach."

CHAPTER XXXVIII

The Plan of Battle

Don Cristobal took a turn or two up and down the sands. Then he paused again in front of Agustin, breathing hard.

"Nothing out of your imagination," said he, "but now continue."

"Should I dare to imagine things—to El Estaban?" asked Agustin, with an eloquent gesture.

He went on: "Don Diego was in a great triumph. He rubbed his hands together and laughed to himself silently. And he said: 'Now the game is in my hands, sir. You must admit that I can take the tricks or leave them, just as I please!'

" 'Ah, Diego,' said Señor Warwick in a great, sad voice, 'I suppose that it is true. We are starving——'

"And here we heard the voice of a girl break in— the voice of a girl, but it had the strength and the hardness of a man's voice, too. And she said: 'Father, will you really tell him everything?'

"Now Don Diego no longer laughed. He began to say in a trembling voice: 'Anne, my dear Anne—do I hear you?'

" 'You coward and ingrate,' said she, 'it is I! It is not true that we starve. Or if we did, we would rather starve than give in to you. Do not try to advance any closer, or we shall close the entrance again and talk no longer.'

"Don Diego retreated a little, still groaning with excitement.

" 'You are in my hands,' said he. 'You must realize that, Anne.'

" 'What a child and what a fool you are, Diego!'

said she and she laughed as smooth and as free as a bird whistling.

" 'You may say what you will, Anne,' said Don Diego. 'You know that I cannot speak harshly in answer, no matter what you use to taunt me. But why am I a child and a fool?'

"She said: 'Because, though you have us huddled here like chickens under a hawk, you forget that there is an eagle hanging in the air over the hawk, Diego!'

" 'Ha!' said he, 'what eagle?'

" 'El Estaban is free!' said she."

"Did she say that?" broke in Don Cristobal softly.

"Aye, señor. That was her word, which was a true word, also! Don Diego made a step or two backward. He was very much troubled, as I could tell even in the shadows beneath the church.

" 'The devil is loose!' said he in a small voice. And then he added out loud: 'But what can one man do, Anne? I have enough here to deal even with El Estaban!'

" 'Others have said so,' said this girl. 'But they have found that they were too sure of their strength. I tell you, Diego, that if we are willing to make terms now, you will be a fool not to accept them. Because you may delay too long, and El Estaban will strike! And then you will have nothing but wounds, perhaps, to pay you for all your work, and your money, and your treachery to us!'

"Don Diego said: 'Anne, what am I trying for except to take what is mine, inherited from my ancestors truly?'

" 'You would never have guessed at its existence if it had not been for my poor father,' said she.

" 'I do not wish to be hard,' said he. 'But tell me what terms you would propose?'

" 'We will give you a third of all that is here,' said she.

" 'A third!' said he. 'One part for me and two parts for you?'

" 'A part for you,' she answered, 'and a part for us, and a part for El Estaban!'

" 'El Estaban!' cried Don Diego, as though that word had been a knife that stabbed him. 'What has he to do with this?'

" 'He has our word to get a share as great as ours.'

" 'I had rather hang,' said Don Diego, 'than see that hungry dog fatten himself here! Besides, he is gone. He has no right. Forget about him, Anne! He has no legal claim!'

" 'He has a claim upon our honor,' said she.

" 'He has gone off and forgotten you,' said Don Diego.

" 'I tell you, he is a man who could never forget what he had pledged himself to,' said she."

"Did she say that?" broke in Don Cristobal.

"She did."

"Oh, jewel of a woman!" murmured Don Cristobal. "Continue, Agustin."

"After that, Don Diego made a little pause, and then he said: 'Why do you trust him so much—that robber and murderer and thief?'

" 'Because he is an honorable man.'

" 'An honorable murderer?' asked Don Diego.

" 'I have said what I mean. And I tell you, Diego, that if you are a wise man, you will beware of him! He is still dangerous to you!'

" 'Do I not know that?' he said to himself. He added aloud: 'I shall make another offer. I shall take a half and leave a half to you and you may arrange as you please with this Estaban. But there is one thing more, Anne.'

" 'Will you haggle like a huckster, Diego? But what is the other thing?'

" 'It is yourself!' said he."

"The dog!" muttered Don Cristobal.

"I could hear this girl cry out in her anger. 'You are a madman, Diego!' said she. 'Do you think that I could ever look at you without scorn after what we know of you now?'

" 'Ann, I hope that you will not poison yourself with malice against me.'

" 'I have seen the truth. Is that poison?'

" 'Anne, if I have committed any sins, they have been more than half for your sake.'

" 'Bah!' said she. 'Do you expect me to listen to such folly? I tell you again that we have made you one offer—one third of the treasure. And that is all that we will offer.'

" 'Let me hear the voice of your father on that point.'

" 'It is true,' said Señor Warwick. 'What Anne says I shall stick by.'

" 'Then you must endure a little more starvation, sir, before you will come to your senses.'

"Señor Warwick cried out: 'Now Heaven take witness against an ingrate and a knave! If there is a death here, it will be upon your head, Diego!'

" 'I hear you,' said Don Diego. 'But what I do is done according to what seems to me honest and good. Heaven forgive me if I am wrong. I ask only for what is due to me!'

" 'What is due to you is pauperism and the contempt of men! Anne, let us go back.'

" 'I shall come here at this same time in three days,' said Don Diego.

" 'You may do as you please!' said Señor Warwick.

"Then, after a moment, we heard a sound as of a heavy stone moved into place with a jar, and Don Diego said: 'Search the place from which we heard the voices. Surely we shall find the underground entrance now.'

"But when we had brought the lights and when we searched, we could find nothing, which was very strange. But as all men know, there is a mystery beneath the church of San Filipo. Have not the bells spoken many times from the heart of the ground, there? Yes, and a man is rash who inquires too closely. But we found nothing with all of our searching, and

Don Diego broke into a great cursing, but still that did not help us to move the stones!"

"Then," cried Don Cristobal, "the three days passed?"

"Yes, but in the meantime the news from San Marino had come to us, and the strange story of how you, señor, had crossed the mountains, and how you had come out from them leading enough men to capture San Marino without shedding a single drop of blood. And how you had sworn to return and make the Sierra San Marino your own country again—and Don Diego sent out everywhere for fighting men, because he said: 'The next place that that devil will strike will be San Filipo!'

"There were other men among us who said that the president and his soldiers would surely catch you, but Don Diego swore that he would not be fool enough to depend upon the actions of any man other than himself, do you see? So he has been gathering his fighters slowly, and two days ago he sent down the river and hoped to have a dozen fighting men back by to-day.

"Yesterday, the third day was ended. Once more we spoke to Señor Warwick beneath the church, and he spoke in a very weak voice. Don Diego would not alter his terms, though Señor Warwick begged him very hard and swore that his daughter was dying of hunger!"

"Merciful Heaven!" breathed Don Cristobal. "What did the dog say to that?"

"He said that if they were in distress the cause was their own stubbornness, and that if Señor Warwick did not surrender, the life of Anne would be upon his own head."

"And what did Warwick say?"

"He said that his daughter was as fixed in her purpose as any old Roman, and that she had vowed that she would destroy herself rather than allow herself to be taken from the tunnel unless good terms were first made, and Señor Warwick knew that she would do what she threatened!"

"Oh, my beauty!" said Don Cristobal. "That there is one such woman in the whole world redeems the whole sex. Now, Agustin, they are nearly starved in the tunnel, are they not?"

"Their voices were already more than half dead, Señor El Estaban," said young Oñate.

"Very good then, we must strike at once, and we must strike hard. Now hear me, Agustin. Here are fourteen of us. Two more men will presently come up from the river, making us sixteen. Sixteen are too small a number to fight forty. Therefore, ride back into San Filipo and give word that Don Diego's fighting men have come up the river, but that their boat grounded on a sand spit and that we have had to come along on foot. And beg him to send out horses to help us into the town, because we are footsore and hot—not being accustomed to travel on foot. At the same time, while he sends out help to us, do you get to the ear of the men from San Marino who are still in the town. Tell them the truth, briefly. And tell them that there will be fighting to-day, but that every man who proves himself a man for my sake will never be forgotten by El Estaban. Do you hear? Subtract the five from the forty and add them to my side. That makes twenty-one to thirty-five. And who has heard of an Estaban who has not been able to win his battles against much greater odds than these? Is it not so, amigo? Go at once. Ride like the devil, and enter San Filipo shouting, 'Help has come! The men from the river are here!'"

"That will be true, but only half true! Now, go!"

CHAPTER XXXIX

The Attack

Agustin Onate wheeled his horse and was off in a streak of boiling dust, and the party under Don Cristobal moved slowly, slowly forward. They had learned from this conversation between Agustin and their leader all that they really knew about the purpose of the expedition, but now, as they marched along, Don Cristobal expanded a little upon what they had picked up so casually.

"Now, amigos," said he, "you understand everything. We come here to strike at the robbers and the cutthroats in San Filipo who have been gathered by this Ramirez to rob an old man and his daughter. We will beat this Ramirez and his men, believe me. And after we have beaten him, we will set the old man and his brave daughter free and take them down the river with us to safety—they and the treasure. And one half of that treasure—which is many millions of pesos—will go to us. We will use that money properly! We will use it to gather men and guns and ammunition and descend again upon the Sierra Marino. There, my children, we will begin to rebuild the things which have been destroyed. We will restore the country to what it was under the rule of my father. Peace will come back. The valleys will be green. Do you understand? We fight for our homeland, though we happen to fight the battle here at San Filipo. Are you prepared?"

The answer was a deep-throated murmur. They were prepared truly. And the little body of warriors trudged steadily on.

They had not gone far before they saw the result of Agustin's mission. Seven or eight riders broke from the ruins of the town and swept toward them leading a score of horses which had been hastily saddled.

They came storming up to the little party with whoops that would have done credit to a war party of wildest Comanches. Their reception was wonderfully strange!

Here were fourteen smiling faces, one instant, and hands that willingly received the horses that were led up. And the next instant, here were fourteen steady rifles leveled at their relievers. And they heard the voice of El Estaban saying: "Now, my friends, this is a very scurvy trick which we have had to play on you. But I am El Estaban, and I intend to charge that town in another moment—and it is necessary to have horses for the purpose. You understand! I could think of no better way than to take the horses of my friend, Ramirez. I am sure that he will understand when the matter is explained to him. For he knows that all good caballeros hate to fight and to journey on foot, does he not?

"Therefore, amigos, tumble out of the saddle— leave your rifles and your revolvers. You are welcome to keep your knives, however, to cut your own throats, if you see fit. Unless there are among you some brave lads who know that El Estaban never leads except to a victory. Now then, if there are any of that cut among you, keep your horses and your saddles and your guns and ride on with us—and prove that your hearts are right by fighting like true men. But as for the rest of you who belong to Ramirez, body and soul, I do not harm you. I give your leave freely to stay where you are!"

When that speech was made, there was no consultation between the men of Ramirez. Each seemed to know instantly what he chose to do. Four of them dismounted and threw down their weapons. But three of them raised their hats and waved them to Don Cristobal, and in this fashion signalized their change of sides.

"Look, my friends," said Don Cristobal, chuckling.

"There has not been a shot fired, but what has become of Señor Ramirez with his forty men? He had only thirty-two, and four of these are out here too far from the battle to be of any help to him. Altogether, we shall be twenty-four fighting men. The odds are hardly against us, and we have surprise to help on our side. Do you hear, friends? Now follow me, and ride with your spurs struck deep. We want speed and straight shooting—and San Filipo is ours. Make for the mouth of the main street!"

They started forward with a sweep and a wild, tingling yell went up to the sun-flooded sky. On they came with a rapid thundering of hoofbeats. And inside the main street, they could see a scurrying of men. Alarm guns began to explode here and there, answered far off. And shouts, near and distant, came up from the town, to tell that the men of Ramirez were at least rallying fast to meet the shock of the battle.

Don Cristobal entered the main street's mouth expecting a burst of gunfire around him—but there was not so much as a shot.

"They have run for cover, and the town is ours!" yelled one of the turn-coats who now rode behind Estaban. "Come on, amigos. But mind the barricade at the next turn of the street———"

His warning had not time to sink into the minds of his companions when the whole body swept around the next bend of the street and found themselves in front of a six-foot wall of old adobe bricks and rubbish—an obstacle solid enough to keep back a man and high enough to keep a horse from jumping it.

Certainly Ramirez had used his time well since he heard Estaban was loose and apt to strike at him. Looking far down the street, Don Cristobal could see a second barrier at the farther end. And from every direction men were running toward the defense of the first.

Perhaps there were not ten men behind that first barricade—but in the hands of those ten men were repeating rifles, and they had a perfect shelter from the fire of Don Cristobal's men.

"Scatter!" yelled Estaban. "Scatter to the side—take to the houses—fight from cover!"

He might as well have called to a cyclone. The charge had to go boiling on until a sharp crackling of rifles began behind the barrier.

One—two—three—and a fourth man fell in half a second before that withering blast of musketry. And then the jumbled crowd of horsemen dissolved and, seeking their safety rather than obeying the orders of their leader, they pitched toward the sides of the street and took shelter in the houses.

But it was a cruel shock to the hopes of Don Cristobal. At least a half of his strength consisted in the force of a surprise attack. But that force was now worse than wasted. Four of his men were dead or badly wounded. And three or four more were hurt with the fire. The men of Ramirez were enormously heartened by their first success, and with shouts of victory were raising the spirits of the whole body of the garrison—and there was the cheerful young voice of Diego Ramirez himself, singing out directions above the clamor of the conflict.

Whatever might be his faults, he was no coward, as he was proving manfully.

Around Estaban himself, on that side of the street, he found a mere half dozen of his men. But he did not wait for more. Something must be done, and done at once. The barricade was held with too great a force to admit of forcing it from in front. But here was Valentin Oñate, steady and cool, wiping the dust and the sweat from his forehead and pointing out that the men of Don Diego held a half-standing house on either side of the barrier. If one of those houses could be forced, the barricade could be fired upon from the rear and it must become untenable.

But to attack men in a house was no easy matter.

"No firing on this side of the street," said Estaban. "Let them think that our hearts are in our boots. Then work up to them slowly, and we'll rush the nearest house from that moldy stack of ruins on this side of the street."

They followed him without a word, crawling snake-like behind him, taking advantage of every covert, as if they were stalking the wild mountain sheep of their native Sierra. So they came to the jumbled ruins of which Don Cristobal had spoken. He gave them a moment's rest, here, and then gave them the word.

"No noise—but run like the devil and get into that house!"

They had not twenty yards to go to gain the cracked and sinking walls of the house before them, and so swift and noiseless was their charge that only one of the little garrison spied them, and with a shout fired in haste and sent a harmless bullet flying over their heads.

Then they were in the house, while the garrison with a confused screeching tumbled out into the street to join their comrades behind the barricade.

There was only one casualty. One poor devil, as he fled from the house, took a bullet through the back and pitched upon his face.

And here were Don Cristobal's men behind safe covert, with the force of Ramirez gathered thick in the street. Ramirez himself knew the danger and strove to meet it. He gathered his men with a shout and a wave of the hand and led them to recapture the house. On his breast Don Cristobal drew aim, but as he pulled the trigger another man leaped in front. That man fell, and in the next instant young Ramirez was safe under the wall of the house.

CHAPTER XL

Jim Gore Returns

There were five cool-headed men with Don Cristobal, but there were twenty tigers striving to force a way into the house; and what can one man do against four?

They forced their way through the broken doorway. They gained the lower level of the house, and here was Estaban cut off with his handful at the top of the ancient house!

Here the battle would have ended even as it began had there not been help from the outside. Don Cristobal, in the wreck of a half-walled room at the top of the house, knelt with his rifle in hand. Up the stairs rushed two men. His bullet dropped the first into the arms of his comrade and both rolled head over heels to the bottom of the steps.

A heavy barrier of planking appeared, with the men of Ramirez pushing it up from behind, and into this Don Cristobal and his companions poured a score of bullets, and brought only one yell of pain from behind it.

Ruin looked Don Cristobal in the face when suddenly he heard a sound far off that was sweeter to his ears than any music that had ever sounded—men shouting with one voice: "El Estaban! San Filipo is ours!"

It was not the cheer of the men down the street. It came from a direction behind the barricade, and he knew at once. Agustin had done his work at last, and had gathered to his side the men of the Sierra Marino who were already in the employ of Don Diego. They came with a shout and a rush. A sudden wild confusion entered the lower region of the house.

"Agustin, Agustin! Have you betrayed me?" rang the voice of Ramirez.

And then a hearty English shout.

"Come on, hearts! The doctor needs us. Take them from the back and he'll jump at 'em from the front——"

The voice of Jim Gore, all of whose timorousness was now forgotten! Wise, wise Agustin to have liberated a fighter of such potency to battle for his old master!

Straight at the shield of planking Don Cristobal sprang with his men behind him. It went down with a crash under that impact. Behind, all was confusion. There was no chance to pick and choose. Rifles were of no avail. All was knife and revolver work as assailed and assailants rolled down the steps to the bottom level again.

Outside in the street came another roar of voices.

The rearmost men, hurrying to the defense of Ramirez, had encountered the last half of Don Cristobal's party as the latter scrambled over the deserted barricade and made for the scene of conflict, and instantly the two divisions were locked in fight.

Don Cristobal, hearing these things, drew back a little from the hurly-burly. It was all very well to fight like a laborer in the thick of the press, but what they wanted to end the fight was the life of one man.

Yonder he stood. And at that instant, Don Cristobal saw Valentin Oñate leap at Ramirez, and struggle with him hand to hand.

Instantly El Estaban was springing for the spot. A wild face loomed before him, with a clubbed rifle swinging high. The rifle and the revolver of Don Cristobal had been emptied the moment before and there was no time to reload. In his hand there was only a knife. But he slipped in like a striking snake beneath the swing of the gun. He struck home beneath the raised left arm, and the man dropped with a gasp, and lay still forever.

Another step forward. It was hard to see, for the

whirl of struggling, stamping, screaming combatants had raised a cloud of dust denser than a fog. But here was Valentin Oñate's broad back as he struggled and fought hard—but in vain.

For suddenly he slipped to one knee. The hand of young Ramirez was fixed in his throat, the clubbed revolver of Diego was raised to deal the fatal stroke —and then Don Cristobal struck home again.

Not with the edge of the knife. To his dying day he was never to be able to tell why he refrained from killing where death was so overdue as in this precious rascal. But he turned the edge of the knife to one side, and struck with his fist, the handle of the knife loading the blow.

Down went Don Diego as though a club had smitten him. And at the same time Don Cristobal saw the form of Jim Gore rushing through the mist of the smoke and the dust with a revolver in either hand, and his face slashed down one side where a knife had grazed him.

He, too, had made for the spot where Don Diego fought, and had arrived only an instant too late to share in the struggle with him.

"Take him and hold him, Jim!" yelled Don Cristobal. "Hold him, and keep him for an instant. Oñate, are you badly hurt?"

He raised the burly form of Valentin in his arms. The grin of the mountaineer was instant.

"In the legs, only," he said. "I'm numb below the waist, but if the bleeding stops, I'll be tough enough to live through ten little fights like this! Ha! Is Ramirez down?"

For the great voice of Jim Gore, heightened and made drunk with triumph, was belowing above the tumult:

"We have the cock of the roost! We have Ramirez! You fools—will you fight for a dead man?"

The fury grew quiet at once. The men on either side had had enough of the struggle in a place where the temperature was that of an oven filled with steam, and where wounds came home terribly from half a dozen different directions at once. They were glad to stop at the first honorable excuse, and in a trice there were bleeding, gasping, weary men dragging themselves out into the purity of the open air, where there were only a few poisonous wisps of gunpowder smoke adrift, and the noise of the battle, the death yells and the screams of victory, could fade slowly from their ears.

And these were the results of that brief and terrible battle in the old town of San Filipo. Of four and twenty men who had fought for Estaban, seven lay dead, and eight more were wounded, some badly. Of the eight and twenty who had fought for Don Diego, nine were dead, but another nine were wounded, though only three of these were helpless. So that of fifty-two men who had engaged in this minute of carnage, there remained at the end only nineteen unhurt!

The old house was dyed crimson, and in the dust of the street there were streaks and spots of blackened red where men had fallen, dead or wounded!

Upon this scene Diego Ramirez with a gasp and a groan opened his eyes and, looking wildly around him, beheld and understood. He was beaten, and there was no hope remaining to him. A hand of iron grasped his arm, and a stern, soft voice whispered at his ear:

"Tell them to bury the dead, Diego. And then tell them to take themselves off, tell them that this is the end of their work!"

Don Diego raised his free arm and waved it. And a groan answered him!

"Amigos," said he, with a wonderfully controlled tone, "we have fought a good fight. But we were prepared to fight men, not tigers. And we were prepared to have honest men with us, not sneaking thieves who would turn to the other side. Do you frown at me, Agustin Oñate? I tell you, you are a cur, and the son and the grandson of a dog!"

"No more of that!" commanded Don Cristobal sharply.

"You have taken my body, not my tongue or my mind," said Don Diego calmly. "I say he is a poisonous rat, and not a man."

"You, Diego Ramirez," answered Agustin. "El Estaban was my master before I had ever so much as heard your name. And he will be my master again, so long as I live. As for the lying things which you say about me——"

"Peace, Agustin!" broke in Don Cristobal. "Will you give your men my message?"

"I shall," nodded the captive. "Amigos, in my house there is my little money chest. There is still more than a thousand dollars in it. Break the lock. Take the money and divide it among you. As for me, I shall not need it. Then bury the dead. Bind up the wounds of the injured—and you may ride away when you will. Adios!"

Rascal though he was, he had given those hand-picked fighters of his such desperate leading in the battle that they greeted him now in his downfall with a hearty cheer. Then they scattered to do his work.

"Tell me, Diego," said Don Cristobal, "why you have no longer any need of money?"

"I shall tell you, Estaban. I have aimed at a star and found only a mouthful of dust. And therefore I want to wash my hands of my hopes. Let them take the money. They have fought well enough to deserve it!"

CHAPTER XLI

The Rescue

Don Cristobal eyed him with a profound wonder.

"You are not shamed then, Diego?"

"Why should I be shamed?"

"Could you keep up your head if you stood face to face with Warwick and Anne?"

"Do you know her so well," said Diego Ramirez. "Do you call her by her single name so soon?"

There was a flash in his eye, but it died at once.

"However," said he, "I have lost my hope of her together with the treasure, and I shall never think of either of them again. I have no shame. If there was ingratitude and evil in me—why, I have let the world see it. I feel as much affection for Warwick as ever. I know that he hates me and that he has cause to hate me. However, he would be amazed to know how much tenderness there is in my heart for him. But that is not a point of importance."

"By heaven, Ramirez," said Don Cristobal, "I begin to admire you. You have betrayed your benefactor, endangered the life of a girl, and tried to steal millions, but still I find that I do not hate you! I believe that you have forgotten your losses already and have your face set toward the future!"

"Señor," smiled Ramirez, "you have a brain and a heart, and therefore you can understand me. When I first saw you, I knew that I had seen a tiger. And I could not tell which I would rather have—a dead Estaban for an enemy, or a living Estaban for a friend. However, you will think that I am flattering."

"Upon my soul, I do not."

"Very well, then, let me tell you that since I have tried to be master and have failed, it remains for me to become a man who serves. You, Estaban, have in your head the conquest of a kingdom. Keep me in mind. I have wits, courage, and the ability to make men follow me."

"And loyalty, Diego?"

"Enough loyalty to know where my interests lie. As long as there is a hope for you to win—and for me to win something worth while under you, I shall fight for you like a lion. The minute that you are beaten, and I can gain anything by betraying you, I shall treat you like a dead dog! Do you understand?"

"Delightfully and perfectly. Ramirez, you are a villain, but you may be a useful one. I think that I must take you south with me. In the meantime, you are my prisoner. Jim, watch him just as if he were a snake. Adios!"

So he left Jim Gore watching this strange youth, who sat down in the shade of the wall and made himself a cornucopia-shaped cigarette and smoked it with the dull, expressionless eyes of content, as though he had not been fighting for a fortune five minutes before —as though dead men did not lie all around him, some of his own killing!

Don Cristobal made straight on for the church of San Filipo. And when he came to the shadows beneath the cellar, he had half a dozen of his men behind him, bearing wine and food. For he could not tell how he should find the sufferers underground.

He found the spring that turned the balance. The great stone moved, and instantly he was down the dark and narrow passage and throwing the light from the electric torch before him; and his voice was flung out, also, with a cheer that raised a hundred briefly leaping echoes down the passageway.

He paused in his haste, and it seemed to Don Cristobal that he could hear a faint answer far ahead of him. He crossed the place where the narrow gap opened above the buried bells of San Filipo, and a fragment of rock, dislodged by his foot, rattled down, and sent back a deep, humming murmur.

He went on, and now a light showed before him— a light that advanced staggeringly—and then a chorus of voices, half-drunken with expectation.

"It is I, Cristobal Estaban——"

"Heaven be praised! Heaven be praised!"

In the dim light they came before him like five wan ghosts. The bearded faces of the men were terrible enough, but the hollow cheeks and the sunken eyes of the girl were what held him.

"He has come, and he has won!" said Anne Warwick. "Did I not say so?"

"Oh, Anne, you have kept the only strength that is

in us through your belief in him. Cristobal, my boy, Heaven bless you!"

"Here is wine in this bottle, and a fragment of bread apiece. Can you walk easily? Are you weak, Anne?"

"Weak with happiness. Ah, but the days have been long!"

"I thought that there was food for three weeks."

"The bread molded."

"Merciful heavens, we should have thought of that, in this dampness."

"It does not matter. But let us know what has happened!"

"Everything is ours. There is a boat ready to take us and the gold and the silver away. There are men to man the boat and fight for us, and load on the money. And then I shall take you wherever you will go!"

"Hurry!" said old Warwick. "I am hungry for the taste of the sun more than for the taste of food. The blessed sun, Cristobal. My flesh aches for the feel of it! Let us hurry on!"

They went stumbling up the passageway, and the three peons came at the rear, laughing feebly, swaying against one another, staggering with weakness and with joy.

They gained the end of the passage, and there Warwick was lifted out, his daughter next, and the peons were pushed up into the shadows of the church of San Filipo, mysterious no more!

And, finally, here was the sunshine—here was food—and in the streets of San Filipo no sign of the battle except the wounded, and the spots where the bullets had carved deep niches in the adobe bricks. For the dead had been removed already.

They led the Warwicks and the three peons to the bank of the river, where the old flat-bottomed *La Mariquita* hove by the banks. There they sat in the shadow of the willows while the workers of the Sierra San Marino trod steadily back and forth, bringing down hundred-pound loads of bullion at each trip.

And the tonnage grew—the bright gold first, and then the blackened silver in heaps and heaps, which was stowed flat on the bottom of the little ship.

Now there was seen one great advantage in her flatness and her width, in that she settled only a very few inches with the two and a half tons of purest gold, and thirty-five tons of fine silver.

Then they gathered the crew. The wounded— Valentin Oñate chief of all—were placed forward, away from the fumes of the engine. And then there entered the ship Warwick and his daughter and their three starved peons, already more than two thirds recovered.

They raised a little jigger sail to help them on their course down the stream. And the man who held the helm, to watch for the sand bars and guide them aright, was none other than Don Diego, late the archenemy!

CHAPTER XLII

Southward Bound

With a fair wind in the jury sail, and the current aiding them, and the engine pumping bravely away at its task, they managed almost nine or ten knots, until the current flattened and widened toward the sea, and finally failed them altogether. As they entered the estuary, Warwick was sitting cross-legged at the side of Don Cristobal.

"Which way are her thoughts, Cristobal?" said he.

And he pointed to Anne, where she sat at the bows, her face raised high to the evening light in the horizon.

"Which way are her thoughts?" said the Mexican. "All I can say is that I hope that they are for the south. I want you and Anne to see the little show which I want to stage in the Sierra Marino."

Warwick smiled.

"Let us be frank with one another," said he. "The question is merely: Does Anne feel that some day she must marry you—and therefore does she wish to sail south with you? Or does she feel that one day she would regret such a marriage—and therefore will she want to sail north."

"Aye," sighed Don Cristobal, "that is the question! Although I should never have had the courage to express it in this bold fashion. But tell me, which way do you think that she tends?"

"I cannot tell."

"Will you not even tell me which way you are influencing her?"

"Which way do I try to persuade her? Oh, north—north, of course."

"I am sorry!"

"Of course you are! Perhaps, if I were a younger man, I should want her to go south—to you and with you. But I am old and crippled. I am afraid of the pain in this world. You are not of her country. And that is one great detraction from a match of this sort. And you would be taking her Heaven knows where in the way of wild adventures."

"She is not a sit-by-the-fire woman, señor."

"No, she is not, I admit. She is a good long distance from that. But yonder in those mountains of yours, you are going to invest millions in the hope that some day you will be able to beat off the Federal troops whom the president of Mexico is certain to set at your heels; and in the hope that you may be able to gather a strong and contented population around you, such as lived under your fathers before you; and in the hope that you will be able to undo the ruin of their works and make the country green again. Well, Cristobal, I give you my best wishes, my respect for the great task that you have before you, my sympathy for your cause, my belief in the strength of will and nerve which you take to the task, my hope that your adroitness may win through for you in everything—but at the same time I do not wish to give you my daughter. I would like to see a quieter future before her."

Don Cristobal bowed and said nothing.

"Are you not going to argue your case?" asked Warwick, half dismayed and half amused.

"I am in the hands of fate," said Don Cristobal, smiling, "and what I try to do with my own single strength is not apt to be of much use, I am afraid. Very little use indeed! Look at that rascal Ramirez trying to teach Jim Gore to gamble! He knows that Jim gets half of my share, and therefore he wants Jim to form the habit of cards—a good habit, that is from the viewpoint of Diego—the scoundrel!"

But he smiled, amused and sympathetic, as one hawk in the exploits of another, at the expense of smaller fowls.

"But poor Jim Gore," said Warwick, "is pouring all his fortune in with yours—in this wild gamble which you are about to undertake?"

"Yes. And I shall make him many times a millionaire for it!"

"You will—or else you will make him a beggar!"

"Exactly. Jim understands that as clearly as I can explain it to him, and he doesn't regret the chance. He's glad of it, because every old-timer is really an old gambler."

"Only—I cannot understand one thing, and neither can my daughter. I think, between you and me, that it is the one bar between her and her acceptance of you, Cristobal. She does not see how it is possible that you should have taken along such a rascal as this Diego, whom we all know so well! It baffles her. And I confess that the rascal is an eyesore to me, every time my glance falls on him. Oh, the bald-faced, scoundrelly villain! I rage when I so much as think of him, let alone when I see his face! Ah, Cristobal, look yonder at the fin of that shark cutting the water—the black villain will follow us for scraps, now, I suppose."

The high dorsal fin of a great shark was seen cutting the water not far astern, and swimming with great speed. Anne Warwick leaped up to see it also. And at the instant that she sprang up, a quartering wave slapped the side of the prow with some solid tons of water and jarred the old hulk violently to the side. Anne Warwick, with a cry, strove to recover her balance, but her floundering was useless. She pitched headlong with a great splash, and before the headway of the boat could be stopped, she was many yards astern, swimming valiantly—and Don Cristobal at her side.

"Steady!" said he through his teeth. "Steady, Anne. We'll make the boat all right."

"The shark!" she gasped, and then swam on furiously again.

In the stern of the boat there stood up a slim figure with a gorgeous scarf about his waist and in that waist a long, murderously curved bowie knife. He waved his hand gayly toward them and then leaped far out, dived perfectly into the back of a leaden-sided roller, and then disappeared.

When he came up again, he was at the side of the swimming pair.

"Courage, Cristobal!" said he. "Swim hard, and all will be well."

He dived again.

Warwick was screaming from the boat: "The shark! The shark! He's coming for you. Do you see his fin? Anne—Cristobal——"

He covered his eyes. The end of a long rope, flung far from the boat, had fallen within the grip of the hand of Cristobal, and now he was being drawn swiftly in, but not so swiftly as the shark clove the water behind him—not a tithe as fast——

And then it seemed that madness seized the great tiger of the sea. He was seen to hurl half of his twenty feet of body from the sea, with a red stream gushing from a gash in his side. He fell, and began to swim in a convulsive circle, searching frantically through the dark clouds of water for the enemy who had stricken him.

And then he twisted in a straight line and dipped down, sounding fast and far. And out of the scarlet welter of the waters where he had sunk arose Don Diego. He spat the water from his mouth and waved toward the boat with a laugh, and the knife with which he had done the deed was in his hand, flashing.

Perhaps, that was why Don Cristobal sat that night beside Anne Warwick and held her hand.

"You were right about Don Diego," she said. "And perhaps you were right about everything else. And—turn the boat south, Don Cristobal!"